HUNGRY GHOSTS

HUNGRY GHOSTS
Susan Dunlap

COUNTERPOINT

BERKELEY

Library of Congress Cataloging-in-Publication Data

Dunlap, Susan.
Hungry ghosts / by Susan Dunlap.
p. cm.
ISBN: 978-1-58243-499-5
1. San Francisco (Calif.)—Fiction. I. Title.
PS3554.U46972H86 2008
813'.54—dc22
2007043827

Cover design by Kimberly Glyder Design
Interior design by Gopa&Ted2, Inc.
Printed in the United States of America

COUNTERPOINT
2117 Fourth Street
Suite D
Berkeley, CA 94710

www.counterpointpress.com

Distributed by Publishers Group West

10 9 8 7 6 5 4 3 2 1

To Erin Williams,
with love

HUNGRY GHOSTS

CHAPTER 1

TUESDAY
5:40 A.M.

I GREW UP in San Francisco, but I'd never noticed this Victorian, much less its turret roof, thrust out thirty-five feet above Broadway. Now, in the eternity between taking position on the steep tiles and getting the cue for my stunt, I was noticing it plenty. The crew had coated the tiles with stickum, but before I could get my feet in place the fog had washed them slick. My legs bowed, feet curling around the curve of the roof, jamming against the tiles. I pressed and released my toes to keep the soles from going numb. A rust-eaten weather vane jerked in the wind; I used it for balance, but it would never hold my weight.

Below, the marquee lights of the strip joints flashed red-bulbed nipples on watermelon breasts. Headlights swept left as cars swung into the detour around the camera crane and the scurrying crews. The first unit— the director, actors awaiting their shot at the post-dawn light—were out of the makeup wagon and gathered around the lunch cart on the sidewalk half a block east. The second unit—the stunt crew—director, other stunt doubles, special effects guys—kept their distance. They would have watched the run-through on this stunt last night when the catcher bag spit Jenny Chin back up and onto the sidewalk. They must have heard the crack when

3

her kneecap shattered. Heard her scream and then the roar of the ambulance racing from the corner where another one now stood.

My hand tightened on the useless weather vane. Maybe Jenny Chin hadn't run a gauge on the catcher bag's pressure; she could have miscalculated the blowup ratio for her weight. I'm careful, meticulous. I wanted to believe she wasn't, that the error had to be hers, not caused by a cheap bag, a bad gauge, or shoddy tie-downs I hadn't even been able to see in the dark.

"Too late now!" I said aloud to buoy myself. But I heard the quiver in my voice. The director called me to replace Jenny because of my reputation from East Coast and L.A. jobs, right? Not because I was new on the books back here in the city I'd left as soon as I could get out. Not because, like coming back home, I had no choice.

Already the nightlife quality of the street was fading; in ten minutes it would be dawn and the illusion of dusk we were creating would no longer be possible. We had one take for this gag. No way could I afford to blow it off. Nor end up like Jenny Chin.

"Two minutes!" the director called.

The wind snapped the short kimono I was wearing against my icy legs. Concentrate! Don't think! Not about San Francisco. Not about steering clear of it. Not about coming back here where every street held memories of Mike; not about his leaving. Focus on the gag. Nothing else.

I stared down. The thirty-five-foot fall would take 1.4755 seconds, barely time to throw myself heels over head, flail for the camera, and stretch out horizontal, spine down to hit the bag and spread the force of impact throughout maximum body surface. Come down curled and you take it fully on your spine—or your head. I brought every bit of my attention inward, mentally ran through the gag, felt my legs pushing off hard, feet pulling free of the gunk on the tiles, the dive into the header toward

4

the bull's-eye on the bag, the twist and stretch. I could feel my back land softly on the bag, could feel a smile spread, could hear the applause of the second unit gang.

"One minute!"

A minute is an eternity when you've done everything already.

The icy wind snapped the gold silk against my ribs and turned the black strands of my wig to razors. Down below, the grips pushing props and hauling dollies pulled up fast. Cameramen shifted behind their lenses. The gaffer switched on the overhead spot on the crane, turning the street black and white. Broadway was dead still: no traffic, no sound. Two blocks away south of me, on a futon above the Barbary Coast Zen Center, my Zen teacher, Leo Garson, was sleeping. He couldn't bear the thought of watching me fall.

I made one final spot check for the red bull's-eye in the middle of the bag, then cut my eye-line to the ground. From now on I'd look only outward. Walling out all thoughts, in that endless minute I stared straight ahead to Pacific Avenue, spotting the *zendo* by its curlicued roof.

"Twenty seconds, Darcy!" the director yelled.

He cued for lights and camera. A gust shook the turret. I grabbed, steadied, straightened up. A huge spotlight began a circle that would end on the turret and be my cue to move. The light, ten times brighter than day, panned across the street along the empty roofs of the Broadway strip joints, the bookstores and offices and decorators' shops on Pacific Street, on a corner of the roof of the Barbary Coast Zen Center.

Lit up a man walking across that roof.

A tall, thin man with red, curly hair like my own.

Mike, my brother, who'd been missing for 11 years.

"Mike! Omigod, Mike!" I pushed off to catch him before he vanished. My foot burned and hit air. I froze, panicked. I jolted back, lurched for the weather vane, grabbed it with both hands. It shook, bent. I pushed my foot hard into the tiles, willing the stickum to hold. A gust flung me to the side. Sweat ran down my back, down my legs, over my feet. I was shaking all over.

"Ten seconds!"

Forget Mike! Concentrate on the gag! But I peered into the dark for the zendo roof. The light had moved away. Mike *couldn't* have been there, but—

The spotlight slapped my arm. I jolted. I wasn't ready, wasn't set. I'd forgotten all about the gag. Thirty-five-foot fall. What was I . . .

The camera was on me! No time to recheck—the light steamed my skin.

1.4755 seconds, the time it takes to snap your fingers. I pushed off hard. The run-through in my memory took over. Silence was thick around me; the light walled off my eyes. For an instant I floated in that magic moment of fullness that mysteriously lures one to jump.

The moment vanished. I plunged, my head straight down. The red circle on the bag raced up toward me. Air slammed my face. I flailed my legs and arms for the camera, pulled my body the way it was supposed to be. Had to be. Hair whipped my face, covered my eyes; I squinted through it, ready to hit the mark I couldn't see. To hit it dead-on perfect.

The bag was like cement. It slammed my shoulder. I bounced. My feet were in air; I wasn't in the bag! I was on the edge. Flying off the edge like Jenny Chin. I crashed onto the sidewalk. Pain shot through me, walled out the world. It was all I could do to breathe. I couldn't feel my legs, my shoulder, my back, nothing but the tsunami of pain. Noise splattered. Someone was yelling.

"What?" I forced out.

"Are . . . you . . . okay?" a male voice yelled in my ear.

"Yeah." I was using every speck of air that hadn't been knocked out of me. My feet burned; my legs felt like crumbling cement. I doubled over, couldn't straighten up. Needed air. My lungs ached. Red dripped from my shoulder. I breathed in as hard as I could, commanded myself to straighten up. "I'm fine." A gofer threw a blanket over my shoulders.

"You nearly missed it!" The second unit director's voice seared with blame.

"Like Jenny Chin?" I was in his face. "Your stunt double blows out her kneecap. Your replacement does it spot-on and gets tossed onto the sidewalk. You looking for blame, Sparto, get yourself a mirror!"

Robin Sparto was a little wiry man with a pale mouth that couldn't decide which way to shift. In another second it'd stretch into outrage. But I'd be out of here then. So much for this job I thought I couldn't afford to blow.

He made some crack about me and the cable car leap, but I didn't have time to deal with that. A cab was about to take the detour. I hailed it and ran.

I had to have imagined Mike up there on the roof. He'd been out of my life more than twenty years. I couldn't let him disappear again.

7

CHAPTER 2

"WHICH AIRPORT?" the cabby asked as I threw myself into the back.

"Just go!"

He shot forward, screeching to a stop at the light.

"Hey, lady, you okay?" He turned full around, a big, round-faced guy who looked like his other job was as a bouncer, like "okay?" meant "able to pay?"

"I'm fine. Drop me at Pacific and Sansome."

"What about the airport?"

"Just go!"

"A two-block fare! Hey, I gotta make a living."

"From all the fares you rejected at this hour?"

"You coulda walked!"

Mike was getting away! "Get going, dammit!"

He pulled a right and launched the cab downhill on Battery, like a sequence out of *Bullitt*. "San Francisco!"

I'm pretty sure I heard him mutter the old local saw about the nuts rolling west, but I ignored it, too busy yanking sweats and sandals out of my bag, jamming legs into pants as we screeched furiously around corners. "Next block, stop!"

He hit the gas, flying west on Pacific, coming violently to a pause at the corner before jolting across Sansome.

I pulled on my sweatshirt. "Middle of the block, the building with the curved roof."

"The old Baytown bordello?" His grin told me he'd watched me dressing in the rearview. Big surprise. What did I expect when I'd hopped in wearing the world's shortest kimono? "Wait for me." I thrust a twenty at him, leapt out, and raced across the sidewalk into a courtyard, eyeing the brick building for stairs to the roof. None. Had to be inside.

The wooden door was huge, like the entrance to a medieval fortress. Without hope, I yanked. It popped open. I ran inside, into an alcove. The room ahead was big, empty, shiny-floored. Stairs led up from the alcove. In two bounds I took the six steps to the landing, pushed off, raced on up to a small hallway with doors on three sides. Leo's boots were outside one.

It wasn't Leo I was after. I pulled open other doors—kitchen, bathroom, empty room with a window at the far end, the street side. I shoved the window full open and swung out onto the ledge. Above me was the sharp curve of the roof. I leapt, caught the corner, hauled myself up far enough to see that the space was empty, as I'd known all along it would be.

Mike wasn't there.

I'd deluded myself, just as I had dozens of times in a dozen cities when I'd spotted lanky guys with dark red curly hair, who pushed off with each step the way he did, red-headed men who wrapped an arm across a woman's back and gave her shoulder that special little pat, only to turn around and once again disappoint me with the face of a stranger.

What did you expect? I asked myself, as I stared at the empty roof. Still, I was crushed. I was also stupid, and hanging over the edge of a roof two stories above the sidewalk. The cabdriver was yelling at me.

The roof behind the façade was plain tar and gravel. Stubbornly, I hoisted myself over the edge and up onto the highest point where I could see other roofs. But there was no red-haired man loping away. Clinging to the last frayed thread of hope, I eyed Pacific Avenue east and west. Nobody in sight. No one but the irate cabbie, that is. Not even a moving vehicle or a lit shop sign. Just one dark window after another.

The man who could have been Mike was gone. He'd had plenty of time to climb down and walk away or drive off before I got here. If he'd been on the roof at all. Spotting him had been so far-fetched, even I couldn't really believe it. If Mike were beside me now, he'd be laughing at his kid sister. "Always were into happy endings, weren't you, Darce? No wonder you want to be a stunt coordinator—control the great illusion." He'd be nudging me, laughing louder, assuring me everything was possible.

The fire escape of the neighboring building was in the back, an easy swing from this roof. So now there was not even a question of how anyone could have gotten up here. I clunked down the metal stairs, stuck with the less-than-comforting knowledge that I would repeat this chase some other year in some other town. I rounded the rear corner of the building into a brick courtyard. The cabbie was still screaming.

I ran toward him. "Did you see a man leave the building?"

"I been watching for *you!* Your twenty, lady, it's gone, and the meter's ticking. I should have left you hanging out the window."

"No one came out of the building?"

"Not that I saw, but like I say, you were grabbing all my attention throwing yourself out the window. I thought I was going to have to scrape you off the sidewalk." He took the bill I was holding out, a second twenty, and said, more calmly, "You're not the first."

"To jump here?"

"It's a real bad vibe place. Jumpers, you hear about them. One was a whore who hit head first, but that was over a hundred years ago. The building was saloon downstairs, cribs above."

I laughed. It was all too familiar. Growing up in the city, I'd heard plenty about the days when law stopped well east of California, and the Barbary Coast was notorious for separating men from their money. "Are you in this area a lot?"

"Yeah, sure."

"Have you seen a guy who looks like me? But older, mid-forties. About six foot."

He stared at me, paused. "That color red hair, that dark?"

I nodded.

"Maybe."

"Maybe?" *Maybe? My breath caught. Maybe, really?* "Either you've seen him or not."

He waited a beat, still watching me. "I'll let you know." He dipped his big bald head and swung into the cab. "Bad vibes."

I grabbed his shoulder. "You know who I'm talking about!"

"I didn't say that." He smacked the door shut. "I'll be back, don't worry."

He'd all but copped to it. What was he hiding? It was all I could do not to try to shake it out of him. But I'd lost leads, or strangers I mistook for leads, before by losing control. I took a breath and went with what would keep him here. "*Bad vibes?* What does *that* mean?"

His hand was on the ignition key, but he stopped before turning it, and for the first time really seemed to be thinking. "You part of this Zen group?"

"Yes." I released his shoulder.

"You do exorcism?"

"No, that's Catholics."

"Too bad."

"Why?"

"It's not just old-time stuff. A fellow had a heart attack right in the middle of the day. Jeweler. Customers in the shop. Splat. Dead."

"People die." *This* was his big bad vibe?

"Then the next tenant's partner sold everything—business, house, car—out from under him. First sign that gave him a clue was when the rent check bounced. After that it all went south."

"Double crosses." I shrugged. And him seeing a guy who could be Mike, that would turn out to be as much nothing.

"So then," he went on, ignoring me, "the place sat empty till now, windows boarded up, and you could hear weird noises inside, and there were *snakes* coming out of it."

"Oh, please! Save it for the tourists! I don't have time for this!"

I'd barely finished when he hit the ignition and sped off toward Columbus Avenue. My twenty, of course, was still in his hand. I stood in the empty street, fuming at him, at me, and, suddenly, freezing.

Dawn was easing into the cold fog of this February day. There was a cement bench across the courtyard. I sat, trying to block out my memories by imagining snakes pouring out of the big double doors, but it was useless. All I could think of was my brother, Mike, who had walked out of the house one day at the age of twenty, when I was sixteen, and had never come back. He's abandoned me to a life with his ghost. I couldn't—wouldn't—imagine him dead, unable to conceive of anything that would justify a decision to slam the door on his entire family, on me, his confidante. I read every story about amnesia victims, lapped up the hope. I had called red-haired strangers, flown across country on an hour's notice to find one who'd been released after fifteen years in a federal lockup, I'd hired a detective, and, after a few years, another. The only endings were dead ends. Above all I had avoided returning home to San Francisco, where memories of Mike might come around any corner but he never would.

But it was Leo, Garson-*roshi*, my Zen teacher, who rounded the gate from the street. He stood in the dim light, smiling. "Where have you been, Darcy? When you jumped off that turret—"

"You came to the shoot?" The shoot seemed ages ago. "You told me you couldn't bear to watch."

"I can't. But I did, anyway. The guy beside me—he was lugging some equipment—almost slapped a hand over my mouth when you jumped. Good move, too. I groaned so loud you'll hear it on the soundtrack."

"I wasn't in any danger. I know what I'm doing."

"But I don't." He had a habit of almost winking that conveyed a meaning, often a joke beneath the obvious, one that was shared with his listener. I wondered if he had any sense of what an intimate gesture it was, and how much more was suggested by it than he intended. He was a gentle man who could spark fury in others. No one seeing him for the first time would have called him handsome. His features were too large for his face, his ears a bit pointed, which, with his shaved head, gave him a slightly extraterrestrial air. His thin form under his jacket hid the musculature honed during six years of country monastery life. That toughness was obvious only in his gnarled hands. The effect of it all was that no one hesitated to approach him about their problems; they just didn't quite believe he'd have an answer.

I couldn't help thinking he seemed so out of place in the city, like an actor who'd walked onto the wrong set. I'd known him only a few months, been with him only two weeks at a monastery retreat in the country. Part of that time he'd been too sick to talk, and the rest, well, at the most normal of times—which that wasn't—Zen retreats don't encourage conversation. Leo had seemed suited to life in the country. But he'd lived in the city here before. Did he have friends here? A lover, even? Zen priests are not celibate. He could have accepted a day job. Priests have worked as secretaries, teachers, therapists, musicians, or cabdrivers. The precepts instruct us to adhere to "right livelihood"—work that does not harm others—but livelihood, nevertheless. It struck me how little I knew about Leo Garson.

I wanted to ask why he'd changed his mind about watching my stunt. He had been so clear on finding no pleasure in simulated danger when I invited him that I could imagine the gaffer clapping a hand over his open mouth. And yet he had dragged himself out of bed before dawn to stand in the cold in unwelcome fear.

But before I had the chance, he got in a question of his own, "So, what do *you* think of our fine digs?" It wasn't merely a pleasantry; he seemed to seriously want to know.

I considered my response. "Like you said in your letter, 'Too good to be true! . . . Our neighbors are big-time lawyers, architects, and gallery owners who pay a bundle for their spaces. We're on the edge of the Financial District, in one of the few brick buildings that survived the earthquake, a place with a sexy history, and a courtyard! Prime property! It'd rent for thousands a month. And the landlord is letting us have it for free. Things like that don't happen in real life. Why give it to us?'"

"Curious, isn't it," he said. "Wait till you see the inside." He turned toward the great red madrone double doors. A dagger of sunlight cut through the fog and vanished. It struck the brass knobs on the door, making them shine like fire. As if even the heavens were saying this place was too good to be true. The sun was as narrow as a spotlight, echoing the one that had shown me Mike on the roof.

"Roshi," I said, "I saw this building from my start point when I was getting ready for my gag. There was a man with curly red hair. Walking on the roof!"

Leo nodded.

"You know?" I said, amazed.

"Yes."

"Who is he?"

"Eamon Lafferty."

Eamon? Lafferty? Had Mike ever used those names? He'd once sent me drafts of stories for a creative writing class he'd taken his sophomore year. Had he used that name for one of his characters? Had he ever known someone with a name even remotely like that? Was there any resonance, in any way? Eamon. I'd have remembered Mike using a name like that. "Eamon Lafferty? Who's he?"

"He's our landlord."

CHAPTER 3

"Leo, are you saying this Eamon Lafferty owns our building? He's the one leasing us this space for free?"

"The same." Even in his traditional black Japanese jacket and loose black pants, he looked like an amused elf masquerading as a Zen priest. His hazel eyes were wide apart, intense, his mouth crooking into a grin. Zen practice is about being alive in the moment, after all, and downright delighted with this moment is how Leo appeared.

But not me. Maybe it was my years in the movie business that made me automatically suspicious, or, more likely, one could say the business and I had been a good fit in that department. In my mind, *too good to be true* wasn't a windfall but a warning. I glanced around the oh-so-desirable courtyard, with its huge pots sporting mature Japanese maples, at the freshly scrubbed brick walls, and those very impressive doors. "Eamon Lafferty has spent money—a *lot* of it from the looks of things—to redecorate this place from whatever was here. A cabdriver just told me about its reputation for eerie sounds, and snakes! He called it a 'bad vibes building.'"

Leo laughed. "'Bad vibes.' I haven't heard that term in years. Whatever, we've got a great place here; you're right, Eamon really got it in shape for us."

Leo's enthusiasm made me all the more wary. "You're telling me he went to some amount of trouble, and no small expense, to take this choice property off the market, forgo an outrageous rent from some law firm or boutique, in order to offer it to you for free? What is he, a Zen fanatic?"

"Don't think he'd know Zen from sushi. Can't swear to that. When I gave him a *zafu* to sit on he cantilevered himself down like he was lowering a grand piano out a window. Like he'd think twice before trying it again. Not that he complained; all he talked about was the lease."

"The lease? What's in the lease?"

"Nothing. No prohibitions, no rent for six months."

"And then?"

"Then we discuss it. That's all. Don't be so suspicious, Darcy. If the rent is too high, we'll pick up the Buddha and move. We don't have anything invested in this location. In six months we'll have a *sangha* of people who'll help us find another place if we need it. If they have to come sit in a storefront, they'll be ready to do it then. It's a no-lose situation."

I shook my head slowly. "Oh, Leo, you so tempt the fates."

He laughed again, but there was a little nod at the end of it telling me he recognized I wasn't entirely wrong. This Eamon Lafferty might be well intentioned, but Leo still was a fate tempter. Had he been the abbot of a Japanese monastery five hundred years ago, he would have been in his element parsing the Heart Sutra: *Form is no different than emptiness, emptiness no different than form,* and seeing the essential emptiness of all things. But in twenty-first-century San Francisco, expounding on emptiness while crossing Broadway would likely get him splattered all over the intersection.

Tempting fate had gotten Leo in trouble before. I knew of three instances, and I'd met him only a few months ago. But here I was, his assistant, and the job of the roshi's assistant is to take care of him. It was good he had in me a skeptical one. "Eamon Lafferty? Where is he now?"

"Gone, I'd guess."

"Gone?"

Leo laughed. "Not *gate, gate, paragate.*"

"Not gone, gone, gone beyond, huh?" I said, roughly translating from the Heart Sutra.

"No gah-tays. He'll be back tonight. That's one reason I'm glad you're here now. He's organized a reception for the Zen Center."

"A reception? Like for a gallery?"

He nodded.

Stranger yet, this guy who was not Mike. "It's not like you've got a cluster of waiting students here. Who are we going to receive?"

"Everyone on the block for a start. Maybe everyone in town. Eamon put a welcome notice in one of the free papers."

"So it really is a wine and cheese event—"

"Tea and sweets. But essentially the same. It's kind of him to do this, to announce the opening of the zendo in a way we could never afford to do." The other side of Leo's fate tempting was the quality of statements like this, the way his years of meditation had shown him how to step back and look objectively before he spoke. He'd made pronouncements before that I'd definitely disagreed with. I'd even once barreled over him when he was too sick to do anything about it. But this assessment of his was different. It was the only time I had ever heard him speak as if he was trying to convince himself.

I stared at the zendo, this suspiciously desirable building. For an instant I could almost see those snakes slithering out under the doors.

Leo had sunk into silence. Suddenly, as if he'd come to a decision, he spoke more directly. "We're here to be available to workers in the Financial district and the Barbary Coast, plus all the people who live around here in North Beach, on the Embarcadero, in Chinatown. It's not like crowds of them will stumble into this courtyard and spot our sign, right?" He nodded at the little black plaque next to the doors.

"Even if they're looking for it."

"The reception is a gift."

It was the kind of gift Mike would think of. When I was in sixth grade, in the throes of middle school and miserable about an eighth grade boy who couldn't be bothered about me, Mike, a big high school sophomore, had staged a birthday party for me in Golden Gate Park with two of his friends' bands. One of them wrote a song for me. Everybody came from my class, plus the vaunted eighth graders, and enough of Mike's friends to make the affair seem very adult to us. Ever after I was "the girl who threw that really cool party."

But this reception, it wasn't Mike's doing. Because no matter how much I wanted Eamon Lafferty to magically turn out to be Mike, that wasn't going to happen. But it made me think better of Eamon Lafferty. "When is this reception?"

"Five to seven."

"Tonight?"

"You can see why I'm so glad you arrived early." Leo turned toward the double doors, then paused and looked at me. "Eamon Lafferty, is he one of your family's redheads?"

There's a bond between a student and her teacher. When I'd moved to New York to study with Yamana-roshi, I had made the decision that I would be up-front about everything. When I was passed over for a gig, I admitted wishing for pins and voodoo. When I dumped a boyfriend without warning or decent reason, I 'fessed up in front of Yamana in a way I'd never done with the guy. When I came home from a set with the gift of Duffy, now *my* Scottie, his first walk was to the zendo. But I had never told Yamana-roshi that when I was sixteen, Mike walked out of the house one Thursday night a few weeks after my cable car leap and vanished.

Two or three times I had headed to the zendo, intending, finally, to reveal this overriding issue of my life, but when it came down to it, I just couldn't. Zen teaches that thoughts are merely thoughts, to see them, feel the bodily sensation, and let them go. But there were thoughts I couldn't bear to face, and memories I couldn't bear to give up.

Leo was my teacher now. I had moved back to San Francisco because he needed an assistant at his new zendo and because I wanted to study with him. Yet though I had already trusted Leo with life and death, I didn't tell him about Mike, either. Nothing more than a passing mention. "No, there's no Eamon Lafferty in my family. My oldest brother, John, is a cop, Gary's a lawyer, my sisters Katy and Janice are married, but not to Laffertys. And Grace, the one nearest to me, is married to being a doctor. So, no, no Laffertys. But I'm anxious to see this guy at the reception," I said, in the understatement of the century. But still I didn't tell him why. Instead I followed him through the doors into the zendo.

Beyond the vestibule, Leo's footsteps paused, like the catch in a hiccup, then resumed. Inside, I saw why. The zendo was a beautiful room: high beamed ceiling, weathered red-brick walls, the wood floor polished to a high gloss. On it lay four round black cushions—*zafus*—on rectangular black mats—*zabutons*. Near the back window, a small teak table held the statue of the Buddha.

I thought for a moment that we would sit *zazen*. Instead Leo turned to me. "I watched you this morning do something that most people would be too frightened to do."

I was about to protest—my training, all my experience—but he held up a palm and went on. "Then the director said something and you looked terrified. You remember. What happened?"

I started, just as I had when Robin Sparto confronted me. If Leo hadn't asked me directly, I'd never have mentioned it; maybe if he'd broached it somewhere other than in the zendo, I'd have avoided it. But now, here, I understood how I kept my hopes and memories of Mike to myself. "He made a crack about my cable car leap."

"You're doing another stunt?"

"No, it was my first stunt when I was sixteen. It's a long story."

He laughed. "Then we'd better sit down."

I followed him up the stairs to his room and settled on a cushion while he sat cross-legged on his futon.

"So?" he prompted.

"It was a Sunday in February, in that one week when suddenly it's like summer, you know? Warm, sunny, suddenly not raining like it has been for the past month. I had to wait weeks for the weather to clear, so I remember well. If I do say so, it was a classy gag: the cable car leap! I've never seen anyone else do it, not before, not since," I said, suddenly back in the thrill of a sixteen-year-old's planning. "Here's the setup: one cable car is going uphill, the other's coming down. Powell's steep there, but at the cross streets it's flat. So you jump onto the roof of the uphill car just as it starts to move off the cross street. Because the brakeman is busy letting out the brake, he doesn't notice till it's too late. By that time I was onto the downhill car. When I touched down on its roof, the momentum carried me across the intersection with the car and gave me enough to jump, catch a tree limb at the corner, swing, and disappear before anyone could react."

"Just like that? All that fell into place for you?" Leo was leaning forward, staring at me.

"Not hardly. The gag looked like three easy steps. But it took me months to plan. I had to check the schedules to see where the cars passed each other. Then find the right intersection. I got a friend to park his dad's truck at the corner. I dented the hood and the roof on my run. Luckily, it had a few nicks already. I spent one entire day timing the streetcars: how long it took from the moment the car came over the rise into the cross street till it stopped; how many seconds it sat if there were no passengers getting off, before it started up again. How long it would take me to run onto the pickup and jump to the cable car, and then where the car would have to be when I started my run. And where the downhill car had to be. The whole thing was a timing gag. Cable car trips can vary a lot. Cars break down, brakes fail, bunches of tourists get on or off and throw the car off schedule, *my* schedule. The day I did the gag I waited so long it was almost dark before everything meshed right. My friend with the video camera had said he was leaving three times by then. Half the people I'd told about it had already left. But I couldn't rush it. Everything had to be perfect. I knew I'd only get one shot at it."

"And you could have fallen under the cars and been sawed in three pieces!"

"Well, that, too," I said, brushing off his comment just as I would have Mom's, had she found out before finding out didn't matter anymore. "But I was sixteen, and personal injury wasn't a possibility. It could have been bad, I realized later, but it wasn't. Nothing bad happened. It did go perfectly. It looked effortless. It was like flying. Like winning the gold. Like, you know, you dream so long about how something will be, and then it not only turns out that way, but better, much better. It changed my life, showed me and my friends that I could do whatever I set my mind to, and, not incidentally, hooked me on stunt work.

"See, it wasn't just about jumping from car to car and down; the key was to make it look easy—that's what stunt work is. It's what made me a star. Well, sort of . . ." I mumbled, suddenly embarrassed by my boastfulness.

Leo was still staring. His expression hovered between shock and distress. He sat there, unmoving.

"Leo, I knew what I was doing. I wanted to impress the guy with the camera and, well, show my favorite brother, who'd gotten awed by a school friend of mine, that I was big-time, too. These days, I would have had the video all over the web, but then I had to make do with letting word slip to the kids who'd do the spreading for me."

"What happened after?" His voice was so flat it hardly sounded like him.

"Nothing." Maybe that was the truth. I could never be sure it wasn't the truth. How could I know?

"Nothing? Really? No consequences?"

"My parents didn't find out till so much later that other things overshadowed it. One of the kids was sure that the cable car company would get me, but the last thing they wanted was to publicize car jumping. The kids were impressed, and I used the video to talk my way into my first stunt job."

He didn't move. Then he repeated, "No consequences?"

All acts have consequences. That's the law of karma. Maybe he meant just that. There was no way he could know anything more. I flushed with humiliation. I felt like my chest was caving in. Leo looked like Dad might have looked, if he had found out before Mike's disappearance erased everything else.

What he said was, "I'm planning to have the ceremony of feeding the Hungry Ghosts." He didn't ask if I saw the connection. "Usually, it coincides with Halloween, and kids—and adults—come in costumes. The priest walks in, accompanied by attendants who shout to get the attention of the ghosts. The kids love that. But, of course, that's not the point. You know what the hungry ghosts look like?"

"Creatures with huge bellies and tiny necks."

"Creatures who are always hungry, who can never get enough. We don't shoo them away; we don't hide from them. We call them. We feed them. We set up a table at the far end of the zendo, away from the altar."

He waited as if expecting me to ask why, but I didn't ask.

"We don't feed them from the altar, from our teachings, from what we want to give them; we feed them what they can accept. We feed them, and then, Darcy, we let them go free. The ghosts are, of course, ourselves."

CHAPTER 4

WHEN I PASSED through the great madrone doors at 4:30 P.M., the zendo was gone. In its place was a startlingly faux zendo, an illusion. A thick woolen rug simulated the wide plank flooring beneath it. Padded folding chairs in floor-length black slipcovers stood where the mats had been. In front of the wall we would be facing as we sat zazen stood a translucent veil that looked like it was made of crystal. Through it I could see the brick wall. With a step to one side, the wall was gone, replaced by mirrors. Another step and it was an opaque silver wall. Servers took positions behind a Brobdingnagian *tetsubin*. Most tetsubin—little iron Japanese teapots—served a single soul or two over a single thought. Tea was poured into delicate cups and sipped with attention. When the pot was empty, more hot water was poured over the leaves for a second, more subtle brew. Tetsubins connected teacher and student, friends discussing the dharma or dreams. The pots were luxuries made to enhance the delicacy of a private moment. This was something on a different scale.

Whiffs of sandalwood floated by and were gone. From the far end of the room came the dissonant notes of a song for *O-koto*, a zither-like Japanese harp.

My mind kept jumping from smell to no smell, expected melody to individual notes, from this carpeted faux zendo to this morning's real one and back, as if trying to discern which was real and which the illusion.

"What do you think?" Leo seemed to have materialized from the ether. He was wearing the same jacket and drawstring pants he'd had on this morning, but now with a white shirt that gave him a more formal air.

"It's brilliant! Life is illusion? A materialization of Zen? Or a dig at dilettantes expecting wine, cheese, and a soupçon of enlightenment—insight without discomfort? Take your pick. Plus, it's gorgeous. The veil alone— reality, self, illusion. I love it! People will be talking about it for weeks. What about you?"

"The artist really put herself into it. It's a lovely gift," he said, looking slowly around again. He was smiling but, I sensed, in the way of one given too great a gift, one with inherent demands.

I wondered what those demands would turn out to be. "Eamon Lafferty," I said, "must have paid a lot for this."

Before Leo could comment, the double doors opened and guests blew in like leaves at dusk. A fiftyish woman with shoulder-length monochromatic blonde hair, wearing a black silk suit—I pegged her as one of the lawyers—was followed by a college-aged woman of Asian descent arm in arm with a big brick of a guy who could have been a central casting thug. Leo stepped toward them and extended a hand. "It was very good of Eamon to invite you. There's tea in the fine pot he's provided and something to nibble on. Look around. Ask me anything you like. I am Leo Garson, the priest here, by the way . . ."

I was impressed with Leo's ability to make everyone welcome, giving credit even as he detached himself from any responsibility for the surroundings, yet at the same time indicating it was his place and he was in charge.

Hands were extended, names given. Dark-suited attorneys with drawn faces mixed with tan-clad architects and languid gallery owners, along with more colorful dealers in antiques, designer furniture, and tribal carpets. I found myself following Leo's example, listening as Jeffrey Hagstrom, who ran a shop down the street, explained why our building had survived the great earthquake and fire that destroyed much of the city in 1906: "Barbary Coast. Built on rock, so the earthquake didn't do much, built with brick, so the fire wasn't bad. That's how come we're standing here, how come this building's still standing." A short, square realtor who made a steady living on the turnover on this block alone predicted: "Be here at Christmas and you'll be the old-timers. The thing . . . is . . ." She stared at the doorway.

Behind us conversations faltered. With everyone else, I turned to the open doorway. I gasped.

Mike.

There he was! Alive, healthy, smiling.

I couldn't breathe; my heart banged against my ribs. I couldn't move; I could barely keep myself from throwing my arms around him and hugging him for every one of the long-gone years, waiting for him to nudge me and do that flicker-of-an-eye thing I had called the cut-rate wink, to tell me everything—how sorry he was, how hard he'd tried to contact me. Memories, emotions, reactions broke over me like waves in a hurricane. Tears welled. Through them, I could see his hair was still as dark a red as mine, but that he was thicker than he'd been at twenty, wore a black jacket over jeans that was more San Francisco–conservative than he'd ever have imagined for himself. We'd go down to the dunes just like we did as kids and laugh about it later.

My tears blurred him. He was slipping out of focus.

I wiped my eyes, and the instant was gone. He wasn't Mike at all, not even what Mike might have looked like, had he chosen a career in real estate or finance. I took a sip of tea and desperately wished my cup was filled with Dad's Irish, the stuff Mike and I siphoned from the bottle "to keep us warm" during our major life discussions out in the dunes beyond the Great Highway.

Behind me people were laughing. The reception had come to life again as if someone had hit Play. The man who had to be Eamon Lafferty moved out of the doorway toward Leo. His walk was not Mike's lope of adventure, but the stroll of the laird. His red curls, tighter than mine, sneaked over his collar. He greeted Leo with a westernized bow, and drew Leo's attention to the room as if asking his opinion. That need for reassurance made me like him better. The guests were talking again, but they hadn't completely taken their eyes off Mike—off *Eamon Lafferty*—as if all of them were as transfixed as I.

Even Leo was riveted.

"Who is she?" asked the short realtor, whom I'd totally forgotten.

Now I realized that the guests weren't enthralled with Mike—with *Eamon!*—but by the woman he was introducing to Leo.

Eamon Lafferty stepped back, opening a clear shot to the woman. All the fuzziness cleared; the picture shifted into its proper alignment. I laughed. The woman was about my height, 5'7", my age, very thin, and altogether stunning. She was Tia Dru, and as long as I had known her—since we were fourteen—she'd had that startling effect on people. She was the only girl who'd ever left Mike speechless.

"Tia!" I said, putting a hand on her arm.

"Darcy? What are you doing here? I heard you'd left the city for good."

"I have a gig in the movie they're doing here, up on Broadway." I could have said, *I'm the abbot's assistant.* I chose not to check Leo's reaction.

"You're still doing stunt work? More power to you." To the men, she said, "Darcy was already a S.A.G. card stunt double when I had a bit part in a film."

"In a couple of scenes that you utterly stole!" I laughed. "The star—I forget her name—was *so* pissed."

Tia grinned. "She was. It was like the dog stealing the show. Bet she never worked with a kid or dog again." Tia hadn't been a kid then, and both Leo and Eamon Lafferty seemed to understand that. The camera veering to Tia: it went without saying.

"What kind of stunt were you doing?"

I told them about the high fall. Be within the moment, Leo would have said. But I was paying scant attention to my explanation, more to the memory of Tia's ability to deflect the spotlight while never losing any light. But mostly I found myself struggling not to stare at Eamon Lafferty's dark brown eyes, his wider-than-Mike's cheekbones, his laugh that was just a bit slower than the way Mike anticipated punch lines. Or maybe it was that Mike had anticipated *my* punch lines.

"While I was waiting for my Go call this morning, the spotlight crossed the roof here, and I saw you walking across it," I said to him.

"Really," he replied, for the first time focusing entirely on me. He hesitated before adding, "And you could still go on with your stunt? I thought stuntmen did a sort of mental dry run right before they started, like athletes."

"They *are* athletes, you clod." Tia poked Eamon's arm and laughed in that way that included everyone in our little group. I felt sure that Eamon had been on the verge of asking something: why I was looking at his roof, or what I'd seen. But, as she'd always done, Tia transformed the situation, and the moment when he might have said more than he'd intended had passed.

Instead, he shifted back to smiling at Tia, as if I didn't exist. I was still half trying to regain the moment when he was Mike, when I was hugging him, when—

Leo raised his voice. "So you met on a movie set?"

"Met again. Darcy and I were in high school together. We were the two special admissions girls in our class, and we steered clear of each other."

I tried to focus, to take in what she was saying, and heard myself slipping into Tia-speak: "But as a kid on an athletic entry into a very serious academic school, I had so little free time I conjugated Latin in the bathroom stall. I still can't hear *'amo, amas, amat'* without having the urge to pee." The rest of the reception guests were talking in groups, but they might as well have been silent, watching Tia; they couldn't keep their eyes off her.

She shifted away from me and I gasped, caught myself, bobbled my teacup, and turned away to cover it all. Tia was holding a cane. I couldn't believe it! It wasn't right! Not Tia Dru! Why would she need a cane? She was magic, meant to soar. How could she be reliant on a piece of metal?

I made a production of getting a napkin for the tea on my hand. Maybe it was because I'd already been knocked off-center by Eamon, but I felt even more out of focus now. Tia Dru, what was going on?

Maybe, I told myself, the cane's only temporary. But it wasn't the kind of cane you get and toss away in a week. I focused on Eamon, then on Leo, all the while trying to see past them to Tia, trying not to stare. She gave the appearance of not leaning on the cane, or on anything else. She was thin in a way that was close to malnutrition, and yet there was always an allure in that near-need for nurture paired with her casual sensuality. Her hair, pale brown, parted in the center, was cut to cup her face. Her khaki shawl draped over a scoop-necked black silk T-shirt, a black skirt, and a little butter-brown leather shoulder purse. That attire should have described a staid, safe woman; instead it looked like clothes she couldn't wait to tear off, to dive off the high board, to race to the beach, to slowly beckon a lover. She'd always had the aura of a woman who'd dare death without a second thought, who'd risk all and never look back.

Her fearlessness, the sense of freedom she projected, had been too much for the rest of us. Incomprehensible, really. She asked for nothing, making anyone else who did want *something*—maybe a lot of it—sure that she was hiding, suppressing, avoiding, escaping a need so gaping that it would swallow her unless we could save her.

It was Mike who summed it up one night when I was supposed to be doing statistics homework and he was standing by the door to my room. "You know the Chinese saying: if you save a man from drowning, you're responsible for him for the rest of his life?"

I'd nodded, forty-five percent of a sample of six thousand questionnaire respondents swept out of my mind.

"You think it's a warning to avoid barnacles, right?"

It had taken me a moment to see the rescued man as a human barnacle attached to the bottom of his benefactor. But I had learned long ago to give my nod well before actual understanding, lest he think of me as a mere kid.

"Untrue. The Chinese were no fools; they knew how seductive it is being the savior. You know how good you feel when you're the one who can set everything right, how hot shit you feel, above it?" He had grinned then. We were both laughing. "Who's saved and who's hooked?" Even then I was startled by his acuity, he to whom his shrewdness so clearly applied.

It wasn't Mike's only observation about Tia. Looking at her now, I realized that he'd talked about her a lot for a girl four years younger, at a time when four years is as good as decades.

But she hadn't seemed sixteen back then, and she didn't seem near forty now. She was tied down to no age, limited to no group. And when saving was foisted upon her, she was always grateful. And she never, ever asked for more. She was the perfect savee, but she never took her salvation for granted.

Once, I knew, she'd had a run-in with the IRS. I never knew what it was all about exactly, just that afterwards one of my brothers walked into the office of a tax attorney friend and was awed by a shimmering glass room divider that Tia had made in thanks.

Art installation! Of course! Tonight's faux zendo was Tia's work! Now things fell into place: why she'd arrived with Eamon Lafferty. Why he'd spent way more money than was necessary and was still smiling. Why there was an ephemeral quality to the work. Why Leo was already talking with her like she was an old friend. And why I felt the same stab of jealousy that had pierced me as a teenager when Tia had charmed everyone, including me.

As if to demonstrate, Tia now smiled at Jeffrey, the guy who'd told me about our building surviving the 1906 earthquake. And, with that surprised smile of a chosen one, he hurried over.

"I'm sure you all know Jeffrey Hagstrom, but I'll do the propers anyway," she said. "Jeffrey is the histo-architectural expert on the Barbary Coast."

He must have been in his early thirties but still had a baby face. He flushed as she spoke. It was hard to imagine him as known, much less well-known.

"He's the consultant to the producers of *Barbary Nights*."

A rouge of embarrassment bloomed on Hagstrom's round, pallid face. "I answer their questions. What they do with my answers—"

"*Barbary* is like all companies." The voice was tenor, the accent was British, the speaker was the central casting goon who'd come in with the college student. Was he part of the movie company? I hadn't seen him this

34

morning, but it wasn't as if I had been eyeing the entire crew at 5:30 A.M. "Our aim is to entertain, not to footnote."

Jeffrey stumbled back, all bloom gone.

"Our real Barbary Coast never loses its intrigue, does it?" Tia said, barely missing a beat, as if that had been the thug's point all along. "No district in all of San Francisco has changed as dramatically as this respectable street. But suppose"—Tia looked directly at the deflated Hagstrom, drawing her hands apart as if she were opening the possibilities—"suppose we were right here a hundred fifty years ago, what would we see?"

"A lot more of you than we do now."

To a one we stared at Hagstrom, as if to say: did that double entendre come from your little pink mouth? Then we laughed, some of us more than others, the thug not at all.

Tia smiled, perfectly comfortable with her barnacle. "So Darcy and I are ladies of the night?"

"It's the nineteenth century; there aren't any other kinds of women here," Jeffrey said, his color returning.

"And you gentlemen?"

"Eamon, you're just off a freighter back from the Far East. You're still lurching from two years at sea and all that gold banging around in your pockets. You can't wait to spend that money—"

"On us?" Tia asked with a wink at Eamon.

"You and drink, not necessarily in that order," Jeffrey answered for him.

"And the abbot?" She gave a smile to Leo and let it linger a moment. She seemed the Tia of old, delectably at ease in her utter control. But I couldn't help notice her hand tighten on her cane.

Jeffrey accepted a cup of tea from a passing waiter. "Abbot, of course you'd be a preacher. There are a few missions at the edges of the Barbary

Coast, though it's such a lost cause you'll be focusing on the heathens in Chinatown."

"Converting them?"

"Ultimately. But, more practically, setting up safe houses. Life is much, much better for the white prostitutes here than the Chinese in Chinatown. No, really—" he held up a hand to forestall my comment. "If you're Chinese, you were kidnapped or sold by your family, shipped to a strange country, plunked into a crib on the street, and screwed until you're too diseased to be worth anything. When that point comes"—he paused for effect, and a sip of tea—"your pimp carries you to a room with no window, maybe an underground storage space. He lays you on a slab, places a pot of tea and an oil lamp next to you, and walks out. You hear the door lock. The only light is the dimming glow from the lamp. You just hope you die before the oil burns away."

I shivered and clutched my teacup tighter, trying not to feel the agony of a woman abandoned and waiting for death in total blackness. It was a moment before I realized that Jeffrey had stopped talking, that a horrified silence had descended on our group. Tia's hand jerked and for the first time she actually leaned on her cane. She was looking at Jeffrey, not with horror, or even distress as he stood in the damning silence, but with the kind of panic I had seen only on the faces of other women. After what seemed ages, she walked, now relying on that cane she had been careful to appear not to need at all. She went to Jeffrey's side and put her arm through his.

Her sweet gesture resuscitated the group. Eamon signaled the waiter to bring tea. "And you, Jeffrey?" I asked, taking pity on him, "what's your job?"

"Me? Well, I'm a small man, of the sort that needs money to protect them. I, uh, I own this building, this saloon. This room here—back then it actually *was* a saloon. So I own the saloon and you ladies are hustling drinks here and guiding our guest upstairs, since the entire focus of the Barbary Coast is to separate a sailor from his booty."

"Surely a sailor—Eamon—couldn't spend it all in one night, even on one of us." Tia's laugh sounded only a bit forced. She freed Jeffrey's arm and let her hand rest in his pocket, as if to assure him she was still there.

"Even on both of us," I said.

"I'll have a helluva time trying," Eamon said, grinning at Tia.

Jeffrey didn't smile. "Not spend, Eamon, be relieved of. You're lured in here by my barker." Jeffrey nodded at the thug. "Darcy entices you upstairs. Or maybe—sorry, Eamon"—now he did smile—"you don't even get that far. Maybe my bartender gives you a Mickey Finn and drops you through— You know back then the Bay was just a few yards from here?"

"You mean it's all filled land for the next four blocks to the Bay, right?" Tia asked helpfully, without looking up from fumbling with her cane and purse and shawl. She gave Jeffrey a small pat on his side, the way a mother might to assure her child he was fine, then she moved far enough to be out of his limelight.

"Filled land is a slippery concept," he said with a little grin. "This—my saloon—was—is—on the waterfront or close to it. Let's say close to. Close enough for me to invest in a subterranean alley from the basement to the docks. For the likes of you, Eamon. I knock you out, drop you through a trapdoor onto a cart waiting there, on top of the other victims. The cart rattles down the rail and dumps the lot of you into a ship's hold. By the time you wake up, all you see is the Golden Gate slipping away behind you and the whole Pacific ahead. You've been on land for an hour, max." Jeffrey Hagstrom was back in his stride now, as if Tia's touch had transfused him.

"Shanghaied," Leo said.

Everyone laughed. The volume of its sound made me aware that our circle had grown, with Jeffrey now holding court before half the guests.

I had assumed that Tia was with Eamon. They had walked in as one; they looked perfect together, their contradictions creating balance: his tall sturdiness grounding her fragility, her plain khaki shawl and long skirt grounding his expensive jacket with the narrow band of navy and char-treuse handkerchief just peeking from the pocket, her understated beauty reflecting back on his flair.

"The way to the dock was just large enough for the carts," Jeffrey went on. "Luckily the ground slants downhill to the Bay."

Jeffrey had that about-to-make-it look as he held forth on the tunnel.

"It's still here, isn't it?" Leo asked.

"Oh no, those carts—"

Leo grinned. "No, no. I mean, the tunnel. It's still down there, right beneath us, right?"

CHAPTER 5

THERE WASN'T even time for Jeffrey Hagstrom to offer Leo directions to the old tunnel. Instantly, Eamon Lafferty led the charge out of the zendo into the courtyard. The light in the hall was slightly brighter than in the zendo, marking the edges of Tia's body as I walked out behind her. She used her cane, and I could see the slight quiver in her arm as she leaned against Jeffrey, letting him support her in a way that would once have horrified her. She paused at the door, turned back momentarily, then moved on. Her jaw was tighter than I'd ever seen it.

In school, I hadn't known her well, but I'd run into her a lot, at the kind of parties we didn't mention to parents, at track meets and tests, and, for a month our senior year, in a play. Not once had a wrinkle of hesitation lined her face. She had skated on her ability to see things before they changed and to adjust so fast that she was on to the future while those around her were clambering out of the past.

But now it was not that she had seen the end of the tunnel, rather that she'd realized it had an end.

I felt so sad for her. Or was I imagining her distress? Truth was, I was still so unnerved from the instant of "seeing Mike," I was hardly a decent judge of anyone else's emotions.

We all kept walking, out the door into the courtyard.

The potted trees threw fingers of darkness across the stones as our group followed Eamon behind the building to the fire escape I had used this morning. There were fewer than a dozen of us left now.

"It'll be back here," Eamon announced, and the rest of us piled up behind him. He moved sideways, hands behind his back, scanning the base of the back wall and murmuring monosyllables that suggested impending discovery. I kept expecting Jeffrey to take over again. But Jeffrey seemed content to let Eamon drag out his failure.

It was Leo who spotted a grunge-encrusted half door behind one of the tree pots. Eamon leapt forward to do the pulling, and the effort took all of his body weight and the help of a crowbar someone fetched. The door was only thirty inches high. A tiny flashlight materialized and its straw of illumination shone into a shaft narrowed with slick, hardened black substances. It looked about ten feet long. I'm not claustrophobic, but what came to mind were those grim stories of children falling into wells and fire departments lowering ropes and drilling parallel holes and none of it ever able to save them. Similar foreboding thoughts must have crossed half the dozen minds here as we all peered down into the blackness. One woman said something about wearing high heels, a man muttered about it being better by daylight, someone else stammered of dinner plans and made a beeline for the street. Flashlights glistened off slimy walls. Jumping into that chute would be like going through a mummy's wrappings with a hole in the bottom. As unappealing as it looked, still the seduction of the tunnel's lurid history kept us poised on the edge, that and the unwillingness to be the first to admit fear. I glanced hopefully over at Leo, but there was an odd look of determination on his face. It wouldn't be Leo who'd save us. Tia tottered at the edge. Her jaw was set, her gaze unwavering, like the Tia of old. "It can't be more than ten feet down!" She pulled off her shawl and thrust it into the nearest hand.

I couldn't let her do it. "Make way!" I called out. "Professional here. Stunt double into the hole!" I held a hand out for one of the torches.

"Stop!" Jeffrey called from behind us. "You're in the wrong place. The entrance is here."

I stepped back so fast I smacked into Leo.

"It's over here, on this side of the courtyard," our expert insisted.

We hurried to the front of the courtyard, in the corner behind a five-foot-high brick wall that connected to the entry arch. Two of the potted maple trees stood on the metal doors. Relieved as I was, a dull wave of disappointment washed through me at the sight of this prosaic entryway, the type of loading hatch found in sidewalks in all big cities.

"Then what was that back there?" Tia demanded sharply.

"Sewer, probably." Jeffrey bit his lip. "Or just a hole. This area is sprinkled with little holes like that, particularly here where rock meets fill. Tunnels made it worse."

"You've been in the tunnel?" Tia demanded.

"Well, no." He moved another step back. "You know I'm not crazy about closed spaces. The entry to the tunnel's here. I can tell you all about it, but, well, I'm not going to go down there with you."

"You could have told us before Darcy almost jumped into God knows what." Tia grabbed her shawl from his hand and nearly smacked his face with it as she flung it around her shoulders. It was almost as if all her concern for him earlier had never been.

"Here! I've got it open!" Eamon pulled the big metal sheet up, letting it clank open to the cement. Again the flashlight circled around, but this chamber was the size of a boxcar, with a metal ladder—clearly a later addition—on the wall. Tia was over the edge so quickly the metal cover was still reverberating. Lowering herself onto the same leg step after step, she steadied herself with arms that were working over capacity. Eamon followed, then I, and Leo and four others, till the tunnel was crowded and the small rhomboid of dusky light wasted in illuminating our own bodies. The odor of must and decay was so thick it was hard to breathe and made it seem as if everybody who'd passed here on his way to death had left a part of himself, a part I was pulling up my nose.

"To your right," Jeffrey called down. "The tunnel slopes toward the Bay. If you look down, you can still see track marks from the carts, I know."

"Uh-uh! I've seen enough," a woman said. "I'm not staying in any grave till I have to." She grabbed on to the ladder and was up over the edge before anyone reacted.

A narrow band of light shone on the damp earth and stone walls. The stone was encased in an unnatural grime that must have been the residue of the nineteenth-century traffic and its passengers' blood and vomit. The still-damp mud clung to our shoes, as if trying to hold us here in the same earth as the long-dead sailors and dying prostitutes. I started to breathe through my mouth, but it didn't cut the stench. Someone aimed a light around the edges of the floor and ceiling and held it overhead to scan the tunnel roof for signs of the trapdoor. The dark sucked up the tiny beam of light and the chill echoed the icy water of the Pacific.

"There it is!" The light shone on scratches in the ceiling two yards along that must have been the trapdoor from the saloon-turned-zendo.

"Sheesh! Do you think—"

Suddenly Tia was running down the tunnel. The dark engulfed her. Her heels and her cane clattered erratically. There was a thud—and then a scream.

"Aim the light at her!" Eamon ordered the man who had the other flashlight. But the beam was eaten by the dark in less than two yards.

"Tia?" I called.

She didn't answer.

"Tia!" I yelled. "Give me the light!"

The man with the flashlight started toward me, but a hand grabbed it and vanished into the dark.

I started after.

"It's okay!" It was Leo. "I've got her! Here!"—he aimed the light back so it made a dim path. "Help me get her out of here!"

"I'm fine. Just hit my head," she murmured unconvincingly as Eamon and Leo half carried her, their own feet sliding in the damp mud. Jeffrey was at the top of the ladder, and Leo passed her to Eamon partway up, then with one arm hoisted her far enough for Jeffrey to pull her up and steady her on her feet.

"Get away!" She rammed both fists into Jeffrey's shoulders. He jolted, veered over the edge of the hole, and jerked away. "Just get away from me, Jeff!"

Behind me someone gasped.

"She must have really hit her head," I said, without turning around. The whole thing was so unlike Tia, or at least the Tia I used to know. Never had she come close to anything so uncool with a boyfriend; it would have humiliated her. What was going on?

But by the time I waited my turn and got up the ladder, she had her cane and was barely leaning on it. She was shivering a bit but smiling at Leo, nodding in apparent thanks for something as he walked off.

Eamon patted Tia's back and took off at a lope, leaving her pulling the miserably damp, muddy shawl tighter around her thin shoulders. The stench of earth and decay clung to the shawl.

I grabbed her arm. "Tia, what's going on with you?"

"I'm fine!"

"Really? Lucky for Jeffrey you didn't send him flying down there."

"Jeffrey?" Her face went blank momentarily. "I didn't . . . He wasn't that . . . I wouldn't have let him fall," she said, looking more herself. "He's fine."

I caught her eye. "Listen, you whack your head and you're not always the best judge of what's what. I speak from experience, *experiences*."

She laughed, but it was a forced sound. "I've done worse and survived."

"What I'm saying is—"

"Where are you staying in the city? With your sister . . . with Grace?"

I gave up. It was her life. "At Mom's. But Gracie's living there for now."

"Do you have her phone—"

Eamon pulled up to the curb and waved.

She squeezed my shoulder. "Gotta go. Eamon's driving me home." She turned toward the car, took two unsteady steps, stopped so suddenly she had to grab the cane with both hands. "Come to lunch tomorrow?"

It wasn't an invitation one declines. "Sure."

"Noon?"

"Fine. I'll get you Gracie's number, but if you've got signs of concussion, don't wait to ask Gracie. Heads aren't her specialty."

She laughed, and this time it sounded real. She pulled a business card from her pocket and by the time she extended it to me Tia seemed as in control as she always had. "I'm really looking forward to lunch, Darcy. It's time you came home. So, I'll see you tomorrow." She walked slowly, but without weaving or using her cane, across the pavement, folded up the shawl, and slid into the green convertible.

In the open car, Tia looked just like she had at that high school track meet, sitting next to Mike, grinning as the fog-laden wind blew her silky hair off her face. Eamon hit the gas, and as they drove off, a gust wafted her hair and she leaned in toward him and smiled as if the past ten minutes had never happened, as if the last twenty-five years had dissolved.

I followed them with my gaze, suddenly unable to move. Concern for her, loss of Mike, that glorious moment when I believed Mike had come back, Tia so undone: the whole swirl of emotion engulfed me. I didn't dare take my eyes off the car, lest I come apart.

And then the convertible turned the corner onto Columbus and was gone.

Slowly I retraced their route back to the curb in front of me. But now the parking spot was empty. No car blocked my view of the chair boutique across the street, and Jeffrey Hagstrom running around in the window like a crazy person.

Chapter 6

I was across the street and banging on the shop door before I had time for second thoughts.

Jeffrey Hagstrom looked worse than Tia. Half hidden amid shiny gumball-colored accent chairs, he looked like a disoriented mole frantically rooting in a dahlia bed.

"Did you drop something?"

"What?" He jerked upright, pale round face flushed, eyes quivering as he took me in. "No. Well, nothing important. I was just . . . What are you doing here?"

"I figured you'd lost your mind . . . and you were looking for it." I held my breath.

But I'd guessed right. After a slow double take, he mustered up a shaky grin. He glanced around at the tangle of chairs, hesitated as if about to apologize, then shrugged as if putting his emotional state into words was beyond him. The color was draining from his face now. Seeing him in this light, I realized he was taller than I'd thought, and thinner. But he looked like he would be fat—or should be. His short sandy hair seemed almost painted on. His shoulders sloped so steeply when viewed straight on, his arms seemed to sprout from just below his neck. Everything about him murmured: *Pay me no mind, or if you'd prefer, kick me.*

47

Which was just what Tia had done.

He let his fingers linger on the armrest of a brass pipe throne in the window as if it were the only friend who could be counted on to help him. "Jeffrey," I said, "is the coffee shop down the street still open?"

"I guess."

"Come on, we're going. Coffee'll be the thing for both of us."

"I don't—"

"I was too busy at the reception to eat anything. I'm starved, and I need coffee. You can't refuse me company."

He stood, fingers tightening and releasing the tubular armrest, as if weighing the danger of trusting me as he had Tia. Finally, he jerked his hand free. "Just let me straighten things up." The shop was small for a business with such a narrow specialty stock. To survive in this pricey area Jeffrey would have to sell a lot of chairs made to please the eye rather than the butt. But he hadn't crammed in stock. Each piece stood as if it was the focal point. The effect was to create an awed urgency in the viewer as if he were at a cocktail party of the stars. Even now, well after closing time, Jeffrey moved methodically adjusting chair after chair. The arrangement had to be a work of love, and of art. No wonder Jeffrey and Tia had connected.

But by the time we finally stepped outside, I was thinking, *No wonder he drove her crazy.* Pacific Street was as empty as a back lot at night. No traffic, just swaths of curb with no parked vehicles, no one walking but us two. And no lights from the café on the corner, either. "Damn! It's closed!"

Jeffrey made an odd noise I took to be a laugh. "I've got a key."

"You *own* the café?"

"No. Renzo's the block's keeper of the keys. He's got one for my shop, your place, too. Handy when you forget or the alarm goes off. He gives keys to us regulars, you know, in case of emergency."

"Emergency? You mean *food* emergency?"

"Huh? Oh, yeah. Well, for Renzo, there are only two kinds of emergencies: earthquake and lack of coffee. Not in that order." He unlocked the glass door of the Barbary Caffè, a space even smaller than his. Three tiny tables with two round chairs each and a bar packed it.

"Are all these tables ever full?"

"Huh? Oh . . . yeah. But you don't slide your chair back without apologizing to at least three people. Coffee? Food?"

"Is there any?"

Jeffrey managed a laugh. "That would be the third emergency: no food. Focaccia?"

"O-kay!" I sat while he took charge of the espresso maker and put the focaccia bread in the toaster oven. I had the feeling he was glad for the counter separating us, giving him time to pull his mind out of the store— or away from Tia—and focus enough to carry on a conversation with me. The familiar tasks seemed to calm him. He didn't look at home behind the counter, but at least like he was visiting home. With the blinds down and the smell of garlic mixing with the aroma of coffee, the place seemed cozy, particularly after that wretched tunnel. Still, I was shivering, and when he brought the espresso I held the cup to my sternum till it nearly burned.

He passed me the plates with the puffy, steaming bread and we wolfed it. Eating the warm bread together gave the occasion the illusion of normalcy, as if Tia hadn't just lost control or Jeffrey had not been prowling his shop like a crazy man. I wanted to ask him about her: was she on serious pain meds? And the cane! Why was Tia Dru of all people walking with a cane? I took another bite of focaccia.

Before I could swallow, Jeffrey leaned forward, inhaled, and started flinging out questions. "How do you like your Zen space? It's a real coup, don't you think? I tried to get Eamon to turn it into a period bar. He could make a bundle from the tourist trade. The courtyard's a big plus; tourists adore drinking outdoors. But the key is the tunnel! People just eat up that kind of history, I told him."

"You and Eamon are friends?" I asked, amazed. He didn't respond, not at first. In the flurry over the tunnel and Tia, I'd almost forgotten my original question about our too-good-to-be-true zendo site. "He gave us the space. He did a lot of work—"

"He got some breaks," Jeffrey now answered slowly.

"Breaks?"

"Permits and things. You know, the kind of breaks you can get when you're related to the police."

The police? My brother John, the detective? So that was his real question. "Do people assume he's related to my family, the Lotts?"

"He never says that, but if building inspectors make that mistake, he doesn't feel called upon to correct their misapprehension."

I took a sip of espresso and then another, feeling the rush anew. He was fingering his cup but not drinking. "Jeffrey," I said slowly. As he looked up a wary tightness flashed on his face and I wondered which question he was afraid of. "Why did Eamon renovate that space for us? It's a very generous thing for someone to have done, someone who isn't interested in sitting zazen."

"Maybe his reward'll be in heaven."

I laughed. "He'll have to celebrate alone. We don't have heaven."

"Well, then, you're in the Barbary Coast tradition." He almost smiled. "I don't mean to badmouth him. It's his money. And he does let me use the tunnel for storage."

"Storage? It's way too damp and the smell . . . It's like a tomb down there."

"Appropriate. It'd be for stuff of my father's that I don't want but can't throw out . . . yet. Lower it down; forget it. My dad died a couple of years ago. Auto accident. Eamon understands. He knew my father back East; he was a recruit helping Dad close up the lab at Fort Detrick. I was still in high school, so it's not as if I really knew Eamon then. He was just another of Dad's grunts."

"It's nice you have someone to talk with about your father."

Jeffrey's cup stopped halfway to his mouth. He gave an edgy laugh and his cheeks colored again. "Sorry," he muttered. "Thing is, I didn't like the old man. Eamon wasn't crazy about him either."

"Really?" I prompted.

"Dad was military research, weapons-grade. You only need to look at me to know I'm not weapons-grade. In his eyes I was a chronic disappointment, except when I was an acute disappointment. But"—he laughed with a sort of victorious bitterness—"if he could see that I took my inheritance and opened a frivolous chair shop and it's making decent money . . . You know, I'd give up a year of my life to see his reaction."

"That'll be *your* reward in heaven."

He was still a moment, then laughed again. But somehow the act of laughing unsettled his hold on the present and I had the sense he was back in his shop worrying about the arrangement of chairs on his floor grid.

"Jeffrey," I said, pulling him back, "what's going on with Tia? That whole thing in the tunnel—"

"What happened down there?" Suddenly he was all alertness.

"She ran off into the dark, hit her head, and freaked. You saw her carried out. And then, for no reason, she shoved you. Is that in character for her now?"

He leaned forward over the small table. "No. No. I've only known her for a few years. But no."

"You've been dating all that time?"

"No . . . no. I . . . I was going to say we've been friends for those years, but really it's that I've been her friend. She had a temp job at Letterman in the Presidio when I was working there and we saw a lot of each other. When she moved on, we'd get together for coffee every couple of weeks. I was the confidant, the sidekick like in the movies, the pal the girl tells about the guy she's hung up on. There was always some guy. It was like Elisabeth Kübler-Ross's Five Steps for the Romance-Addicted: new excitement, getting serious, things are nice, getting bored, gone."

"What step is Eamon?" The words were out before I thought about how unkind a question it was.

"Eamon? Oh, she's not attracted to him," Jeffrey said, as if discussing her taste in porch furniture. "He's peaked; he has no potential. It's potential that hooks Tia."

"But he did drive her home."

His eyes widened, and it was a moment before he could force out, "After the tunnel?"

I nodded. Damn, how insensitive was I? But I needed to know what the hell was going on before I turned up at Tia's house for lunch the next day. "Tia's accident, Jeffrey, what was it?"

"You don't know? I thought everyone knew."

"No."

He lifted his cup, drained it, and looked coldly at me. "A cable car hit her. She fell and it rolled over part of her pelvis."

"Omigod!" I couldn't . . . anything. I couldn't move, couldn't think. Everything stopped. The paralyzing shock and horror of it turned me icy cold. The scene rushed over me: the brakeman frantically pulling back the lever, passengers screaming. *Lucky to be alive.* The trite phrase floated in my mind. Lucky? Maybe. Lucky because she *made* herself be.

"You okay?" Jeffrey was asking.

I stared down at my coffee. Finally, I managed, "How? Why?"

"How come it hit her? She was running and she slipped."

My cup was rattling now. Running and she slipped; it was too mundane. "How—"

"She said a man was chasing her."

"Who?"

"She insisted she didn't know."

I was still staring, but now I was seeing Jeffrey more clearly, and the distinct lift at the corner of his nose. "But you don't believe she didn't know."

"Oh, no. I do not."

"What do you think happened, then?"

Jeffrey put down his coffee and looked directly at me, as if he was suddenly seeing something he hadn't quite expected. He gave one of those little nods that indicates decision. "You want to know what I really think? I think she did it on a dare—"

"Someone dared her to run in front of a cable car?" I asked incredulously.

"Not someone. A sort of self-dare, to see if she could. Maybe it was a spur-of-the-moment thing; maybe she was running from someone, and when she got near the cable cars she saw a tow truck with a slanted ramp, and on impulse she ran up it and leapt for the top of the cable car. And missed."

I dropped my cup. The heavy ceramic bounced once. The dregs splattered. I watched, numbly. My great cable car stunt.

Jeffrey was saying, "I don't know why she even thought she could leap on a moving cable car."

I knew why.

I had made it look easy.

It's possible that there were worse moments in my life, but I can't remember one.

CHAPTER 7

EARLIER, LEO GARSON had watched Tia Dru drive off with Eamon Lafferty and he had wondered. Then he watched Darcy go off with Jeffrey Hagstrom and noted the pang in his chest. Ghosts come in different forms, ghosts of the past, ghosts of the hoped-for. He hadn't realized that he had assumed Darcy would hang around and that they'd celebrate the opening of the zendo with a stroll into Chinatown for the kind of dinner he'd been dreaming of for six long years. Assumptions, the ghosts of the future.

Now the zendo was empty, the rug and chairs and giant tetsubin gone, the room cleaned, and the zabutons stacked in one corner. The cleaners had waxed the floor before their departure and the smell of lemon wafted invitingly. He could light the oil lamps and the candle and sit in meditation, sit with his ghost.

It was tempting to linger here in this beautiful room with all its potential still ahead. As Eamon Lafferty had said in his initial letter, *With a location like this, on the edge of downtown, a block from the Financial District, from Chinatown, from North Beach, a meditation hall could serve hundreds of San Franciscans.* The letter had not added the obvious: Its abbot could become quite the powerful man, not merely in the city, but in the Zen hierarchy. Lafferty might well have assumed that Leo would be anxious to get even for his six-year exile in the woods. Leo smiled. How often had he told students that guilt does not erase a person's desire for revenge, however undeserved; it merely makes the guilty work harder to justify their desire. He had learned that by looking in the mirror. *To study the Buddha is to study the self. To study the self is to forget the self.*

He let the heavy door shut behind him and stood in the courtyard watching the fog push in like a rug being unrolled across the sky. Fringes of it were beginning to cling to the potted trees—as if he needed reminding of the ghosts of the place, the ghosts of his desires.

Most religions had stories of hungry ghosts, huge-bellied, toothpick-throated creatures—some who fed off the living, some who robbed the tombs and ate the bodies of the dead, but almost all were driven blindly by their greed and thwarted by their self-deception.

All along he'd sensed this site was too good to be true. But he hadn't been able to swallow that truth. Now there was nothing to do but what he had said when he believed he had a choice left. *Don't assume.*

CHAPTER 8

IT WAS 10:00 P.M. when I let myself into my family house. I had one goal: to get to my room without human contact. I couldn't bear to talk about Tia's accident, and at the same time couldn't handle chatting about anything else. The only being who could help me now was Duffy, and as soon as I'd arrived yesterday, Mom had scarfed him up and headed for the Russian River. "A Scottie needs time near the water," she'd declared, as if San Francisco were not on a peninsula.

As I eased through the living room I could hear John, Gary, and Gracie bickering in the kitchen. A normal night chez Lott.

"Dead body," John was complaining. He'd be straddling one of the red vinyl chairs, arms resting on the back, finger ready to point. "Of course it came to us in Homicide, but it's not a homicide. Just another homeless guy with the bad luck to swallow who knows what and do it standing next to a third-floor railing of one of those nineteenth-century staircases, the oval ones."

"What?" The sharpness of Grace's voice meant she was standing by the stove heating stew from the pot Mom always left for hungry kids. She'd be staring at John, as if the force of her gaze could compensate for her being not quite five feet tall and nowhere near one hundred pounds.

"What?" Gary, the lawyer, always pounced on generalizations. Gary was

57

Grace with charm. He'd called her a bulldog; she'd labeled him an opportunistic lapdog. Then he'd laughed at her for her *graceless* terminology. More than once strangers had said the two of them looked like Russian stacking dolls. They were thin, sharp-featured, with straight black Lott hair and the pale blue eyes Mike had called "executioners eyes.'" With them time would grind grooves between the eyes and creases beside the mouth, dividends of anger, long hours of work, or just determination. They also had overlarge earlobes. Mom thought it an adorable trait, but both of them were sensitive about it, which had been a serious mistake for middle children. Now Gary's focus would appear to be on his bowl of stew, but he'd be noting John's every move. "Well, the poison ought to be easy. If your vic swallowed it and dived off the landing, the bottle can't have gone far."

"Gone when we got there. It's not a high-honesty building. Neighbors had hours to boost anything Norris McMahon, that's the vic, didn't crush in the fall. By the time they got around to notifying us, the guy was stiff. Picture it: the vic's lying at the bottom of the stairs for eight, twelve, twenty-four hours, with all of them stepping around him like he was a pile of shit."

"So what did make them call?" Gary asked.

"Huh?"

"Why then?"

John had a way of inhaling like he was dragging mud through a grate. "They said—wait'll you hear this—they said he fell, just then. Whole bunch of them in on that one. Like the guy got rigor on the way down." He let out a huge, world-weary sigh. "And they thought we'd believe it!"

"But if there was a poison—" This from my sister.

"You're missing the point, Gracie! It's not that the vic finds a bottle of lye or who knows what and pops it down—the coroner'll find out sooner or later; it's hardly high-priority—the point is that the neighbors can't be bothered to report a dead body lying by their front door." John let out another great, oldest son sigh. "Forget I mentioned it; you'll never hear about this guy again."

It all seemed so normal, as if Tia Dru had never heard of my cable car stunt and never tried it. I wondered if they even knew about Tia.

WEDNESDAY

I barely made it into the zendo before Leo rang the bell at 6:40 A.M. The only other person there was a fellow sagging into his chair like he'd found a good place to keep warm until Renzo's opened. He looked as sleepy as I was.

They say that one of the reasons for sitting in full lotus position—legs crossed, right foot on left thigh, left foot on right—was so the monks could fall asleep and not topple over. I pulled my legs into position, placed my hand in a *mudra*—left on right, thumb tips barely touching.

My eyes closed; reality slipped away. I was back with Jeffrey Hagstrom listening to him saying he didn't believe Tia when she insisted she didn't know who had chased her. That jolted me awake. I inhaled deeply, hoping the breath would keep me conscious.

But my eyes closed again. I was Tia leaping for the cable car and missing. I snapped awake, inhaled, and focused on my breath till my dream-panic settled.

My eyes closed yet again. I was the homeless victim falling dead over the railing. I bolted awake. After that I wished for sleep, and sat with new waves of guilt. The period lasted an eternity. The guy across from me must have been as relieved as I when the final bell rang. He was out the door before I finished fluffing my cushion.

I blew out the candle, trimmed the wax, stirred and tamped down the ash in the incense bowl. Straightening the mats took only seconds. I took a last look at the too-good-to-be-true zendo and headed upstairs toward the room I had yet to move into.

Leo was crossing the upstairs landing. He'd changed to jeans, black sweatshirt, and a watch cap. "Busted! I've got a coffee date."

I raised an eyebrow. "You've been back in the city how long? You don't waste any time."

He laughed but didn't respond to my tacit query. "There was something else you were going to ask me, right?"

I hadn't planned to mention it, didn't want to at this hour, didn't know where to begin. I swallowed and leaned back against the door to my room and wished I could sink through. "Leo—Roshi—you remember the stunt I was telling you about yesterday, the cable car leap?"

"Yes?"

"And you asked, and I insisted that it didn't have any consequences?"

He nodded.

"Well, I didn't intend this, not in any way. I mean, I never even considered the possibility. But still, well, the thing is, after I did it one of my classmates—well, uh, Tia, from last night—I think she tried it. A couple of years afterwards. I never knew. I was gone by then. She tried to jump the cars. That's how she was injured. The cable car, Leo, it ran into her." I swallowed harder. I thought for a moment that he'd interrupt, give advice, give solace, but he waited so quietly he was almost not there. "She tried it because I made it look easy."

He said, "You don't know that."

"Leo, don't comfort me!"

He inhaled and waited till he caught my eye. "I'm not. You don't know; you only think you know. Maybe your guess is correct, but maybe not. Don't assume."

"I'm going to lunch with her, today. How can she look at me and not see that cable car?"

"Don't assume." He put his hands together, bowed to me, and left.

Don't assume was small comfort. But then, Leo hadn't meant it to be.

I found a gym and worked every machine. Then I downed the strongest coffee I could find. At noon I was outside Tia Dru's flat, still nervous and guilty and trying not to assume. How do you apologize for creating an illusion that ruins a life? *Don't assume*. Still . . . like the header from the turret, I'd push off and deal.

Tia's flat perched on the peak of Pacific Heights, the second-story front of a vintage fourplex that must have cost a fortune. Location alone would have done it, but the heavy-on-the-charm couldn't have hurt. The day was warm for February; the sun was just shoving back the fog that had been tucked around the city. By four this afternoon it would be rolling back across Pacific Heights, heading toward the Barbary Coast to the east. But now, sunlight sparkled off the miniature red roses and the glossy leaves of succulents on the wide tiled steps to Tia's door. *All these steps to pull herself up!*

Don't assume.

The door was open. "Tia!"

"I'm in the kitchen. Come on in!"

Inside, it was all yellows, and padding: over-wide cushioned armchairs in sunflower prints, thick honey carpet, lemony upholstered ladder-backs at the glass dining table. A foot-square ottoman stood between the armchairs where a person more interested in food and drink than comfort would have stationed a coffee table. Vases of bright red and violet freesias were here and there as if left carelessly by someone with armfuls of flowers, and their deep sweet smell came in whiffs. The whole room was a cheery cocoon created to support Tia the way her cane had outside.

Don't assume!

She walked steadily to one of the armchairs. Had I not seen her last night, I would have thought only that she walked with more awareness than other people. Nothing, not the set of her slim hips in the long brown cotton jersey skirt that was a twin of the black one she'd worn last night, nor the swing of her feet in her narrow-strapped sandals, nor her wide smile suggested she'd had to focus on every step. Had I not studied the out-takes of failed stunts to spot the misplaced foot, the bad angle, the ill-timed acceleration, I wouldn't have picked up on her deliberate foot placement. I held my breath, waiting till she was seated to say what I had to.

She swung like a dancer into one of the welcoming armchairs, her chin-length brown hair giving a final sway into place, and before I could broach anything, said, "You must have just about dropped your teeth when you first spotted Eamon Lafferty. I sure did."

Smiling, she had jerked the rug out from under my plans. I'd forgotten that habit of hers, infuriating but so intuitive that you ended up thinking she was just saving you trouble. But I wasn't ready to talk about Mike or pretend not to while discussing Eamon. And I couldn't shift enough to deal with her accident, my guilt. I said, "Tia, what made you leap into that wretched tunnel?"

"It was your fault."

"My fault?" For an instant I thought she had read my mind about her accident. But the tunnel, my fault? "I never—"

"I was looking down that first hole, the one in back of the zendo that went to the sewer or whatever, thinking, *anyone would be mad to jump in*, and then you shoved forward insisting you were the professional."

"That's crazy. I never *wanted* to jump in, I just thought—"

"But you looked like you would. You looked great, strong, fearless. So—" She leaned toward me and lowered her voice. "This is so childish. You know, Darcy, I wouldn't admit this to anyone but you, but after that bit with the hole, when I saw the ladder down into the tunnel, I knew that was something I could do. My arms are strong now, stronger than anyone might imagine."

Strong enough to compensate for her mangled back! "Oh, God. Tia, I am so sorry." I reached for her hands. "If it hadn't been for me doing that cable car—"

"Forget it!"

"If I hadn't—"

"It wasn't about you." She didn't pull her hands free; they lay cold, unmoving, in mine.

I was an idiot. I wanted to tell her how bad I felt about stealing her dignity, too. I wanted . . . I was just an idiot. I sat, sweat lathering my back, waiting for her to move.

She remained still, neither looking away nor even shifting in her chair. "It really wasn't about you last night, Darcy. It was about Eamon." Then she eased her hands free. "Like I said, this isn't super-mature. But I was tired from standing, I hobbled out of the reception, and I didn't want Eamon to leave with the impression that I was a cripple. I had to change the story line. It worked, see?"

I had to jam my teeth together to keep from saying I was sorry again.

"Darcy, listen to me. It's not your fault. Believe me! I'm almost insulted you think it is! No, don't answer. I've made my choices, I live with them, and—" She led my gaze around the room—"do it damn well, in Pacific Heights. But I don't take foolish chances."

"Yeah, well," I contradicted her. Her mouth tightened ever so slightly, ready for the obvious comeback about her accident. I went on. "What about running into the dark in the tunnel and hitting the end?"

She laughed, relieved. "Okay, not often."

"Why'd you do it?"

"Why not?"

"No, really, Tia, why?"

A small jade frog stood guard next to her glass; she ran a finger up its lumpy back. "What did you think?"

"You were crazy."

"Crazy loco, or crazy tough?"

"Both."

"Good enough." She smiled and caught my eye in a way that said my "good enough" mattered. "Listen, Darcy, I'm glad you're back. We could have been friends, in school, if . . ."

"If Mike's disappearance didn't destroy everything." The words were out before I realized it.

She nodded slowly and rubbed her finger gently back and forth across the jade. I understood the comforting gesture, and that she had trusted me with things she worked to conceal. And there was something about her that made me trust her with what I hadn't even revealed this way to Leo. "Mike walked out the door into the fog over twenty years ago, and it's like yesterday. There's not a day I don't think of him. He was my buddy, my protector in the family. And when he vanished, every-thing stopped. No one in the family talked about him, not after the ini-tial flurry. He was totally gone. And I was utterly alone. It seemed like only I cared."

She laughed.

"Tia?"

"Sorry, I'm so sorry, really. It's just that you couldn't possibly have been more wrong. Gary and John, they never let up. You must know that now, right?"

"No, I don't. I'm stunned. I don't— They— They never said anything to me. Never let up how? It's like I've walked into an alternate San Francisco and the real one is over to the left somewhere. I didn't even know you knew my brothers." I looked down and realized I was digging my fingers into the armrest.

But Tia wasn't watching out for her upholstery; her whole attention was on me. Without moving, she seemed to be reaching toward me. "*Know* is too strong a term. Except for Gary. John found me the summer between junior and senior years in high school, the year after Mike disappeared. You were still around, so I just assumed you'd know. I was out of college when Gary called. I had the impression he thought he could ferret out more than his brother had."

Despite everything, I laughed. "That's Gary, all right. And Grace? Did my sister hunt you down, too?"

She eased back in her chair. "Grace was a fluke. She was a resident in the ER when I had my accident. I was so scared I was looking for anything to distract myself. I saw her name and, oddly, remembered you saying that you and Mike were the curly redheads and the rest had the straight black hair. Hers was long, tied back, and dead straight. So I asked. And then she asked."

"Did she ask you about Mike, too?" Grace had never mentioned this. None of them had.

"Oh, Darcy, I don't remember. They all came at it from different directions."

I was still clutching the arm of the chair. I eased my fingers off the fabric. "Tia, this is going to sound silly, but I'd like to know those directions. I've spent years searching for Mike. I've hired detectives, tracked down his college friends, chased strange red-haired men down city streets, but no one else—" I swallowed. "Well, I assumed no one else did, that they just accepted that he'd gone. It's because no one ever mentioned his name, so, see, I don't know who knew what when, if anything." I swallowed and focused on hooking my hair behind my ears.

When I was composed enough to face her again, I had the sense that she'd been about to say or do something comforting, then thought better of it. Now she was shifting into the back cushion. She put down the little frog and said, "Sure. I kept a diary back then. I probably wrote down every question, or at least my reaction; my answer, their reaction to *me*. It's packed away in a box in my garage downstairs or I'd get it for you."

It might have been the awkwardness of my admission or her shifting her weight, either to give me a moment of privacy or maybe because she couldn't sit in one position longer, but I understood that she was cutting to the chase because there was something else she really wanted to talk about, the things she'd actually invited me here for.

"But for now," she said, "here's what I told them—"

"No. Tell me what you *didn't* tell them."

Tia shrugged. "You always did see between the lines. In high school that made me very nervous. I'll bet it's had that effect on lots of people."

"Not so they mentioned." I grinned.

She smiled. "Your brother John, the cop, caught me coming out of school. He was—excuse my saying this—young and taken with his authority."

"One out of two. John was born middle-aged. Now, probably, he'd admit he loved flashing his badge back then."

"He was a cute cop, though, and I didn't want to seem like a silly high school girl who had a crush on his brother, a guy I barely knew. Mike and I did a little pas de deux watching a track meet of yours, but it led to nothing. That was unusual for me. I have to admit, I was affronted. So I set out to show him the error of his lapse—in the nicest possible way, of course. That's how come I called you to borrow homework I'd already finished, and came to your house for it. Do you remember?"

66

I laughed. "I figured you had to be desperate."

"The whole ploy was a failure. Mike was on his way out, and then I had to spend an hour copying your equations, which weren't all correct, either!"

"Hey, you could have clued me into that. I wasn't distinguishing myself in advanced math at that point."

"I owe you." She motioned toward the dining room table. "So that's what I did not pass on to John."

I was surprised at how essential she made me feel, as if I were the long-lost friend who made her whole. No wonder guys were so enchanted. No wonder Jeffrey Hagstrom kept coming back after her flings. Like Jeffrey, I knew she'd invited me here because she wanted something. But I was glad she had, glad to help, glad we were going to be friends. I stood and gave the lunch a closer look. A pass-through counter had been cut into the wall between the main room and kitchen. On it was a clear bowl piled with calamari salad. Garlic bread sat atop a wooden slicing board. Two cups on heaters held melted butter. And three bottles of white wine awaited inspection. "What about Gary? What didn't you tell him?"

Tia didn't respond. I turned back and was startled to see her struggling out of her chair, good leg braced against the far foot of it, both hands on the near arm trying to get enough initial thrust to swing herself up. Her hip jutted out, bony, with the idiosyncratic musculature of the injured. Her jaw was clenched and her face drawn in lines of frustration and fear.

I gasped. It was all I could do not to race over and pull her out of her chair. Stepping aside was my penance. I'd gritted through my own injuries, broken legs, ribs, vertebrae, combinations thereof, and I'd known plenty of other stunt doubles on crutches, in wheelchairs and casts. But the worst temporary injury is joy compared to the most minor permanent one, and Tia's was not minor.

I turned quickly back to the table and tried to find something to say. "Last night, at the house, all three of them were there, bickering like always, this time about a dead body of John's. Apparently the guy had gotten poisoned and fallen three stories down in the middle of one of those nineteenth-century oval staircases and either lay in the lobby till rigor mortis set in or went stiff as a board on the way down, and John . . ."

I turned again in time to see Tia walking to the table as if nothing had happened. It was an impressive accomplishment. She moved with the same measured gait as she had at the door. The lines of frustration in her face had vanished. The reversion was so remarkable that for an instant I questioned what I'd just seen.

"And John," I hurried on, "was all pushed out of shape because the neighbors were trying to tell him the guy went stiff before he hit the ground."

"You know what, Darcy?" She came to a halt at the table. Only the slightest coloring on her cheeks, plus the shine on her forehead, betrayed the enormous battle she'd just won. Her hair had swung back in place, cupping her face. Was the reason she'd got that cut not understatement but practicality? "Give me a minute to look for those diaries. You can be moving the food to the table."

I didn't dare offer to go down for her.

"Oh, and remember, I wanted Grace's phone number? I need to talk to her. Not about this," she added with a dismissive glance at her hips, as if to dispel any thought of possible angling for free medical advice.

"Sure. She's living at home. I'll write it down for you."

"Then how about serving up the lunch? Feel free to start. Pretend it's the freshman trough!"

I didn't look at her as she made her way to the front door and on outside. Had she always had that self-control, or was it a side benefit of learning to hide pain? I remembered her at that long freshman lunch table in school, tossing back food like everyone else to grab a few extra minutes to gossip, flirt, or take a last scan at test notes—and before the hard and important tests, I remembered her laughing.

The serving bowls were ready so I shifted them to the table and began scooping out salad. It would be hard for her—for anyone—to understand my family's attitude toward Mike's disappearance. I could remind her that John was already a patrol officer at the time and his colleagues had interviewed us all. And then there was the reporter. I added a slice of garlic bread to each plate. But still, there were always reasons. At first Mike's being gone was unbelievable, an alternate universe that had settled on ours and would certainly lift any minute, leaving us crowded in the kitchen like always. It wasn't possible at first that he could be gone.

Then possibility seeped in and I felt like the biggest traitor in the world. I couldn't mention it; I couldn't be near anyone who mentioned Mike's name. I couldn't read, study, hold a conversation, do anything but run track, take gymnastics classes because they were so hard with my tight track muscles, and try out for basketball, soccer. I never rode the bus in those days, but bicycled or roller-bladed. I moved fast, as if I could outrun the truth. I was too busy avoiding to wonder how anyone else was handling things.

But John had been thorough enough to find an acquaintance of Mike's as distant as Tia. And, years later, Gary had been looking, double-checking. I sank back into one of the padded dining chairs. It let out a *huh!* The briny smell of calamari mixed with the overly sweet freesias. In the kitchen the refrigerator groaned on. My stomach roiled and I thought I wouldn't be able to eat and that that would be so rude after all the trouble Tia had gone to. Learning my brothers had been looking for Mike for years, I should have been relieved, but I wasn't. What did it mean and how could they be doing more than I had when I was the one who cared the most? Sweat coated my face. How could they have searched for Mike and not told me? Gotten leads, hopes, and not let me have them?

I saw John sitting at the dining table holding out his plate for a slice of ham the Easter after Mike's disappearance, asking about the traffic detour on 46th Avenue; Gary showing off his new Mustang when I came home at Christmas my freshman year in college. Now they seemed to me entirely different men, as if strangers had hijacked my memories. Rational explanations, common sense were way above me and I could only feel the small, poorly weighted anchor of my family being hoisted out of the water and flung aside. Thoughts swirled, emotions, recriminations, more emotions. I felt fifteen years old, not thirty-nine. I wanted badly to get out of here, and I was equally desperate to know what Tia had recorded in her diaries.

Finally, I got up, went into the bathroom, and flung cold water on my face, leaving a great circle of damp on Tia's yellow towel. I saw my watch face: 12:35. I'd gotten here exactly at noon. Tia and I couldn't have talked more than ten minutes. What had happened to her? Had she gotten distracted by a neighbor? Fallen in the garage? I opened the front door and raced down the steps. "Tia? Tia, where are you?"

No response. "Tia!" The garage doors were closed, locked. The courtyard was empty. I spent the next five or ten minutes pulling at the garage doors, running down the walkway between buildings, poking behind the shrubbery. But all along, I knew that she was gone.

Just like Mike, she had walked out the front door and vanished.

CHAPTER 9

"I'M IN A TIME WARP. Tia was about to tell me about Mike. And then, just like he did, she walked out the front door and vanished." I'd finally managed to get through to my brother, John, at the police station.

"She's been gone half an hour? Darcy, she could have gone to the store for milk, got caught in the line, forgotten her phone, and be on her way home right now."

"She walks with a limp now, John. We're on the top of Pacific Heights. There aren't mom-and-pop stores on the corners here."

"Maybe she got sick of you!"

"She invited me for lunch. The food's still waiting on the table."

"Darcy, we can't take missing persons calls from acquaintances. Even from family there's a required waiting period of—"

"She said"—I suddenly remembered that this call could be recorded and made my comment more vague—"she had a diary she kept in high school, a thorough diary."

"I'm on my way. I'll call you back."

"My number is . . ." I was talking to myself. How was he going to get back to me? Of course, my number would have come up on his screen, would be recorded in the police log: start time, end time, location. Knowing John, even though I'd never called him on my cell phone or given him the number, he already had it.

For a moment I sat on the steps, watching the traffic on Broadway burst forward an instant before the light turned green. Obviously John remembered Tia Dru. And something she might have noted in a diary got him moving. Right now he'd be headed to his car. Which meant I had five minutes to find that diary before he grabbed it and dangled it out of reach as he had dolls when I was five, letters a decade later.

The side-by-side garages comprised the ground floor of the duplex. Breaking into Tia's would be bad enough, entering the neighbor's—a stranger's—worse. It would be made lots worse by the arrival of a police detective.

I peered through the windows, hoping for an indication of which one was Tia's. One unit held boxes, plastic bags covering lumpy things. In the other sat a white Volkswagen bug. If you live this close to downtown, you're better off without a car. There's always a bus or a trolley or a cable car within a couple of blocks. To most folks in this gentle climate garages are storage rooms, driveways home to cars.

For Tia, a couple of blocks up the steep San Francisco hills would be like me scaling the Transamerica Building. I pulled out a tiny skeleton key and stuck it in the U-lock. In his speedy departure from the location set, Duffy's former owner abandoned not only Duffy but what we all assumed to be Duffy's dog bag. I figured I had inherited balls, blanket, dog shampoo, dog treats; instead I got a tiny skeleton key, larger skeleton keys, and other items for which I couldn't guess the use and didn't dare ask about. The smallest key I had dubbed the universal skeleton. It had yet to fail.

I slipped inside the garage. My five minutes was down to four. If John caught me, he wouldn't throw me in jail for being inside a friend's garage, but he might well create the kind of aftershock that would reverberate through family dinners for decades.

A window in the back gave just enough light to show that this garage was neater than any I had ever seen. The little car was parked inches from the right wall, leaving its owner, who undoubtedly was Tia, ample space to get in and out of the driver's seat. In front of it were ten cardboard banker's boxes, in two rows one atop the other. They were even labeled. If the diary was here, she could have been back upstairs with it in two minutes. She also could have grabbed it and left.

My phone rang. "Hello?"

"Darcy, I'm on my way."

I shouldered the phone and pulled open the first box. It was labeled Taxes, and that's what it held. "John, how come you interviewed Tia about Mike disappearing?"

He was silent so long I wondered if he'd hit a dead spot. But when he spoke, his voice cracked just slightly—but hugely for a police detective. "I did what I could."

"But why Tia? What even made you think of her?" I opened the next box—books—and the next—dishes.

"He mentioned her."

"Mike?" Saying his name, forcing John to respond, made the thread to Mike seem real in a way it hadn't in years. "What did Mike say about Tia?"

"He was thinking of asking her out."

"Really?" I yanked open the last of the top boxes—folders of bank statements, phone bills, printed documents. "Did he talk about girls with you much?" John was the last person to whom I would have mentioned a boyfriend. Rigidity and sarcasm are not appealing traits in a confidant.

"He only told me about the girls who'd impress me. It's not unnatural for a boy to want to impress a father figure." His voice had taken on its familiar tone of righteous defensiveness. *John, the Enforcer, a father figure!*

He must be delusional. I clamped my teeth together and kept searching Tia's boxes.

As soon as I could conceal my own sarcasm, I asked, "And what did you say about her?"

"Reminded him she was sixteen years old."

I shoved a box over and peered into a collection of sweaters, scarves, two stones with circles on them, and a couple of perfume samples. "What did she say when you saw her?"

"Darcy, it was ages ago. I can't remember."

This from a man who'd remembered my most venial sin long after I'd forgotten it. This from a sib who'd searched for Mike for years and never once mentioned it, never talked of leads, hopes, never let on that he, too, was living a half life till Mike came home. I swallowed hard; now was not the time to be vomiting out recriminations. Rather, it was a moment to choreograph as I would a stunt, to give the illusion of . . . "Doesn't matter, John. I'll just read what Tia said."

"You have no business—"

"I'm here, John, with the diary. I'm just giving you a chance to offer your version first." I looked into the last box—blankets. No diary.

"Darcy, you're in someone else's house. I can't condone you reading her private material."

"I know, I'm 'putting you in a very awkward position.' That threat worked better on Mike than me, remember? Last chance, that's what I'm offering you."

"Listen, I'm not kidding—"

"Never mind. I can read for myself." I hung up, checked the car through its closed windows, and tried the trunk. When has a trunk ever sat unlocked while the doors are locked?

I was out of the garage and headed back up Tia's steps when the phone rang, as I knew it would. John had had time to give in without admitting defeat. In our family, defeat was never admitted; setbacks were merely sustained and guerrilla attacks continued long after the enemy had forgotten the war.

"I'm going to save you the trouble of reading trash," he said. "Whatever Tia said doesn't matter, because she's a liar."

"Really?" Liar was the last thing I would have called her. Charming and in control as she was, Tia had never needed to lie. "A liar then, or now?"

"She was then. No reason she'd change."

I barely caught myself before snapping back. I liked Tia. I'd liked her in high school. Her utter gutsiness racing so fast into the dead black of the tunnel impressed me. And, maybe most of all, her taking her injury in stride had me in awe. *Think like you're choreographing a gag, dammit! Keep your eyes on the landing spot, and your mouth shut!* I swallowed, and waited.

"Darcy, when I interviewed her, I already knew Mike'd seen her three times total. He'd told me. At the track, at our house, and once on the bus when he couldn't get a ride downtown. She pretended there was more, that they had dated. I can tell when a girl's looking to make herself important. It's what she was doing."

"That's crazy! She was already popular. She didn't need to lie. And she was too smart to lie to the police." What she had told me about not wanting John to think her a silly high school girl made a whole lot more sense.

"She did!"

"Prove it!

"Darcy, you're very defensive—"

"Prove it, John."

The unmarked car screeched to a stop. He was out the door before it was still. "The proof is," he said into his phone as he climbed the steps, "that she had no proof." He clicked off his phone and stood, hands braced on hips, as they had been braced against his equipment belt all those years he'd been on patrol. His clipped black hair topped suspicious hazel eyes. Over the years, he had squinted and pursed his lips till permanent lines bisected his forehead, dug in beside his nose and mouth, and channeled over his chin. Now he leaned against the porch pillar and said, "She said Mike had a Celtic cross tattooed on his groin, as if she'd seen it, as if there had been plenty between them. But I saw Mike coming out of the shower the week before and there was nothing on him. The girl was a liar."

"Maybe she just wanted to be rid of you. Why else would she tell you something so easily disproved, that disgusted you, and made you think she was lying?"

"Because, Darcy, that's what liars do. I know. Liars are—"

"—your bread and butter? What can I say to the great authority on human misbehavior?"

He peered in the doorway.

"She thought you were cute, John."

He stopped still, then turned, a look of disgust pinching his face. "She was sixteen!"

"Teenage girls thinks guys are cute, John. They even discuss those guys with their friends." I had forgotten how great was the temptation to tease John.

"Yeah, well, she didn't discuss Mike with anyone on the list of friends she gave me."

"You checked up on *her?* Did you figure she was that central to Mike's disappearance?"

"No."

It was an un-John-like no, a word that wavered rather than hammering. "Not central, but you thought she knew something she wasn't telling you, right?"

"Everybody keeps secrets. Question is: is it *your* secret?"

"Was it?"

He glanced back inside the house as if checking for eavesdroppers. It was another minute or two before he admitted, "I don't know."

"Then you're not through with her, are you?" The battle wasn't over; merely a setback would have been sustained.

"I am."

"You figured she had a lead to Mike and you let her keep quiet?"

"I'm a police officer. We don't harass witnesses."

"But—"

"We don't harass witnesses—"

"John, what did you assume she knew?" *Was that what she invited me here to discuss?*

"I don't have all day. I only came out here as a favor to you. I was in the middle of an important report. A hostess walking out on her guest is not a crime. But I'm here. I'll check around . . . as a favor to you."

"What? You'll keep looking through the front door? John, she's not here. You don't need to look. You need to have cops out there," I said, waving both arms toward the surrounding streets.

"Don't tell me my business." He peered in through the door, pulled it shut, and headed down the stairs. "I'll let you know if I hear anything."

"Like you have all these years, about Mike?"

"Darcy, don't—"

"Forget it!" I so wanted to stalk off, but he was in the way. I could manage only a weak "Just forget it," as I watched him get to do the stalking to his car and tire-squeal off.

John was going to do zip. So be it. I would find her myself. I was dressed for a run anyway, in my "dress sweats." *Don't assume.* Maybe she wasn't really gone. Maybe she circled back inside while I was in the garage and didn't want to deal with John. Strange, but hardly stranger than vanishing. I felt foolish, but I knocked. Of course, there was no answer.

I loped along Broadway, glancing into apartment lobbies, up stairs of flats, into narrow courtyards. At Octavia Street I turned uphill, then east on Pacific toward Van Ness, the thoroughfare where the dynamiting had finally stopped the fire after the great earthquake of 1906. Ahead was downtown and the mixed neighborhoods of Polk Gulch, Russian Hill, North Beach, Chinatown, and the Barbary Coast, behind were the great Victorians and mansions of Pacific Heights.

Van Ness is a crowded, traffic-clogged, four-lane thoroughfare with bus stops at corners and as good a chance of hailing a cab as a pedestrian has in this city. I ran two blocks in either direction, but there was no sign of Tia. I checked a couple of blocks of Polk Street east, peering past fringed lampshades into antique shops, through the tinted windows of cafés. Two blocks farther down I spotted a woman with short, light brown hair sipping from a paper cup in a coffeehouse and was halfway across the room before I knew she wasn't Tia.

When I emerged, the California Street cable car rattled by a couple of blocks away. If Tia'd gotten on it, she'd already be at the Ferry Building. Like New York City, San Francisco nurtures pedestrians. There were a dozen ways she could have gone. Giving up, I headed back to her apartment, but when I got there the door was still locked and everything looked unnervingly normal.

I wanted to scream.

Instead, I ran. As I jogged in place at the red light back on Van Ness I wondered how Leo, Garson-roshi, the teacher with whom I came back here to study, would tell me to handle this. He might go for the traditional: all is impermanence, and this interlude is part of that impermanence.

I crossed and headed along Broadway toward the little tunnel that sucked cars out of the staidness of Russian Hill and spit them into the bright red and gold of Chinatown. As had my old teacher, Leo's mentor, Yamana-roshi, Leo might say, "We see through our own eyes." He would mean I was looking at Tia as if she existed wholly in connection with me, with Mike, with my family. He would be telling me to stop viewing her as the ghost of my own hopes and assumptions. He would advise me to see her as she really is.

As I looped up around the tunnel, I wondered if Leo . . . Then I pulled out my cell phone and dialed. "Leo, it's Darcy."

"Are you sick?"

"No, I'm running," I panted.

"Are you okay?"

"Yes, I have a question, I mean for you, as my teacher."

"You're calling me from the street, while you're jogging, for a *dokusan* question?"

"Well, yeah," I said before I could quite tell whether Leo was seriously appalled at the way I'd transmuted the centuries-old traditional private interview in which the student comes to the teacher in a room where a candle is lit and incense burns, and asks a dharma—teaching—question.

"Be aware!"

Zen is a practice of awareness of everything. But I suspected Leo meant the traffic. I plunged in with the tale of this afternoon. "We were putting lunch on the table. She went downstairs to get me a diary she wrote when we were in high school. And she never came back. You don't just walk out on your guest. You don't leave with the food on the table."

"You don't know her as well—"

"As you do after a few minutes in a reception?" He sounded just like John.

"As well as you think." His voice held none of the frustration of mine. He was merely clarifying.

"Sorry, I didn't mean to snap at you like that." I came down harder on my front leg, pushed off faster. "Oh, okay, 'don't assume.' Listen, I'm not just assuming." I stopped. Stopped speaking, stopped running. Stood panting. "Leo, I'm not assuming about lunch. I'm not even assuming that she looked at me and resented my walking on two legs without a cane."

"Tia's not one to lie. If she told you it wasn't about you, believe her. So, you can choose to assume that at the center of her accident and her pain and her sudden departure is *you*. Or you cannot assume, and see things as they are. Your choice."

Don't assume. I was still panting. *Don't assume.* "Okay, but . . . Leo, how do you know . . . ?" Leo had hung up. My teacher hung up on me! The zendo was a couple of blocks away. I pocketed my phone and ran. Hang up on me, indeed!

But I'd barely hit Columbus Avenue when I reconsidered. Okay, I *was* assuming some control over Tia I'd never even come near having. Just as I was assuming she'd, in fact, gone out for her diary. Had she? She'd left, but she could be sitting in a neighbor's kitchen. I had believed that she walked with a limp, but I only had her presentation.

And what about the liar issue? John insisting she was, Leo sure she wasn't. Was each of them merely seeing through his own eyes? Was John himself lying? And how did Leo get to be so sure about Tia so quickly? Luckily, in a minute I could ask him just that.

The light was green at Columbus and Broadway two blocks above the zendo. Running downhill, I moved fast. Double-parked by the zendo was a mob of police cars, light bars flashing.

CHAPTER 10

PATROL CARS BLOCKED off the street at Columbus. Their pulsing lights turned the white buildings scarlet, the brick ones to dried blood. A crowd three-deep angled to peer over the hoods, stretched to see above the car roofs, pressed into the spaces between bumpers.

Leo! Injured?

"I live here," I puffed to the cop at the barrier.

"Driver's license."

"I just moved in."

"Proof?"

"I *said* I just moved in."

"Yeah. Like I haven't heard that one before. No proof, no passage." He was small for a cop and thin. He lifted his equipment belt; when he let go it bounced on his hip bones, cell phone, flashlight, and night stick clattering. Behind him, beyond the barrier, a small crowd waited.

"Ask Leo, the abbot of the Zen Center, in the middle of the block, he'll—"

"Anything else I can do for you? Tea while you wait?"

"Sarcasm is the kind of bullying that elicits an unnecessarily negative response to a city's police force," I said, repeating a particularly stodgy line from recruit training I'd heard from John.

The cop stared. "No proof, no passage, *ma'am*."

"Leeeee-oooooooooooh!"

The crowd inside the barriers turned. "Quiet!"

I recognized the voice. Demanding quiet on the set. "This is a *movie location?*"

"Well, yeah . . . *ma'am*."

"Robin!" I called to the one person whose name I knew. "Robin, it's Darcy." It had been pre-dawn dark when I'd met Robin Sparto yesterday. Since I was an emergency replacement for a double who'd been injured the previous day, he didn't waste time on my credentials. Once I'd assured him I'd done high falls and had an S.A.G. card, he'd moved on. I wasn't sure he'd even recognize me in daylight.

"I did the gag yesterday," I called to him. "Remember?"

"Yeah, but we don't need—"

"I live on this street, but I don't have a wallet. Vouch me in."

He turned back toward the crew, grumbling. "The damned consultant hasn't shown up. We've been waiting half an hour. The light's only going to hold so long, you know."

"Hey, I live here! What do you need to know?"

"Yeah? Huh." He nodded to the cop, who knew when he was beat and stepped aside smartly.

I was desperate to check on Leo. But, I reminded myself, there was no reason to assume anything had happened, other than his hanging up on me. The biggest danger now was from the impatient talent and the crew standing on the protected side of the vans.

Robin wore a frustrated expression. "There's a tunnel somewhere—"

"Over there. Behind the courtyard wall. That's where I live. Are you using it?"

"Probably. Final sequence: Ajiko is led into the death room with the oil lamp and tea. We were going to do it back in L.A. Sealed room is sealed room, you know? But then I heard about this tunnel. It's like a room, right? Damp dirt walls, no exit. Who owns it?"

"The tunnel? Eamon Lafferty, I assume. The building's his."

"Then that's okay. Keys," he called to one of the gofers. A younger, smaller version of Robin raced over, extending a ring.

"You know him?" I asked.

"Everyone knows Eamon."

"Really?"

He stared at me, as if he were watching a knobby brown beast transform into a woman, or vice versa. "You of all people must know that. What are you, Eamon's sister? No wonder he was so hot for you to have this job."

"Eamon Lafferty got me the gig?"

"Oh, don't—"

"No, really—" I shut my mouth and shrugged. There's a time for truth, and a time for silence. Eamon Lafferty had gotten me this job, the same Eamon Lafferty who'd given the zendo the building. How did he even know I was a stunt double? Why would he care, much less find me work?

"Aren't you his sister?"

"That one." I pointed to a large brass key on his ring.

"You know the key? You've been in the tunnel?"

"Oh, yeah," I said, as if Eamon and I had played there as kids.

"Take me down. Ajiko!" He was calling the female lead.

Ajiko Sakai was a star in Japan. This was her first American film, her first step to stardom here. She was black-haired, tiny, and gorgeous. She was also polite. She stood waiting at Robin Sparto's shoulder, her head barely that high. Compared to her, I was a baboon.

There's a reason stunt doubles are near-twins of the actors. Just how much pull did the universally known Eamon Lafferty have? I needed to get him one-on-one, this guy who walked off last night with the prize of Tia Dru. I needed to figure out what was going on with him and just who he was—*if* I could ever get beyond him not being Mike. But not now. Now was for connecting with Sparto and making sure the next time he needed a stunt double he'd remember me. I took the key and unlocked and pulled up the metal door.

The fog had rolled in, turning late afternoon to a murky dusk. The crew was wrapped in wool and down. In my sweats I was already shivering. The hole looked like a fresh grave; the stench of mud and putrefaction oozed up from the entrance.

"You want to check it out, Ajiko?" Robin was asking.

I turned in time to see her shake her head. She was in character as My Yen, young, alone in a strange, barbaric country, terrified but resigned, on the threshold of the vile room where she would die. I glanced at the actress, but she was staring at the dark hole, sucking in the horror, cultivating dread.

"Okay, then!" And when Sparto turned toward me, I swung myself with bravado down into the tunnel.

The subterranean space couldn't have been more different from last night. Then Tia had run so fast into the darkness she'd nearly knocked herself silly against the wall. We'd all stood stunned, in part by her, but also by the lingering sense of the tunnel's evil history. Now a bank of lights was lowered down, illuminating the mottle of gray rock and mud shot through with sick-yellow clay. The crew was all business.

"Great! This is terrific!" Robin said, coming down behind me.

"Hard to find anywhere more claustrophobic," I added. And hard to find a place to set a scene where he was less likely to need a stunt double, dammit. The space was useless for me, but not so for Tia. What *had* she been looking for down here? I needed to buy some time to find what she had nearly knocked herself out to get to. "This far wall, Robin, it must have been open to the Bay once. I mean, it's a tunnel; it had to go somewhere."

"Shine that spot down here, man!" Robin trotted closer, as did I. The wall appeared solid, though horridly damp. I rapped randomly, creating slight indentations in a couple of places, scraping my knuckles on rock in two others, getting nothing but dirty. Sparto shrugged. He was already losing interest. In five minutes he'd be out of here and his bank of lights with him. I ran my eyes over the rear wall again, scanned the low ceiling. There was no nook where anything could have been hidden.

I scanned the side walls near the end, but they were the same. What was Tia's game here? The whole thing was crazy. I would have dismissed the entire episode if she hadn't disappeared on me. Was she just wacko? I took a shallow breath, trying to ignore the wretched smell. Whatever she was after had to be right around here, the place she'd run to, the reason she'd smacked into the wall. Had she hoped to find and pocket it before the rest of us got the flashlights on? Had she even known exactly where it was? I stuck a finger into the wall, but hit rock almost instantly. I clasped my hand and smacked the wall from one side to the other, splattering mud and bruising my hands, but no nook revealed itself. Nothing, just nothing.

"Okay that'll do it. Let's clear out of here. Come on, uh . . ."

"Darcy, Darcy Lott," I said automatically, as I did a last-ditch search for some reason to extend our stay. Sparto was already starting for the ladder. I grabbed his arm.

"Uh!" He flung me off.

I hit the wall. Mud splattered.

"Wha—?" But he wasn't looking at me, he was staring at a big lump of mud, about eight inches wide, seemingly just dislodged from the entrance to the extension of the chute we'd peered down last night. "Where the hell does that lead?"

I moved closer. Did the mud lump have a tail? Was it a dead rat? Or a live one? It was too dark to tell. "Bring the light over here."

A lighting tech obliged and I aimed it into the opening. The chute above led into the hole below, comprising one long narrow tube that passed by the corner of the tunnel on its way to wherever. I bent down, ear to hole. "Could be water."

"We're blocks from the Bay," Robin scoffed.

"Sewers."

He took a step back. "Do you think this hole was big enough for a woman once?"

It was definitely big enough for Tia to have pulled something out of. That would mean it wasn't deep. "Could be, Robin. A small woman like My Yen could look like she was wedged in there. It would be awful. But I could manage it," I added quickly. Setting a scene here would give me a chance to check this hole and its contents. "Really awful," I repeated, choosing not to think about the awfulness aspect at all.

"No way to shoot it." He was across the tunnel and up the ladder before I stood up. And by the time I did, the lighting tech was at its foot waiting for escape.

I walked back as slowly as possible, trying to spot something, anything Tia had dropped, used, anything. Trying, failing. Resigned, I climbed the ladder.

The fog had flooded in now. It was rush hour and the traffic on Columbus was muted to red and white flowing lights. Fog sat in the courtyard smoothing the corners of the zendo, blending the red madrone doors with the brick siding. I hurried in and up the stairs. "Leo, it's me!" I called as I hit the second-story landing.

He didn't answer. I checked my watch. Oh, gee, it was 6:20; afternoon zazen was still going on. I was supposed to be there. Showing up at

86

zazen was the least the roshi's assistant could do. But not draped in mud. I slipped into my room, took off my clothes, and wrapped them into a ball. Grabbing clean ones, I went to the bathroom, where I could hardly run the shower above the people sitting zazen. I sponged off, put on the dry clothes, and waited to hear Leo come up so I could explain. I listened for the bells ending zazen, but they didn't ring. I thought surely I'd hear the large one used in the service, but I didn't. When it got to be quarter to seven and I hadn't heard Leo's footsteps on the stairs either, a shot of fear went through my body.

Maybe something *had* happened to him after all. It made no sense, not logically, but still. I knocked on his door.

No answer.

"Leo!"

I hesitated, then opened his bedroom door.

Tia Dru was lying on the floor.

CHAPTER 11

"Tɪᴀ! Wʜᴀ—?" I flipped on the light. "Ti . . ." Her skin was whiter than I'd ever seen skin. Blood surrounded her, more blood than her delicate body could possibly have held. Her throat gaped open.

Leo! Was he dead, too? "Leo!" I stepped over Tia, right over her, and pulled open his closet door. Nothing there but clothes, robes, suitcases. "Leo!" I yelled.

I raced down the stairs, into the zendo. The room was dark. The tiny kitchen beside the entry was dark, too. Outside I yelled again, "Lee-ooooooh!"

"He was heading downtown last I saw him." Eamon strode in from the street. "Are you okay?"

"No! Omigod, Eamon, Tia's dead! Upstairs. There's blood all over."

"Blood!" He ran for the stairs. For a moment I couldn't move. Oddly, I thought I'd remember later his automatic concern was for his property rather than for the woman he'd taken home just last night. He turned all the lights on and as I followed him upstairs, bloody footprints sprang out at me. It wasn't till I reached the top that I realized they were my own.

He was standing outside Leo's door. "Have you called the police?"

"No."

"You have to call them. Never mind! I'll do it."

89

"No, wait—"

"What?"

"Nothing. Go ahead." I was going to say I'd call John, but since he hadn't involved himself this afternoon, what was the point of trying to rope him in now?

I stood in the doorway, not wanting to see Tia's body, yet not able to pull my gaze off it. She was wearing the same clothes she'd had on at lunch. For an instant I heard her calling, "I'm in the kitchen. Come on in," saw her walking toward me, her hands extended toward me, saw her smiling, surrounded by the yellows of many shades, smelled the freesias.

Now her hands were striped with red, her T-shirt caked brown with blood, almost the same color as her skirt. It looked ludicrously like an ensemble. The long skirt had been pulled up in her fall, revealing the misshapen leg she'd worked so hard to disguise. Her arms had flopped at her sides as if she had clutched at her throat, at the hand dragging the knife across, clutched until she couldn't.

Tears were swelling in my head, but my eyes were sandpaper-dry. She was lying on the hard floor, inches from Leo's narrow futon. Her blood had hardened on his blue sleeping bag. It was thicker than the smear on the floor because . . . because the killer had wiped the floor, wiped away shoeprints. I leapt back, as if it wasn't already too late not to trample any signs of the killer's departure. And then I started to shake.

Suddenly Eamon's arm was around my shoulder and he was saying, "Let's wait on the landing."

I was glad to let him guide me down the six steps to that half landing where the staircase turned, glad to have the feel of a comforting arm. "Eamon, did Tia give you any sense that—"

"That she was going to be murdered?"

"No, no. I mean that she was worried, I mean, you know, anything strange?" I was shaking so hard my voice was quavering. Eamon's hand tightened on my shoulder, pulling me against the firmness of his ribs, and I was glad for that, too.

"I just met her. She felt bad about ditching Jeffrey, but she didn't act like he'd come after her with a razor." He sounded as undone as I was.

"Leo? What about Leo? Have you seen him?"

"He was racing out of here when I pulled up. Just before you came out of the tunnel."

"Right, the tunnel. Robin wants to do a shoot there."

"That's fine. I just caught him and settled things. It'll be fine." I could hear the constriction in his voice that mirrored my own.

"I'm sorry," I said. "You must have planned to see her again, to have something with her. It must . . ." I swallowed, but I couldn't force out more.

The gulp of a siren pulled me back. Leather-soled feet pounded up the stairs. The face I saw coming toward me was that of an Asian American who looked about my age but was probably older. His suit screamed Plain Clothes Shop.

"Detective Korematsu," he said, extending a hand to me and to Eamon.

"Whatever I can do to help, Detective," Eamon said, as if welcoming him to the grounds.

I wondered if he knew my brother John. His name sounded vaguely familiar, but that made no sense. I'd barely seen John since I got back, and never to talk about his job. I'd heard more about it from Grace when she visited than from him.

Korematsu looked in Leo's room, called down to someone to order up a crime scene unit, and took down our names. "Eamon Lafferty," he repeated. "Did you discover the body, Mr. Lafferty?"

Eamon hesitated and I had the feeling he wanted but was unable to phrase his reply in a way that would be more helpful to me. "No, I came to help Ms. Lott after she discovered the body."

The detective nodded. "Okay, Mr. Lafferty, Officer Greiss will take you downstairs while I speak with Ms. Lott."

"Just a moment," Eamon insisted. "Darcy, I have a good lawyer if you need one."

"A lawyer!" Fear washed over me. Tia, the police, Eamon—it all seemed unreal, and now a lawyer! Only a fool opens her mouth to a cop—my brother the lawyer and my brother the cop had both proclaimed that more than once. A fool and her freedom are soon parted. But this was different. I needed to get this interview over with so I could find Leo. Where was he? Why had he been racing out of here? I'd never seen him move faster than a stride. Had he seen the killer? Was he following? Foolhardily? A fool and his life are soon parted . . .

I was losing it. Concentrate, Darcy! "I'm okay, Eamon." To the detective, I said, "What do you need to know?"

As Greiss followed Eamon downstairs, Korematsu motioned me into the nearest room, which was my bedroom, and asked for my address.

"Here, I guess."

"You're not sure?" he said in a tone that suggested domiciliary confusion was quite the norm.

"Here."

"Do you know the identity of the deceased?"

"Tia Dru. We went to high school together."

"Does she have family here?"

"Maybe. I think she lived with an aunt or someone—not parents—back then."

"Husband? Brothers, sisters?"

"No. I mean, I don't think so. I just don't— What I know is, she was here last night for a reception. I was at her house for lunch today. Before we could eat she went out to get something out of the garage, and she disappeared. There should be a record of my call about that," I said, hoping to cover everything pronto.

"Do you recall to whom you spoke?"

Whom! Korematsu must be the most civilized cop in the SFPD. "I called my brother, John, at the Hall of Justice."

He had been leaning against the doorway. Now he turned toward the hall and let his instructions float over his shoulder. "Excuse me for a moment. If you'll just wait here." He walked partway down the stairs and I couldn't make out what he was saying into his phone.

A line of uniformed officers moved up the stairs and into the crime scene. It seemed both ages and no time at all till Korematsu returned. Vaguely I wondered if I was in shock. It was almost the same sensation I'd had in Tia's dining room when I'd realized the truth about my brothers hunting for Mike. But one thing I was clearheaded enough to see was that there was no way I was going to let Mike's name come into this investigation.

Korematsu walked back in, propping himself against the doorway. There was a studied quality to his expression. He was slight, with hair that was long for a detective. I wondered if he was about to be rotated into an undercover job. He looked undercover, not homicide. He was way too sexy for homicide. I could see him half sprawled in a dark bar, setting up a buy, see his hair hanging over his eyes, down around his chiseled cheekbones.

I flushed. I really was losing it. I stared down and inhaled slowly. Still I found myself thinking that he was one of those guys who hold their college looks till they're fifty. Was he that old? When John was that age, he was already a force in Homicide. Had Korematsu joined the department late? "So, Ms. Lott, you said Ms. Dru disappeared about twelve-thirty."

"That's right," I said, yanking myself back to the question.

"You talked to Detective Lott at twelve forty-eight. Then what did you do?"

Broke into the garage was not the answer I wanted to share here. I sobered up quick. It was what they call in the stunt business "death curtain time," the moment the assumptions are shattered and you know you're going to die if you don't get out that very instant. I'd had a few of those moments in car chase gags; each time I'd bailed I'd ended up with a broken pelvis or a collapsed lung—instead of a coffin. Now I saw in Korematsu's face the deadly eyes of a homicide detective. *Whom.* I forced myself to stay still—no straightening of shoulders, no intake of breath, definitely not an iota of change of expression. "I waited for him. I wanted him to find her, but, well, there was nothing he could do, was there? Officially, I mean."

I thought for a moment he would say, "Whom do you mean?" but he merely nodded for me to go on. Not so much as a smile for John Lott's sister. "I ran the neighborhood, checked each side of Broadway, the blocks around, Van Ness, Polk, and then went back to see if she'd come home." I looked past him across the hall into Leo's room. All I could see of Tia was her arm flung out palm up. I turned away, squeezing my eyes shut to hold back a torrent of tears.

"That was what time?"

"I don't know. But then I ran back along Broadway to here and had Robin Sparto, the second unit director on the movie, get me through the barricade. The officer there may remember the time. Robin might have some idea."

"And then you came up here?"

"After showing Robin something, yes."

"And you went to the priest's room? Why was that?"

To ask why the bell hadn't rung as it always does to end the evening sitting, to find out if there had been an evening sitting at all, and to ask what could have been so important that the priest misses the evening service on the second day the zendo is open. "To say I was back."

"His door was shut."

"Yes."

"You knocked?"

"Yes."

"And?"

"There was no response, so I went in."

"The door was shut and the priest didn't say anything to admit you, but you went in anyway? Is that normal for your relationship with him, Ms. Lott?"

I looked Korematsu in the eye. "It is." At the monastery where I'd met Leo I'd had to protect him, and going in and out was part of that.

"And you found a woman in his room."

Oh shit! "She was dead."

"There are footsteps, in blood, leading down from the crime scene—"

"Mine. I went to get help."

"Uh-huh."

"Uh-huh." I followed his eyes to the wad of clothing on the floor with the dark stains. If he tested them, he would discover the stains were mud. But by the time he got the results he would have dusted Tia's apartment for prints and found mine. And then there was her garage, also full of my fingerprints. *Whom!* Now I remembered where I'd heard Korematsu's name. He was a new instructor in the academy when John was in charge. As the least senior guy, Korematsu was assigned to teach recruits how to write reports. John had gotten him busted back to wherever he came from for the sin of focusing too heavily on grammar. *As if,* Grace had told me, *writing a sentence clear enough for the D.A. to understand was going to be a blot on the department.*

The guy would have to be a saint not to relish John Lott's sister with a corpse in the next room and blood all over her shoes.

Again I looked him in the eye, and said, "Detective, I am a police detective's sister. My brother joined the force when I was four years old. You, of all people, know how opinionated he is about police behavior, and about the stupid things civilians do in the face of the police. Can you imagine if I were to kill someone, I'd leave bloody footprints and then call you?"

For the first time, he smiled. He said, "We'll talk about that at the station."

I waited till I caught his eye. "I don't think so."

CHAPTER 12

I HATED to have to summon one of my big brothers, but, dammit, Korematsu was not going to haul me to the Central or whichever station he worked out of and leave me twiddling in an interrogation booth. Possession is nine-tenths of the law and I was damned if I was going to be possessed. I pulled out my phone and called Gary. He said exactly what I could have scripted for him: *Why didn't you call me immediately! Korematsu!! Don't say another word, not to him, not to me!!! Korematsu! Shit! Not a word, even about why that bastard is there!!!*

I sat silently. Korematsu stood silently, with the expression of one who's swallowed a hot coal of fury. I wanted to say: Tia is dead in the next room, and the big issue here is your petty feud with my brother! Or: Why would I kill Tia! I was happy to see her; she was going to make my return to San Francisco fun. I figured today's lunch would be the first of many, that we'd talk about old times, but more that she was my friend.

How could I have imagined she'd walk off the way Mike had or, worse, that she might ever end up dead? The parallel chilled me. She was so entwined with Mike in my mind. But she wasn't dead because of Mike. She had her own life, had had it for years, and something in that sprang up to slice her throat. I shivered and suddenly I couldn't stop shivering. The horror of it washed over me like her blood all over Leo's floor. Sweat, icy now, coated my skin. My clothes were meant to cool the body, not warm it. I was remembering Tia in her long skirt swinging her body into her living room chair with a bravado that covered her pain, or almost.

Korematsu shifted. Without moving my head I could see him through my eyelashes, his forehead wrinkled, his brows peaked over his dark eyes. He looked toward the closet, seemed to reconsider, glanced toward a shawl hanging out of my not-yet-unpacked suitcase, hesitated. I sat unmoving, waiting, in this still moment of suspended investigation, this oddly intimate moment.

My phone rang. I just about tossed it across the room. Gary said: "Tell Korematsu to let me through his damned cordon! No wait, let me tell him. Hand him the phone."

I did, and waited while Gary handed his phone to the cop outside.

Korematsu stared down at me. "Your brother! What are you, a twelve-year-old?" He handed back the phone, his fingers brushing mine.

"No, I'm not." I held his gaze, and my response shifted to a near-tease. The moment, the very inappropriate moment lingered, and promised. I was almost glad when the heavy door banged open downstairs and Gary's feet pounded up the stairs, and the question of who would look away first vanished.

"You okay, Darcy? Has he threatened you? Intimidated, touched you in any way?"

Korematsu only looked at him coldly and stepped out into the hall, calling for a subordinate to bring a notebook. He held it out to Gary. "Ask your client to list her activities today, by the minute, with names and addresses of corroborators." Then he was gone, leaving a uniform to watch us.

My brother stood holding the pad, looking as stunned as I had. He bore no relation to Mr. Take No Prisoners on the phone. He was staring beyond the uniform into Leo's room at Tia's body. "Oh, Gary, I'm so sorry. Did you know Ti—?"

"Rabbits!"

I stopped instantly, heeding our old ritual of warning our siblings of approaching parents or John. Gary looked like he'd taken a medicine ball in the gut. His eyes wrinkled up; for a moment I thought he was going to cry. Of course he didn't want the cops to know he'd known Tia. And I was horrified that I'd damned near fallen into Korematsu's trap, forgetting there was a uniform outside. It was such an old cop trick.

I followed my brother's gaze back to Tia's body. Eight hours ago she'd made me lunch; now she was lying in the next room with her throat slashed. It was like parallel universes, as if I had stepped through a crack into the wrong one.

I was glad to have this clerical task to focus on. I thought it would be done in ten minutes, but it took much longer, even recording the easy stuff:

Sat zazen with Leo Garson and one stranger: 6:45–7:20. *Who was that man who looked like he'd chosen the zendo as a place to keep warm until the Caffè opened up?*

Gym 8:00 to 10:30. *Not long enough to keep in stunt shape.*

Walked to Tia's: 11:30–noon.

Each memory settled in the lap of my mind, wanting to be examined. And then there was the time at her flat before I realized Tia was gone, and the time after, both of which I needed to account for in ways other than the truth. At some point Gary stood in the hall and watched the activity in Leo's room. At some later point I realized he was really just staring at Tia's body, staring in a way one does not at an acquaintance but at a friend or lover. When I reached *Called Leo Garson while running around the Broadway Tunnel ~ 5:00 P.M.*, Gary dropped down beside me on my futon. His face was pasty. I hardly recognized him like this.

"Darce, how can she be—"

"Rabbits!"

"—dead like this. I just can't—"

"Rabbits, dammit! Rabbits!"

"—believe—"

"Shut up! Just shut up, dammit!" I slapped him as hard as I could.

"Hey, what's going on in here?" the uniform demanded.

"Call Korematsu. We're leaving." I stood up. Gary never was very limber, even as a teenager, and now he braced both hands against the wall to leverage himself up. Korematsu was in the doorway in what seemed like seconds. I handed him the pad. "It's the best I can do. I'm through here."

I thought he would threaten interrogation, arrest, but he glanced from me to Gary and said, "I could keep you a lot longer. Just promise me you won't leave town." He paused, then added, "Swear on the Buddha."

I laughed.

"I'm serious. This is a Buddhist temple. Swear on the Buddha."

The man really was serious. I didn't know whether to be insulted or teased. But it was the time for neither. "Okay," I said. "I promise to stay inside the city limits, Detective. I could swear on the Buddha, but this is a Zen Buddhist temple. The Buddha is not a god; the statue downstairs is a lovely piece of art but not a holy relic, and the historical Buddha himself was merely a man who realized how to live. Buddha nature is essentially awareness of life, nothing mystical. If I was going to leave town I would swear on the Buddha, hail a cab to the airport, and not think twice about it. But I won't because—"

"It would look bad for your brother, the other one," Korematsu said so automatically I shot a glance at Gary to see what Korematsu was referencing. But either Gary was still dazed or he had enough sense to rabbits himself.

I brushed past Gary, grabbing his hand to steer him to the stairs without making his condition any more noticeable. After Korematsu's comment, I was sure word of Gary's disintegration would be fast-tracked to John and all John's enemies. "It's like living in a village," I grumbled as we hit the street. "An icy, socked-in village."

San Francisco fog is ridiculous. It's like stage smoke gone wild. I glanced at my watch but could barely read the face. 8:15 P.M. Only just dinnertime, and streetlights were gray blobs, the storefronts across Pacific nonexistent. Fog hung off lampposts like Christmas tree snow. There had to have been heavy wind earlier to move this blanket in, but now the air was dead still and cold, like we were wearing wet wool coats with wet scarves.

"Where'd you park?"

"Across the street."

"There's no car there."

Gary came to life. He charged across the empty street, his black hair flying out behind him. "God dammit, that asshole Korematsu had me towed!"

I caught up to him on the curb. "Because you're John's brother?"

"Why else!"

"Red zone, fire hydrant?"

"You don't get towed from a crime scene for parking infractions."

I shook my head. "This isn't a village; it's a preschool. Gary, are you still driving the same car, the big black barrister bucket?"

"Yeah." I remembered now that Grace, who had coined the description, had said he was not amused.

"Where were you when you got my call?"

"Uh, Tadish's."

"Uh-huh." Tadish's Grill, a long-term San Francisco standard for fish and good drinks, was a few blocks to the south, in downtown.

"So you valet parked."

"Oh, right," he said in the sheepish tone that had allowed him to keep secretaries and paralegals and, for longer than he might have, three wives. The tone had never worked on John, and Gary's success with Mom and Dad and Katy and Janice drove John crazy. In John's eyes, Gary was an infuriating joke our parents had perpetrated on him.

"Okay, you're buying me dinner. Plus a stiff drink before."

"I never thought otherwise," he said, which meant that he hadn't thought about it at all.

But when we got there, Gary surprised me. He said to the maître d', "Can I still claim my reservation? It was for seven. I had an emergency."

The maître d' nodded, showing that he, too, knew Gary. He led us through the waiting crowd to a wood-paneled booth.

"I thought they never took reservations," I hissed.

Gary just smiled. But it was a weak smile that reflected his shock. He rapped the bell on the table and when a waiter arrived, he ordered us martinis.

"Gary," I said after the drinks came and we'd both had the kind of swallow that rockets down, assuring you things are not as bad as they seem, "you've seen dead bodies before, right?"

"Yeah. But not people I know." He now took a long, too easy swallow of gin, and I wondered how much lucid time I had with him. "Yeah, I've come across a couple of bodies, but then they're the problem, you know, and I have to figure out my client's response. But this . . . Tia . . ."

"Tell me about Tia."

"You know her."

"Not the way you do," I said, not knowing what that way was.

"Tia." His eyes half shut as he caressed her name.

"What was she like to date?"

He held the glass in both hands and looked into it as if it were a pool of memories. "Like winning the lottery, at least in the beginning. Every moment was exciting. She knew everyone, but she had this way—and I saw it from the other side later—of waving to people that acknowledged them enough to maintain working relations, while she squeezed my arm or whispered something out of the side of her mouth to me. It was a skill. I tried it but," he shrugged, "not me."

I wanted to cover Gary's hand with mine. Instead, I looked into my glass, sipped my drink, and didn't insert myself into his memory. "Winning the lottery . . ." I prompted.

"You know how I am about my work. Workaholic! All my wives complained. They were right, but that's the way it is in the law when you're going up against the best. Okay, I know it's maddening to be the one who ends up eating alone, canceling stuff with people, waiting for hours after your guy swore the third time he'd be right there."

"But Tia . . . ?"

"Tia . . ." He took another long swallow and the warmth of the gin spread across his face.

I took a sip of my drink. Two couples—a white-haired man in a long camel coat, a sturdy blonde woman dislodging a cashmere scarf, and two younger men, one of whom was probably their son and the other his partner—settled in the next booth.

"Tia," he caressed her name again. "We planned nothing ahead. I just called on the fly. That's the way she wanted it. Like when the other side got a continuance and suddenly I had two free days. I called at five. By eight we were on our way to Hawaii. In the morning we woke up with the waves off our lanai. It was like we were the last two people in paradise. We never saw a soul. But meals arrived; everything we needed was there. And Tia was a temptress in b—" Crimson spread over Gary's face.

"Forgot I'm your little sister, right?"

He swallowed the rest of his drink and rang the bell for the waiter. "Should've rabbits that last sentence."

I laughed.

"But it wasn't just long weekends, and wasn't just the sex. If I had two hours for dinner, she knew somewhere new and perfect. Going into the office late meant a morning like . . ." he smiled and I didn't ask. "Even a phone call; it was never the expected. She was game for anything; nothing frightened her. Or if it did, that just made her do it. A double dare. Plus, she always left me smiling."

"And what did you do for her?"

"Grace asked me that, and not as nicely, either. I paid, I was a respectable escort, and I appreciated every single thing."

The waiter arrived with a fresh martini, though Gary hadn't put in the order. He eyed the untouched menus. "We have Oregon clams."

Gary smiled. "Sautéed, then. Trust me, Darce. Allard only deals in the best."

I nodded and the waiter headed off. In his wake a wave of noise—laughter, talk, ice jangling, forks hitting china—washed over us, as if to remind us of our good fortune at having this booth. "So, Gary, I have to ask you, why did it end?"

He put down his glass, leaving his hand on it, finger circling on the sweating surface. "I don't know. Truth is, I didn't take it in for a while. I mean, it was over in her mind weeks, maybe months, before I added up the number of times I'd called and she didn't have time for dinner or even a weekend, or I just got no answer."

"Were you devastated, furious, humiliated?"

"No."

"Really?"

"Really. See, I was too busy. I had just gone solo and I was breaking in a new secretary and discovering I needed three paralegals instead of the one I thought I was getting by with before. I hadn't realized how much support I got from the firm. But on my own everything was a crisis and took more time and I needed to focus a lot more—"

"Just as Tia planned, right?"

"Huh?"

"She gave you the push to go solo, and then when you did, you were too busy to notice she wasn't there. You were happy with your new business. You couldn't be too upset about her after she'd made you do what you really wanted. And you didn't have time to wallow, right?"

"Yeah. But it's not like I never thought about her. I just didn't have time . . . well, like you said."

As if to save Gary further explanation the clams arrived, big luscious disks piled beside thick French fries. I forked one while the waiter was still setting down Gary's plate, dipped it in the tartar sauce, bit into it, and nodded serious approval. The waiter came as close to a smile as the white-aproned curmudgeons here permitted themselves. "Gary," I said after the second clam, "what did Tia tell you about Mike?"

He chewed more slowly, as if masticating my question. He put down his fork. "This may have been Tia's biggest gift as a friend: she never asked 'the question.' You've kept away from here so you don't have to deal with it, but every time any of us in the family makes a new friend, we just wait for 'the question.' We can pretty much judge what kind of friend they'll be by how long they hold off. Sometimes it's 'Have you ever heard anything more from Mike?' or 'What do *you* think really happened to him?'

Then there are the guys after a few drinks who lean in close and whisper, 'You know he's dead, right?' or the ones who ask whether it was Dad who abused him or us or Mom who didn't care enough or—"

"Jeez, Gary, stop!" Mom, who had been so grief-stricken after Mike's disappearance she either couldn't mention his name or couldn't stop talking about him—how could anyone dare to question her love? I wiped my napkin hard across my face to keep from bursting into tears. "I haven't come back here because I couldn't," I said slowly. "I couldn't face being reminded of Mike every time I turned a corner. Every time I saw a guy like—"

"Eamon."

"You know Eamon?"

"Of course. How could he be in San Francisco without any of us spotting him?"

I almost laughed. "Of course. I was just so shocked when I saw him. He must have thought I was nuts."

"Nah, he's used to family reactions. At first we were put off by him not keeping away, but he's become like a pet. Even though it's a jolt every time I see him, he's sanding the sharp edges. Even Mom's accepted him; she treats him like a nephew."

"Tia left the reception with him last night."

"Hmm." Gary forked his last clam and dipped it in sauce. He was thinking of Tia, and so was I. "Gary, when you questioned Tia after John did, early on, did she tell you anything?"

"Only that she had seen Mike at a party where there was liquor and grass, the kind of things that seem sophisticated to a sixteen-year-old."

"John said she was a liar."

"To him, yeah. You know, John can bring that out in people."

"But you don't think—"

"If she is, she's very good."

I didn't correct his use of the present tense. "So what did she say about Mike? In all the time you were with her, you had to have discussed him."

He fingered his last fry, held it up halfway to his mouth, studied it, put it back on the plate. A tray of dishes clattered in the distance behind him. A woman's shrill laugh stabbed through the reverberating chatter. "Tia never said anything about him that I didn't know. But the thing is, Darce, I always felt there was something she was keeping back. Could have been a theory, some fact she knew about him back then, something she heard. I couldn't even get that far in finding out. And, dammit, when I was with her I didn't want to spoil things by pushing. I could have, but I didn't. I kept telling myself that it was only my gut feeling that she had anything at all, and if she did it couldn't be important after all these years. There was plenty of time to ask. But if I did start to ask she kind of shriveled away from me. So I put it off."

What did *that* mean? I wondered.

The waiter came with the bill. "The clams were terrific, Allard," Gary said, laying down four twenties without glancing at the bill.

"Fortunate we hadn't run out during your delay, Mr. Lott."

So that is what it meant. "Your reservation, Gary, that was for you and Tia, right?"

He nodded sadly. "I thought I had forgotten her, but when she called it was the old excitement all over again."

"She called you? When?"

"I dunno, couple of days ago. The day you got here."

"So, the day before yesterday."

"Yeah, because I put her off in case . . . uh . . . you . . . needed anything."

"In case *I* needed? Really?" I was amazed. I'd always been such an add-on in the family, the kid born after the midlife surprise kid, the shock after the afterthought. And I was touched at how hard a time my big-time lawyer big brother, a master of cross-examining witnesses and swaying juries, had had admitting it. Now I did put my hand over his. "Thanks."

We pulled on jackets. Outside the fog was waiting. The valet brought his car.

"I'll drive," I said.

"I've only had a—"

"It's not that. Occupational hazard. I've been in too many car rolls, accidents, gas tank explosions. Most of the time I'm doubling the passenger, sitting in the death seat so that I can spot impending disaster and leap out at the last possible moment. Trust me, you don't want me there while you're driving."

"Okay, but no racing or rolling my car."

"It'll be like riding with an aunt who learned to drive when she was eighty." I had also won the To Hell and Back, the stunt doubles' auto race from the top of a nearly vertical canyon to bottom and back, no holds barred, no route too risky. But I felt it was better not to mention that just now.

Gary's car had all the things I never see on the cars we're about to crash on a set: padded leather seats, air bags, air conditioning, four speakers, and automatic transmission. I twisted the heat knob, another item there's no need for in stunt junkers, and pulled out onto Montgomery Street. Downtown San Francisco is dead after six. I swung across all four lanes of the Financial District's main drag as if I were making a right, hung a left on Market, and focused on avoiding the potholes and streetcar tracks, while Gary fiddled with the knobs on the console.

When he'd found one of the early Radiohead songs, shifted it to the rear speakers, and settled back in his seat, I asked, "Gary, what did Tia talk about when she called?"

"It was weird," he said, as if he'd been waiting for me to get to this. "She wanted to see me. That wasn't the weird part. But she suggested meeting at the old Letterman Hospital, in the Presidio, even though she loathed the changes they made when the Park Service took over from the Army and tore down the high-rise part."

"I thought everyone was ecstatic about the Park Service getting the land, and especially nabbing Lucas Films to be in there. As for Letterman, it was an ugly old building. Wasn't it there during the First World War? It looked like a place you'd have expired in during the flu epidemic of 1918."

"I didn't have time to drive across town, wander through the grounds, and then hunt up a restaurant out there. So I left a message telling her to meet me at Tadish's. I have no idea why she wanted to meet at the Letterman site. You're right, it was pre–World War I, old and bland. But to Tia it was vile."

"Vile! I love it. Jeez, I'm going to miss her. Not merely pedestrian, or ugly, but vile! If the Park Service could only hear that. Vile! Gary, did she give you any clue what she wanted?"

"Not really. The thing is, Darce, I haven't talked to her in a while, so I could be wro—no, I'm not! There was a touch of desperation in her voice. I mean, I was pleased and I was insulted that it took that kind of crisis to make her call. Still, I know how much she hated driving downtown and hassling with parking, and I figured if she was willing to come to the heart of the Fnancial District, she really needed to see me—"

"About?"

"I assumed she'd tell me at dinner."

I nodded resignedly, not that Gary was likely to notice in the dark. We had passed the Castro District and were going up the steep part of 17th Street now, over Twin Peaks. Even Gary's moose of a car was panting its way up. Had it been daylight on a rare day when there was no fog at all, we could have seen all the way to the end of the avenues, across the Great Highway to the Pacific, or at least imagined we could.

As it was, I headed down into the thicker fog, watching our cones of light extending less and less far from the grill and listening to what I took for foghorns, and realized was Gary snoring. I was very glad to be away from the zendo, the crime scene, going home. I was even more glad that Mom was still gone and I wouldn't have to tell her about Tia. I knew I was numb—that tomorrow Tia's death would hit me again, harder—but now I noted fuzzy red and green lights in the fog, found myself compulsively checking both sides of the street for pedestrians bursting from between cars, motorcyclists cutting me off, squad cars squealing in front of me. As always, my left foot was poised on the brake.

Soon I'd be sitting in the kitchen sipping a bit of Powers, wishing I had room for some of the stew that Grace was heating up. Soon everything would be all right.

I pulled up in front of the house, poked Gary awake, and got out. The house was dark. The only light inside was above the note board in the hall, where messages had been tacked as long as I could remember. Now it held a single sheet with my name. I unfolded it:

Darcy,

1. Call Jeffrey Hagstrom.

2. Robin Sparto wants you for a stair fall at 5:00 A.M. Grant & Francisco. He said to be on the set at 4:00! Eamon can take you then—no earlier. I told Sparto you'd be there at 4:30 and he should be thankful!

3. I called Jeffrey Hagstrom, left message that you had a pre-dawn gig and you would have to get back to him later. Okay?

I laughed. And then remembered laughing with Tia.

I reread the note. *Eamon* could take me at four in the morning? Did he live near here? Was he staying *here?* The ride downtown would take about twenty minutes. Good thing, because I had plenty to ask him about the zendo building and about his drive home with Tia.

Something had shifted in me. For the first time I had thought about Eamon not as Mike, but as our landlord, as, perhaps, the last person Tia had trusted.

Chapter 13

Leo had raced out too fast to bother with a jacket. Now the cold bit into his skin. He was alone, but that wouldn't last. This was just a respite before the barrage began again.

He closed his eyes and listened to the tight flow of his breath, to the whir of the air, felt the cold metal on his spine. He should plan his next move, consider his options. He smiled, almost laughed. That wouldn't take long. But no, he would not do that.

He recalled a night colder than this one, foggier, in which he had felt more desperate. In Japan, at the monastery, when he couldn't make the grade and couldn't go home to America, couldn't . . .

It was Yamana, his mentor, who had told him the story.

A monk came to see the roshi in dokusan. "Roshi," he said, "it is time that I leave and study with another teacher, as is our custom."

"Go with my approval," the roshi said. "But first I will give you a gift."

Leo remembered the surge of excitement he had felt at the idea of a special farewell gift chosen by the exalted head of the great monastery for this young monk.

The roshi picked up a pair of tongs, plucked a hot coal from his fire, and held it out to the monk.

The monk stared at the red-hot coal. Then he jumped up and ran out.

But he couldn't leave the monastery, not without the roshi's blessing. So he sat in meditation for a full week. He tried to figure out the meaning of what had just happened. How had his teacher expected him to react? How could he have accepted his teacher's strange gift and still managed not to burn his hands? What did the whole thing mean?

At the end of the week, he marshaled his courage and came back to dokusan.

"Roshi," he said, "it is time that I leave and study with another teacher, as is our custom."

Again, the roshi picked up a pair of tongs, plucked a hot coal from his fire, and held it out to the monk.

The monk stared at the red-hot coal. It hissed with steam. He trembled all over. Sweat ran down his face. He looked over his shoulder to the door, which he could open and run through again. He looked back at the roshi, trying to see the lesson for which this skin-searing coal was a symbol. He knew better than to put gloves between himself and his teacher's gift. There was no way to stall long enough for the coal to cool. No way to get the blessing without the burn.

The monk did the only thing he could. He bowed, put out his hands, and accepted his teacher's gift.

Leo, Garson-roshi, put out his hands and prepared to face the hot coal of what came next.

Chapter 14

THURSDAY

I ROLLED OUT of bed at three forty-five, brushed my teeth, pulled on clothes, and was downstairs before four. In our kitchen, coffee waited hot in the pot—it always did—but I'd get brew three times stronger from the lunch wagon on the set. Instead, I dialed the zendo. I'd wake Leo, and he wouldn't be pleased. But he was a priest; he'd pick up any call, particularly one in the middle of the night when it could be from someone desperate—like me.

Leo didn't answer.

Suddenly I was more awake than if I'd swallowed a quart of on-set coffee. Where *was* Leo? He wouldn't have just wandered off. Panic squeezed me. Had he been killed, too? Could he have . . . No, I couldn't let myself go diffuse with speculation. I forced myself to focus the way I did at the brink of a new gag, looking out over a fifty-foot blind drop or eyeing a junker I was about to roll. I exhaled, felt the tightness. Usually there was a crack.

Through that crack came a new set of thoughts. Of course, Leo couldn't sleep in his room—it was the crime scene. He wouldn't have slept in the only other bedroom, mine, lest I came back. So, he was probably curled up in the zendo. Traditionally monks have slept in the zendo, on their mats. Leo wouldn't think twice about it. And the zendo was too far for him to hear the phone. Leo would be at morning zazen in a couple of hours; we'd talk then. I was so relieved, I headed for a cup of coffee on principle. And so distracted, I almost walked into Eamon Lafferty putting his cup down.

"What are—?"

"Sorry. I must have shocked you. I've got a key."

"For driving me at this appalling hour, you should have a medal," I said. But it did shock me, him standing in the kitchen like Mike, his having a key.

I followed him outside. Unlike Gary's mobile parlor, Eamon's ride was a two-bucket muscle car. I'd barely snapped in the seatbelt when the car leapt away from the curb. At four in the morning, the street was empty. Streetlights seemed to flash on Eamon's face, sometimes revealing a tired-looking stranger, but at instants showing him so like Mike I had to turn away.

I stared through the windshield and the memories of last night—of seeing Tia dead—flooded in. "All that blood! I just can't believe it."

"I know. God, I still can't believe she's dead." His voice was taut and ragged. "This time yesterday morning I was sprawled in bed dreaming of her. I woke up smiling, figuring I'd call her for dinner." He looked over at me. "Darcy, how can she be dead?"

I had to jam my teeth together for a moment before I could even speak. "The way she died; so vicious. So personal. Who could have done that?"

He shook his head. "You were around the zendo before, right? Down in the tunnel with the movie people?"

"Yes?"

"Did you see Jeffrey?"

"Jeffrey? Why him? You don't think that Jeffrey killed her?" I asked, shocked.

"No! I was just trying to figure who knew her best, who'd have a bead on her friends or anyone who had it in for her." He hung a left on Geary and as soon as he was on the boulevard, glanced over at me and added, "I'm not pointing the finger—Jeff's my friend—but Tia really roller-coastered him that night by the tunnel."

"Yeah, what was that all about?"

"I heard you saw him afterwards. What did he say?"

I sat, feeling the heat on my shins, staring out at the dark shop and restaurant façades. "He wasn't angry, at least not at Tia. Really, he was more emotional about how his father treated him and how pissed his father'd be to know he was using his inheritance to sell weird chairs. I guess his thinking of using that revolting tunnel under the zendo to store his father's things says it all."

"He told you that!"

"About the stuff, yeah."

Eamon shook his head. "That's Jeff in a nutshell. He hates the old man, but still he can't bring himself to toss his stuff. I knew his father when he was a civilian in the military lab. He wasn't running on all cylinders even then. He was sure they were out to cheat him. I don't think he ever came up with anything he could patent, but he totally believed if he did, the military would grab the rights. You know how that kind of man is, full of excuses for his own failure: 'I could have been Pasteur or Salk, but what's the point? They'll only snatch the profits!'"

"You worked for him, right?"

He nodded. "The thing is, he wasn't that far wrong about the military in general. They never cared about anyone's potential. Even I could see it, and I was barely out of college. There were some brilliant scientists, with lots of ideas, chomping at the bit to exploit them, just waiting for someone to open the right channels. It was such a waste. What they needed was someone— Sorry. You'll be thinking I'm not so close to sane either. So, Jeff seemed okay? Not upset, unnerved?"

"Not enough to keep him from making me coffee and heating up focaccia. But what about Tia? I mean when you drove her home. What'd she say?"

"Nothing I can—"

"Eamon, something happened before you two left the zendo. She made a point of inviting me to lunch yesterday. There was something she was going to tell me. She'd kept a diary the year my brother, Mike, disappeared. She was going to get it. And then she disappeared."

"Yesterday? She was going to tell you something yesterday?"

"Yes. She went downstairs and never came back. Lunch was still on the table. But my point is, she asked me over there to tell me something and now I have no clue what it was. Did she say anything, *anything*, to you? Even if it seemed insignificant."

He raked his lip with his upper teeth. After a string of green lights and then yellows, we were finally coming to a light I thought he couldn't make. But he hit the gas and shot through as it turned red.

"Surely," I insisted, "Tia must have told you—"

He turned toward me so that he was driving with half an eye on the road. "There's something; it's dangling at the edge of my mind. Not from last night. I'll remember later. But last night I only stayed at her place a little while. She seemed distracted, nervous, I assume, about the way she treated Jeffrey. But she didn't talk about that and it was none of my business. So we just talked about her installation. She was a great artist. It was a knockout installation, wasn't it? I had no idea she was that good."

"So you knew her before you learned she was an artist?" Maybe he did know more about her than he was saying or than he even realized he wasn't saying. "How'd you meet?"

"The usual way." He shot me an assessing glance. "Usual for me. She spotted me in Baltimore and did that Mike double take. I've seen it so often now it's almost like a greeting, but then it was a shock."

"When was that?"

"Oh, six, maybe seven years ago?"

"Funny, she said yesterday what a shock it had been to see you. I just assumed that'd happened recently, I mean, here. Why was she in Baltimore? Some kind of treatment? Johns Hopkins?"

"No, no. She was taking the airporter, and there was a waiting area where I worked."

"Was she there for medical—"

"Nothing like that. It's a lab—weapons research. And anyway, she was just visiting a guy, one of the scientists. They'd just gotten back from some kind of adventure weekend. Both of them had that exhausted, exhilarated look, you know? So when she spotted me, she was wild. She ran across the room."

I could imagine how excited she'd have been. But I had to focus on what I was asking. "What kind of adventure?"

"Darcy, you don't get the picture. She really thought I was Mike. I had no idea what she was talking about. And then, when I did, I was blown away. When I got home I Googled him. The first stories were from San Francisco newspapers, with pictures. It was like looking in the mirror. I couldn't get it out of my mind. And then I kept watching for more, hoping, you know, like it was half me that was missing. Every year or so there'd be a story, always with pictures: once with John in uniform by a patrol car, another with Grace when she was the city liaison at the Letterman lab, and the last time with your mom outside the house—pictures to jog Mike's memory if he had amnesia. Katy told me that later."

"My sister, Katy, planted stories?"

"To keep him in the news. All the stories had his picture. Didn't you ever see them?"

I shook my head. He couldn't have seen that, but he didn't ask again, and

I felt a rush of gratitude when he went on. "When I ended up coming out here, one of the first things I did was check the library just in case I had missed something en route, an article about him being found. I was really hoping—" He swallowed. He was looking ahead now, not so much concentrating on the road as not looking at me. "Darcy, I'm so sorry he's not back. I keep wishing, not like you do, I don't mean to say that, but just . . ."

No wonder the family had welcomed him into the fold. No one else cared this much anymore. I wanted to keep talking about Mike, to know about every news article, bask in every mention of him as long as I could. There was so much I didn't know. So much I didn't know about any of them—Mike, my siblings, Eamon himself.

"Eamon, ten, fifteen years ago you were a lab grunt, right? Now you own a building in the Barbary Coast. How'd that happen?"

"Not own, lease." He looked toward me and grinned. "Still a big step. And your family's made everything easier. But I am good at bringing people together, seeing connections. You know, I'm actually grateful for that tedious time in the lab. It made me keep an eye out for a connection, like seeing who could be better off somewhere else."

"So, you're a head hunter?"

"More like a head spotter—spotting heads that go together."

Was it just modesty? Or was there more to moving these lucrative heads around? I remembered Jeffrey's observation about him letting the building inspectors think he was related to John. But that was such a small deception. "Still, you lease this pricey building and then you give it to the zendo—and you're not even a Buddhist." I tapped his shoulder and waited till he looked over. "So, how come?"

He stretched his fingers and took his time placing them back on the wheel, as if using the time to come to a decision. "Don't go repeating this. Agreed?"

"Okay."

"I did it as a favor to John."

"My brother John?"

"The same."

"Why? The world would come to an end before John Lott would ever sit himself on a zafu."

Eamon threw his head back and howled. "Too true! It definitely wasn't that he cared about meditation. The thing was, he heard Leo was leaving the monastery in the woods. Leo had to go somewhere. He knew you were his assistant. And your mother wanted you back here."

My mouth hung open. "It's all for me? I'm the reason for the entire zendo? There was no need for a zendo? It's just there so I would come back to San Francisco?"

"Not no need," he said quickly. "People are coming already, aren't they?"

I nodded. My thoughts swirled. I hoped Leo didn't know the Lott family was behind his being here. Mom wanted me back that much? And John . . . I could barely take it in. And Eamon's incredibly generosity. "That's a huge favor you did for John. I've heard it called a bad luck property. Someone was telling me about it being boarded over, about ghosts and snakes—"

"Portland! That's it! I knew there was something Tia said about Mike! It was in the back of my mind; I just couldn't get it. If we hadn't been talking about coming home, I would never have made the connection. Tia said she had seen me getting on a plane in Portland. But the thing is, Darcy, I've never been in Portland."

My whole body went light. "Really? Did she think she really saw Mike?"

"She did at the time. He was getting on a plane, so there was nothing she could do about it."

"A plane to where?"

"She didn't say?"

"Didn't you ask?" I demanded.

"I should have. I'm sorry. The conversation went in a different direction."

Damn! "Did she say when that was? What year, even?"

"No." His voice was ragged; he dragged out the word as if he was raking through his memory for any scrap of a clue. My stomach was leaping, my skin quivering. It was all I could do to keep from grabbing his arm and shaking him. "I can't tell you why, but I have the feeling it wasn't recent, because . . . wait . . . because she didn't say she couldn't get to him because of her leg; she just sounded like he'd been unreachable. But that's just assumption on my part. I'm sorry. I wish I'd jumped on this, but at the time . . . and I'm really sorry, but the thing is she didn't say she was thinking it was Mike, she was couching it like she'd seen me but she couldn't be sure because I was getting on a plane. I'm sorry, but here's the truth: I just thought she was flirting."

I felt like a thousand pounds was crashing down into the seat. So damned close! I took a breath and forced myself to take what there was. It wasn't Eamon's fault, really it wasn't. "It's okay," I forced out. "That means he's alive! I've always known it! But this, this is proof! This changes everything. Omigod!" He braked. We were at the set—already. I hadn't even realized we were in North Beach. I looked out at the roadblock, then at my watch: 4:35 A.M. I was already late. "Damn! Where will you be later?"

"Around the zendo. But I told you every bit I know."

"You might remember more."

"I won't. I'm sorry. But I don't want to get your hopes up. That's all—"

"Finally!" Robin Sparto was rapping on the car window.

I held up a hand to him and turned back to Eamon. "Thanks for everything. Really." I shrugged at Eamon and got out.

Sparto had moved away from the car and it was a moment before I realized he'd seen Eamon and backed off. But now it was just him and me, and he was yelling. "Come on! Did you think this was a 10 A.M. call? It's fucking twenty to five! We've only got the site till six. And then there's the light. This is a night shot, dammit!"

"So, where's the staircase?"

"I thought you lived here. Don't you know your own city? It's over there."

I hurried over to the circle of light. The staircase was still lit only by streetlamps, but even so I could make out the steps. They were cement, the railings metal with supports every six feet—just far enough to get up enough speed to smack them hard—and the staircase had no landings. It was three stories unbroken.

This was the stair fall from Hell.

CHAPTER 15

"WHERE DO I get padding, Robin?" The set was empty but for the second unit and the general support guys. The cameras were staked at the top and, presumably, bottom of the staircase and one had been suspended beside it, on a runner line, to follow the action. The street, lined with flats and small apartment buildings, had been blocked off and the company's vans and wagons were double-parked behind us. Their lights were off and they stood as dark rectangles in front of the larger dark rectangular dwellings. The permit the company had gotten would require as little light and as much silence as possible at this hour, before residents were awake. The location set looked deserted.

"Costume wagon's over there," Robin said, pointing downhill and behind us to a van the size of a weekender for an intimate couple. "Just get the wig and the outfit. It's a skin shot. No place for pads."

"No padding! All that saves stair falls is padding."

"What saves them is skill. If you're not good enough . . ."

I didn't have time to waste arguing. In the costume wagon I slipped on silk drawstring pants, made to be worn lower on the hips than any nineteenth-century Chinese courtesan ever dreamed of, a camisole with all inessential cloth in tatters, and the black wig. No shoes. Even with long camera shots, there was no way to pass my sturdy stands off as tiny aphrodisiacs. There was no makeup because the camera would never be on my face. It would catch the rolls, the arms and legs flailing, the slams into the steps and the pole railings, the head over heels, the exposed skin. And if they were lucky, the blood.

It was 4:50 A.M. I strode to the top of the stairs. "Flashlight?" I asked the bulky blond lighting tech who was adjusting the bank of night lights.

"Don't have!"

"A lighting tech without a flashlight? On a night shoot?"

The guy shrugged.

What kind of operation was this? I had had some question about the catcher bag placement in my last gag, but that could have been just a mistake. Now, when the crew didn't have the basic equipment . . . I was on the verge of demanding, "What if that fine bank of lights started to wobble? How would you check the stand?" But I didn't have time to waste on him. I barely had time to scope the stairs and do a practice run. I needed a torch. But there was no time to comb the set.

After last night in the dark tunnel, I'd grabbed the smallest of the family stash of flashlights. I hadn't expected to need it so soon. It was meant to illumine a door lock or show a woman the makeup in one quadrant of her face. I flashed it on the steps. Unadulterated cement steps: no padding on the edges, no thin foam cover, not even a sprinkling of leaves and mulch to prevent the cement from scraping skin. Robin should have made sure the edge of every step was padded. I illumined the pipe railing uprights. The crew should have been here an hour ago spreading a strong temporary glue on the uprights' "north side"—the side invisible to the camera—to hold a strip of padding the same color as the pole, just thick enough to cushion the blow when I rolled into it. There was nothing: no padding, no glue.

"Robin!" I yelled as I stalked toward him. "What the hell is going on here? There's no padding anywhere. As long a shot as you're going to have to take on this, you could have padded the hillside."

"This is not the spa; it's stunt work."

"It's incompetence! Either get some padding on the uprights—"

"Hey, if you're not tough enough—"

"You'll what? Call the crowd of applicants you had waiting if I didn't call you back at eleven o'clock last night?"

"You want to have any rep in this business—"

I lowered my voice. "I already have a rep in this business, and it's for doing things right. We don't have much time. Get me glue and pad strips, and I'll do the setup myself."

His hands were weaving back and forth, lost in their emptiness. "Fine! You set the whole thing up, but plan to do the gag in one take, because the sun's not going to wait for you to cushion every edge." He stalked off, followed by an assistant.

Why was this crew so hostile? They hadn't been this way two days ago. Not friendly then, but not hostile. Robin, himself, had been normal last night, happy for my help in viewing the tunnel. Now he was off the deep end. The lighting techs had abandoned their posts, leaving the staircase in shadows. On a normal set, before the shoot began there would be scurrying, whispering because of the neighbors, but lots of talk. This one was dead quiet. A normal second unit crew is close-knit; we know our success, our jobs, and at times our lives depend on each other; we're looking to help. This crew was anything but.

Common sense told me to drop the supply box and walk away. But stunt work values the tough. You triple-check every knot and hinge, but you never let on you're afraid, never ever even hint there's a standard stunt you won't do. That goes double for a woman.

The night wind whipped up the hill, channeled between the buildings. It slapped the strands of the long black wig against my face. I shivered in the skimpy costume. I could still walk away.

But dammit, I was not about to give Robin the satisfaction. I turned and nearly stumbled over a clear storage box of supplies: glue, pad strips, scissors, torch, tape, magnifying glass. Hoisting the box, I strode to the top of the staircase. There wouldn't be time to pad every step and post. I had to map my route for the fall pronto. I could hear Leo repeating the kernel of Zen instruction: *Don't assume. See things as they are, not through your own eyes.* I pushed aside my questions and focused on the route. The uprights were about six feet apart on the left side of the staircase. I would hit every other one, do a "react," a roll, change directions, and aim for the next upright. Hard as the uprights were, rough and sharp as the edges of the stairs were, they were the only momentum brakes. Stair falls are like driving downhill when your brakes fail; you slow yourself by scraping or bouncing off the things that will injure you the least, but if you want to live, you have to check your momentum. Ideally, stair falls are done in segments, and as close to slo-mo as reasonable. The film can be speeded up later. Ideally.

I didn't fool myself about this gag. I flashed my light down the steps, painted glue, cut a padding strip, and pasted and moved on. The light on the staircase grew dimmer as I descended away from the streetlights. Two of the path lamps were out and thick foliage half-covered two others. I flashed my torch on the steps, then the uprights, and back to the steps, watching as I moved for cuts or brakes, knives of rough cement in the edges of the steps, protruding branches, debris.

"Five minutes!"

There was a landing about four feet long at the bottom, then a drop to the street. If I hit the last upright before it with the fleshy part of my hip, that would spread the force of impact in both directions, toward my head and feet, rather than bouncing it back. From there I would stagger across the landing and back, and have time to set up a clean drop to the sidewalk.

My shot would end and the next thing the viewer would see would be the actress sprawled on the sidewalk.

"Three minutes!"

I walked slowly upward, eyeing each step one last time. At the top, a woman started pulling on my wig, and another shifted something about one sleeve. The script supervisor waved them away and motioned me to the start point. She showed me a photo of beautiful Ajiko Sakai at yesterday's close on this sequence. I took the same stance. As the script supervisor fine-tuned it, I ran my sequence in my mind, eyeing the first upright, feeling my shoulders pull forward just before I hit it so I could be into the rollaway before the impact.

"Lights!" Robin called.

The banks came to life behind me. The brightness would glimmer off my clothing and pick up the shine of the wig.

"Camera! Action!"

I burst forward, taking two short strides to the edge of the staircase, leaning into the fall. I bent my legs, letting the shins flutter as my feet came up. At the first pull of gravity I rolled, and came down on hands and feet facing the steps. I rolled right, hit the upright hard, but the padding helped, rolled left, flailing arms and legs as I passed over the middle of the stairs, pulled in as I hit the other side, and let the momentum carry me a foot over the wall onto the soft underbrush. Keeping my head tucked, face protected, I somersaulted through the leaves and branches, landing so softly on my back I would have come to a stop had I not pushed off to roll across the steps again into the next upright. Grabbing it, I swung myself up, feet on the edge of a step to give the appearance of almost regaining balance, only to have my feet slip. I angled forward so my body slid down the steps, spreading the impact and allowing me to use the hand on the upright and the other one, hidden under my body, for control. When my feet were fully on another step and my body upright back to the camera, I'd fall backwards, arms flung wildly. I kept my knees bent till the last moment, pushed off toward the railing, caught it with my right hand, and guided my body into the next upright.

The padding was gone! My shoulder banged hard into the metal, sending shots of pain through my head. I couldn't see straight. I couldn't stop. I flung myself across the steps to the shrubbery. One more move and I'd be on the landing with an instant to regain control before the final drop. My head was throbbing. I pushed off, upright again, side to the camera as if staggering sideways down. My feet hit the landing and slid.

The landing was wet! I sailed across and off the edge into the drop.

Using every ounce of abdominal muscle, I yanked my chest forward as my feet flew backwards into space. My arms and head hit the cement. I grabbed for traction. My hands slid; my head was beyond the edge, into air. I bent my knees. My fingertips slid over the edge. I dropped into space.

I hit the sidewalk at an angle and staggered back. No one caught me. My head was spinning, throbbing. I thought I was going to throw up. My arms were bleeding, my knees were raw, and I knew I would be black and blue on all sides. I couldn't think straight. How? Who? The padding had been removed from the upright. And somehow the landing that had been dry five minutes earlier was covered in water.

Most suspicious was the absence of people around me. When a gag goes well, the second unit is elated. Everyone applauds because everyone had a part in it. But here, no one applauded; no one was watching the drop in case I needed to be steadied once I was off camera. No one was there at all except the paramedics. Even the camera crew was keeping its distance. The only person moving toward me was—

Omigod! Detective Korematsu! What was he doing here? How did he know I would be here? Maybe he wasn't after me. Maybe he was just walking to work or— Get a grip, girl! Whatever he was doing here, he was the last person I intended to deal with now.

To my left, under a canopy of live oak branches, were steps that led to the staircase. I raced up as fast as I could make my aching legs move. Each step activated a new area of pain—stomach, thigh, knee, ankle, foot. The leaves and branches swam. Once on the staircase proper, there was no overhanging greenery to conceal me. My abdominal muscles shrieked—I had torn them, I knew, and each step tore them more. I needed to stop, to bend over, to wrap my burning middle in ice. I focused on each step, just making it through the next step, one after another after another, not looking up, definitely not looking behind me. If Korematsu called out to me, I didn't hear him over the shouts of my own pain.

After an eternity, the stars in front of my face vanished. I was at the top of the staircase. I sighed but didn't stop till I was in Robin Sparto's face. "The padding was ripped off! The padding *I* just glued on! I could have been killed! What the hell is going on here?"

"You—" He gulped back the accusation.

"Listen to me! Safety is your job. How could you let someone rip off the padding? There was five minutes between the time I glued that padding and the start of the gag. In those five minutes someone ripped off the padding and sprayed water on the landing. They could do that because it's dark down there, because, Robin, you had no security, no crew down there. If I'd been maimed, I could sue this company into bankruptcy and everyone in the business would be pointing the finger at you. So, tell me, how did this happen, huh? Who did it?" I yelled.

He shrank back, looking over my shoulder for help.

I grabbed his arms. "Who, Robin?"

"The police?"

SUSAN DUNLAP

What was he talking about? Out of the corner of my eye I saw Korematsu.

I let go of Sparto and faced the detective. "Yes?" I snapped.

"I need to talk to you. When you're finished here."

"About?"

"When you're finished."

I turned back. But I was finished. Sparto was a couple of yards away, surrounded by people and moving away fast.

"Hey!" I yelled after. Yelling at him was my first mistake. Sparto picked up his pace. Malice or incompetence, he wasn't about to tell me which. I glared back at Korematsu and made my second mistake. "Obviously, I'm finished! So what is it you can't wait for?"

He pulled a picture out of an envelope. "Do you recognize this knife?"

"Yes. We use it to trim the candles on the altar. The blade's a little long for that, but . . ." My whole body went cold. "Omigod! Is that what killed Tia?"

"When did you last see it?"

"I don't know. I mean, I just got here, to the city. I've only been to one sitting and I didn't do the candle afterwards. We don't trim them after every sitting," I said, trying to remember when I had seen that knife with the green and black handle that Leo liked so much. "I don't think I've seen it here at all."

"But you've used it to trim candles?"

"No, I've seen the people assigned to care for the altar using it."

"But not here?"

"No," I said with relief. "Not here."

"Then you haven't seen it since you were with Leo Garson in the monastery up north a couple of months ago? But you saw it there?"

Oh, shit!

132

CHAPTER 16

KOREMATSU OFFERED ME a ride to the zendo. I declined. Bad enough I'd let him question me when I was still shaken from the stair fall sabotage and riding my fury at Robin Sparto. At least I had the sense not to let him get me alone in a police car. I'd already incriminated Leo—and me—plenty.

Leo! I needed to warn him. The zendo wasn't far. I slipped into the wardrobe wagon. As I changed back into my own clothes—sweater, loose pants, good leather belt, thick black nubby vest—reality slapped me. Furious as I'd been with Robin Sparto, the full import of what had happened hadn't struck till now. Someone had tried to kill me! Or close to it! It was only because of luck, or skill, that I wasn't lying at the bottom of the staircase with my brain all over the sidewalk.

Who? Who even knew I was going to be here? Who had I told? The film crew sure wasn't friendly or careful, but kill? That was a huge leap.

If not them, who? And how? But that part was easy. In the dark there'd been plenty of time for someone to come up from the bottom of the staircase, pull off the padding, and splash a thermos of water.

Suddenly the bruises on my shoulders, back, hips, arms, and legs throbbed and I felt woozy all over. I had never been panicked in a stunt. Even after stunts that went bad, there was always technique to focus on, the next shoot to worry about. But now, with nothing to distract me from the cold truth that someone didn't want me alive, I stood and shivered.

I knew I should check the staircase for evidence, though I also knew there wouldn't be any. Anyway, there wasn't time. Korematsu could already be knocking on the zendo door. Leo wouldn't fall into the trap I did—answering questions in the heat of emotion. Leo would tell the truth without considering the consequences. He'd look at the photograph of the altar knife and say, yes, that was his. One of a set of two he liked, not just because of the smart green and black pattern on the handle, but because knives used to trim candle wax tend to get dull, and the blades on these held their sharpness. He'd tell Korematsu what he'd told me: "They cut better than any knife I've had."

I yanked on my shoes, jumped down from the wardrobe wagon, and raced full out for the zendo. My knees shrieked, my shoulders screamed, and everything between hurt. Sweat ran down my face, covered my body. I crossed Broadway once again—was it just yesterday afternoon that Tia was still alive?—and ran downhill the two blocks to Pacific, expecting to find Korematsu's car dead in front of the zendo.

But it wasn't. No car, no light anywhere. "Leo!" I called as I took the steps two at a time. No reply. No Garson-roshi. Where was he?

It was naïve to assume the cops would have cleaned up: there was still black powder all over the doorjambs, and Tia's blood, maroon now and caking on the floor of Leo's room, shocked me. Was she so unimportant that her blood was left for us to walk on? Poor Tia, she deserved better than this. And Leo, who'd only been in this beautiful zendo a couple of days and had only met Tia yesterday: he deserved better, too. But their disregard was his good fortune. Of course he hadn't slept here. Was he at one of the other Zen centers in the city? Or did he still have friends here? Maybe he was with his luncheon date?

I grabbed a rag and bucket and started cleaning. Despite my bruises it felt good to be doing something finite, ordinary, and useful. I tackled it as if it were a work period task in a *sesshin*, focusing on wringing out the cloth, wiping up a swath of soot, wringing out the cloth, noting my thoughts, letting them go.

At 6:30—ten minutes before zazen—the downstairs door creaked open. Leo was cutting it close. I sighed with such relief that I dropped the towel. I hadn't realized how worried I was. Or how tired. I hurried down to tell him I would be lying low for a while.

But the figure in the vestibule wasn't Leo. It was the grizzled guy who'd been here yesterday morning, the one who squirmed so much I'd decided he was just keeping warm in the zendo until he could find a place for coffee. Where was Leo? For the first time it struck me that I had no idea how long he'd been gone. Did he even know Tia was dead? Or did he know only too well by now?

"Are you Darcy?" the man asked.

"Yes."

"I have a message for you. The priest here, Leo Garson, left it on the machine at the Caffè." He must have seen my confusion. "Renzo's. I'm Renzo."

"Oh. Thanks. But why didn't he call my cell?"

Renzo shrugged. "What he said was, *Ask Darcy to lead the morning sitting. Ask her to mention the Hungry Ghosts Ceremony.*"

"Where is he?"

"Dunno. Somewhere noisy." He glanced into the zendo. "Not like here." When I didn't respond, he asked, "Is there going to be zazen this morning? I mean, can there be without Leo?"

"Of course. Zazen is just sitting, in this case sitting together. Having the priest sit in the zendo with you is very nice, but it's not necessary. We'll start in five minutes." I caught his eye, glanced around the empty zendo, and smiled at him. "Sit anywhere."

Where was Leo? Did he even know about his knife? And what about its duplicate? Was it still in the box of altar-cleaning supplies in the hall closet where anyone could snatch it? It was too late to look now. Now I had to hit the wooden clappers to call people to zazen, and decide how to explain the Ceremony of Feeding the Hungry Ghosts. Like Day of the Dead ceremonies and memorials, the Hungry Ghost Ceremony deals with honoring those who died during the year, but its focus is on letting them go. Hungry ghosts are ravenous, yet they can never get enough. They are consumed with wanting, with insatiable greed. The ceremony itself— But I realized I didn't know just how Leo would do the ceremony.

When I walked back into the zendo, Renzo had been joined by three other people I'd seen at the reception: the lithe Asian woman, the blonde I'd taken to be a lawyer, and Benton Stallworth, the one I'd thought of as the archetypal thug. I nodded to them as if they were old hands here and walked into the dawn-dark zendo. Everything was as it must have been after the evening zazen last night: black zabuton mats lined up on the floor, four along each wall, folding chairs by the door, waiting for the stiff-hipped or those who had already blown out their knees.

On the altar the Buddha sat cross-legged with his hands in the teaching position, one on his lap and the other on his right knee, fingertips touching the earth or, in this case, his stand. In front of the altar was a thick kneeling mat. I stood at the end as Leo would have, bowed to the altar, stepped around to the other end, between it and the altar, bowed again, lit the candle and the incense, aware with every move of Leo's absence. I moved to the seat opposite where Leo should have been sitting and bowed to it, and when I turned to bow to the room, the crowd had doubled. I sat, adjusted myself on my cushion, giving them time to do the same, then rang the bell.

136

The soft, sweet sound floated across the room and for an instant seemed to connect everyone in it.

Unlike yesterday, people sat facing the wall, as is traditional. Renzo's long narrow face, half-closed brown eyes, and ponytailed brown hair, thin on top, gave him the look of a coffeehouse San Franciscan with time to ponder, hold forth, and bob in each wave of change that washed across the city. One thing he'd changed was his clothes. In place of yesterday's rumpled jacket and slacks were new jeans and a black fleece jacket so new the tag was still on the back.

I sat in front, facing them, eight in all, and wondering how many were here to sit zazen, how many to check out a murder scene.

The shadow of the altar flowers danced on the wall, like a tall couple too in love to move their feet, swaying minutely as the last chords died. Like thoughts dissipating into the air. I let my own float off too and just sat, listening to the sounds of breathing, the crackle of wax, the swish of cloth, feeling every new pain from the aching in my shoulders to the excruciating soreness in my tailbone. And when the forty minutes were over, I rang the bell and said, not what Leo had instructed about the Hungry Ghost Ceremony, but this: "Today's service will be a memorial to Tia Dru, who was my friend. Please feel comfortable saying something about her. Then we will offer incense and chant the Heart Sutra."

Usually at memorial services one or two people speak briefly. Usually one of those people is the one who asked for the service. I stood, fluffed my cushion, turned to the group and took a deep breath. But before I could start, Benton Stallworth said, "I hoped she would return to films. She could have, despite her limp. Couldn't convince her, though. Pity." He shook his head. "Pity."

I found myself staring at him, amazed that he had known Tia since before her accident.

"Had hoped," he said softly as if the words were escaping through a barely open window of his heart. They hung in the midst of us and seemed to echo the others' feelings.

"I had hoped, I really thought, that she would be okay," Renzo said. "I was there at her accident. That's how I know her. I thought she was going to die, mangled as she was, blood all over, skin hanging off her. I thought . . . But then, you know, I hoped, I wanted to see her like she was before, and I believed—yeah, it wasn't just hope, I really believed—she would walk out of the hospital without a cane. There was just something about Tia that shouldn't have been tethered, you know?" Renzo inhaled sharply and swallowed. He looked like a man who was looking beneath what he had assumed. "I didn't see her often. But it was always like we'd just talked yesterday. I told her about this place, the property, I mean. I told her. And now . . ." He pulled out a handkerchief and blotted his eyes. It was gray, looked as if it had been meant to peek out of a pocket of a tailored suit, and yet it didn't seem odd now for it to have been in his jeans pocket.

"She . . . Tia . . ." the blonde woman cleared her throat and tried again, "Tia . . . was the most . . ." she swallowed. Her hands were shaking. I was two seats away from her, too far to offer a hand of comfort. But now I saw that her face didn't have that stunned look of grief but was pinched in nervousness, as if what was constricting her was not Tia, but fear of what she intended to say. "Tia," she said softly, "was the most daring woman, no, daring *person*, I ever met."

Benton Stallworth jolted forward, toward her, then caught himself.

Renzo made no pretense of eyes-down. He was staring at both the blonde woman and Stallworth. And the woman herself had gone dead pale.

We all waited, but she said no more. The silence of the room seemed to close in around her. Her words hung, as if daring had a meaning beyond what we knew.

Renzo blew his nose—

But it wasn't him blowing his nose; that squeak was coming from behind him, from the doorway. The door to the vestibule was open only an inch. Leo? I was holding my breath.

The door didn't move. Not Leo. Someone else out there. The idea of someone standing out there, listening to us, to Renzo's remorse, infuriated me, and it scared me. The blonde woman looked terrified, as if the eavesdropper were here because of her.

I breathed in as I had learned in acting classes and said as calmly as I could, "Please come in. It's not too late to join the service."

The door creaked slowly, as if things had shifted to slow motion. In our group no one turned around, but eyes moved. The door opened and Korematsu stepped in. He was wearing the same dark jacket and blue shirt he had had on an hour ago on the set. To me he reeked of cop, but to anyone else he must have looked like a guy nervously pushing away a thick swath of hair that hadn't quite fallen onto his forehead, so he could get himself together enough to speak. In my peripheral vision I saw a hand start to reach out to him. He looked like a guy who could have dated Tia.

But he was a cop, the investigator on this case, and I knew damn well what he was doing, lurking around the memorial, vulturing for suspects, as if it were some sort of mob funeral. Dammit, he was taking advantage of the grief of these people in our zendo. I'd been sitting in the front seat, the only seat that faces into the room; it had been my job to watch their backs during zazen, literally and figuratively, and I was not about to let any one of them be emotionally mugged now.

I took a breath, stared him in the eye, and said, "We have been speaking of Tia, as you heard. Now that you're here at her memorial service, what is your remembrance of her?"

Chapter 17

I never thought Korematsu would answer my question. I had just wanted to make him as uncomfortable as Renzo would be when he realized his emotional comments had been overheard by a cop and now would become part of the investigation report. But Korematsu stood as thoughtfully as the others had. The only difference was that when he spoke he watched their reactions, and mine. "I didn't know Tia. Mostly I read about her. I only"—he paused, eyes looking up as if searching right behind the skin of his forehead for the words he needed—"came into contact with her twice. The first time was at the accident scene. I was on patrol; I took the call."

The blonde woman jolted back as if she'd been slapped. Benton Stallworth shifted his bulk to face Korematsu and looked him over as if the police officer had suddenly become worthy of his attention. The lithe woman glanced at her watch, and Renzo had no reaction. He, of course, had been around last night and must have noted Korematsu on the scene then. Renzo was taking in my surprise. I should have been impressed at Korematsu's honesty, but I remembered John saying over and over as I grew up: look for the secondary motive. A good cop always has a hidden reason. What did this one have to gain now?

If Korematsu was staging his comments for us, he was doing an Oscar-worthy job. His gaze was to the floor now, his head slightly bowed. He thrust his hands in his pockets as if to get them out of sight. "I thought she was dead. Like you did. Her back . . . very bad. I was sure she wouldn't make it." He inhaled slowly. "But she did. It was a testament to her, to medicine, but really to her. I always read the blurbs in the paper about her, I cheered for her, you know, like I was a proud parent." He inhaled again, more slowly. The rasping sound of his breath cut the silence. He said, "The second time I was with her was last night."

It was hard to disbelieve that level of sincerity. But Benton Stallworth had managed. He didn't harrumph, but his muffled cough gave the same message. I wondered if he saw something I'd missed.

The Asian woman glanced at her watch again.

The vestibule door opened. My brother John glared in. What was he doing here?

Before he could speak, I reached for the bell. "Normally we each offer incense, but this morning we will just end with the chanting of the Heart Sutra. I'll pass out cards with the words."

Chanting always begins raggedly in a Zen center where few have been trained. Zen attracts individualists, and nowhere is that clearer than in the chanting of sutras. For the voices to mesh, women would have to go an octave higher than the men; women are not about to do so, perhaps not anywhere, definitely not in San Francisco. Men could go lower. They don't. They have their reasons, too. Hearing the first lines of the Heart Sutra chanted is an invitation to experience the gap between desire and reality.

I chanted the title: *Prajna Paramita Hridaya Heart Sutra* and was poised to motion people to start when Benton Stallworth's full baritone rang out. For a minute he rang forth into stunned silence, then one by one voices joined his, their shakiness covered by the rich certainty of his. By the time we reached *Form is no other than emptiness, emptiness no other than form,* the words seemed to encompass us and Tia Dru, life and death. At least to me, and I didn't look up from them to observe anyone else. John would be glaring at Korematsu. Korematsu would be ready for him. They'd both be eager to get to or from me whatever it was they wanted at the location set. I didn't dare look up. This might be as much of a memorial service as Tia got. I wanted to prolong the moment for her.

But when the service was over, what I wanted was to snag the blonde woman who'd had such a strong reaction to Tia and to Korematsu. She must have sensed I was after her. Before I extinguished the candle, she'd straightened her mat and shot through the door. I couldn't follow, not without getting snagged by the lurking policemen. Besides which, I was the roshi's assistant here in his zendo.

Benton Stallworth turned out to have sung professionally, which was why he'd picked up the chant right away. He'd never been in a zendo before yesterday. He'd come back today because he had met Tia at a cast party the last time he did a shoot in the city. While he was telling me this, my brother and Korematsu were outside together. The Asian woman seemed to know him and nodded as he spoke in fine British tones. I was half listening, as I tried to gauge whether Korematsu was in the entryway doorway or outside, whether I could get into the closet and check on the spare knife without him seeing me. Whether I could check on it before he looked for the altar supply box.

"Lori Okira," Stallworth was saying to me. "She brought me here."

I looked at her: she seemed sulky.

I began to get the picture. No business has sugar daddies like the movies. He must be on the producing team and clearly, he hadn't been ladling out enough of that sugar. But our movie was young; there was still time to find her a small part. Now she glowered at me, too.

"You're pretty banged up. I guess that's what happens when you've shot a stunt to hell."

"Wha—"

"You looked like a sack of potatoes rolling down the stairs, right, Benton?"

"Hey! What do you know about that? Were you there?"

"No!" she said, sounding petulant, as if watching a gag in the pre-dawn cold was a treat denied.

I wanted to smack her. But I did the right thing, swallowed my outrage, and asked, "What did you hear about it?"

"You screwed up the setup, insisted the crew stay away and—"

"*I insisted? Who told you I insisted?*"

"Oh, puh-lease!"

"Ladies!" Benton Stallworth grabbed her arm and turned, virtually lifting her off the ground as he moved her out the door.

In the moment that his bulky body blocked the doorway, I started after the two of them, heard John and Korematsu arguing outside, remembered that I needed to check the hall closet. I could grab Lori Okira and demand an answer, or I could see if the duplicate knife was in the altar box. Threat to me in the stair fall? Threat to Leo from the detectives? I had to choose.

I slipped into the hall closet, held the door open long enough to see the box, an open four-by-eight cardboard affair. The ash sifter was there, and the tweezers used to grab the ends of stick incense that had burned down into the ash. Scissors, flattened tablespoon with handle bent 90 degrees to even out the ash—there, too. But no knife. Both knives belonged in this box. One had been used to kill Tia. Why was the other one gone? To incriminate Leo?

Leo and the knife were both gone.

I considered telling Korematsu about the missing knife, briefly, very briefly. Instead, I waited till I heard the big police V-8s pull away. Then I walked down the street toward Renzo's Caffè. I needed to figure out why Lori Okira believed I'd sabotaged the stunt myself and who the hell she was, anyway. What did the missing knife portend? And what was going on with Leo? I was too tired. I needed to sleep, but I couldn't go back to the zendo, and I couldn't go to Mom's house. Korematsu or John would find me either place. If either of them got me, they'd grill me for hours and I'd end up revealing something. Even if I watched my mouth much more carefully than someone who right now couldn't remember the beginning of her sentences, I'd give myself away with a gesture or a sigh.

I stepped into the Caffè and saw the first good thing of the morning: Renzo holding out two cups of espresso and nodding toward a window table. "How did you know?"

"I saw you on the sidewalk. Like walking with your mind, you know? Coffee, that's the thing. Coffee's always the thing. *My* coffee."

The coffee was dead black against the white cup.

"Milk?"

I laughed.

Renzo smiled. "We will be friends."

I took a sip of his espresso. "Believe it." The post-dawn hour that belongs to the zendo was over. No longer did flocks of birds sing just for us in the last moments of city silence. It was early commute time now. On Columbus Avenue, twenty feet away, cars, buses, delivery trucks spurted from traffic lights. But this block of Pacific is a civilized street. Architects might be drawing by eight, but lawyers rolled in around ten, and antique shop owners would be wasting their time unlocking portals much before noon. The only pedestrians were drivers who'd managed to snag street parking and were rushing off to jobs or meetings elsewhere.

Here in the empty Caffè, on the empty street, it was like sitting in a dream. I took another swallow of espresso, too big a one for a devotee. I could feel the spreading heat, the jolt of alertness, and see the opportunity sitting in front of me. But before I could phrase my question about Tia's accident, Renzo put down his cup and said, "You knew Tia in high school?"

I nodded and sipped. When could he have learned that? "How—?"

He smiled, a sly curl of the lips on a long narrow face. "Eamon," he said. "Eamon always knows first. It's a hobby with him. Cute."

"Cute?"

"Yeah, cute. A grammar school girl thing. Little hand with a pink brace-let popping up first."

I sipped coffee.

"Didn't mean to offend. I know Eamon's close with your family."

"Did he tell you that, too?"

"Yeah, but I could have figured. I've seen some of them around. Gary used to have offices a couple of blocks away. He considered a live/work space on the other side of Broadway before he moved to Romain Street. Then I saw you—you're peas in a pod, you and Eamon."

I started to take another sip of coffee and realized the cup was empty. It was a little cup, but even so I had made fast work of it. The top of my head felt like it was attached to one of those billed caps with a propeller.

Renzo nodded in approval. "Another?"

"Please. How about a pastry, too? I've been up for hours. Thanks."

"Doing the stunt." So he, too, had known I was there. Regardless of what he said about Eamon Lafferty, Renzo was the collector of facts, and he made me feel distinctly queasy. Like cops, collectors don't give away parts of their collections for nothing.

Renzo set down a black plate holding a round flaky pastry topped with glazed pear, redolent with the scent of almond. He smiled proprietarily, leaning back in his flimsy chair as if it were the guard post to his collection of gossip, and he was preparing to deal. What was he after? What could he think I had discovered in my day and a bit back in the city? The sweet scent of the tart made me ravenous; it took all my strength not to dig right in, but it was food or information. "Renzo, you were at Tia's accident. How did that happen?"

Eyes that a moment ago had been assessing me now were cast down. "Wrong place, wrong time."

"Did you know her before?"

"No. Just happened to be walking by. Heard the brakes, people screaming. Then I heard the crack—you think when someone falls like that it'd be with a thud, but this was a crack. Like a rifle shot. She snapped her pelvis: that was the crack. And the other bones. I thought she was dead. I was frantic to call the police, but you know that saying about never a cop when you need one? Not true this time. They were right there, I mean, *right* there. That brother of yours, he must have heard the brakes and all, too. He came running, panting up the street. And then the other guy, the one who was here today—"

"Korematsu?"

"Yeah, him. He was there in a couple of minutes. Took charge of the scene, or as much as your brother would let him. I gotta give it to John, he double-checked everything, even though it wasn't his scene."

"John was first at the scene? Came running up?" I asked, horrified.

Renzo nodded and reached down for his cup that he had already taken to the sink. "The accident was terrible, just terrible. Tia got a big settlement, really big. No one thought MUNI would ever pay out like that. Even she was surprised. Good thing for her."

Suddenly, out the window I saw the blonde from the zendo crossing

Columbus. She looked as disoriented as I had felt, like she'd raced out so fast she'd gone the wrong way and was retracing her steps.

"Gotta go, Renzo. I owe you!"

CHAPTER 18

I CAUGHT SIGHT of her half a block from the Caffè. "Wait! Hey, wait, don't run. I'm Darcy, from the zendo."

She cut north, up Columbus. Bad move. Downtown with its plethora of cabs, trolleys, buses, and the rapid transit station was to the south. North leads to Broadway, with strip joints, closed at this hour, and North Beach with cafés, also closed. I swung around the corner and started north.

The woman had vanished.

I ran past the architectural bookstore. It wasn't open, of course. I stopped, peered inside—dark—and kept moving.

I almost overran the alley.

She was pressed against the wall.

"What are you doing, running away from me?"

She looked at me, her face scrunched in fear—or something else? She wasn't a natural blonde and her complexion was too dark for the hair color, giving her a hard look at odds with her protectively hunched shoulders.

"Come on back to Renzo's—"

"No, not there."

"Okay!" That had seemed the most comforting setting for talk, but from her reaction I might have been suggesting the downtown lockup. "Here's fine, then. Tell me about Tia."

"I shouldn't have said—"

"But you did. There's no going back. When you called her daring, just what did you mean?"

"I shouldn't have—"

I grabbed her arm. "She's dead! The time for squeamishness is gone."

She gasped, and for a moment I thought she was going to burst into those annoying tears that create a protective wall. I shook her. "Tell . . . me . . . now!"

"It was . . ." She swallowed. "It was just a game, a kid's game. I only played once. I would have more . . . but . . . I wasn't good enough, not like her. She was the . . . fearless one."

"Truth or dare," I said, so disappointed and disgusted that I dropped her arm, and she stood there staring at me. She looked insulted.

"It wasn't what you think. Not the party game. Not 'I dare you to ask Bobby Higgins to the party.'" Her hands rested on the ledge of the big black leather purse hanging from her shoulders. It was the closest to hands on hips she could manage, but it carried little defiance.

If I hadn't been so furious, I would have laughed. "What was it, then, this big, terrifying game of yours?"

"Not mine, I said it wasn't mine. I was just a tryout, a washout."

"So?"

"Maybe it started as the party game years ago, but by the time I knew Tia she was an adult, and so were the others. It wasn't about sex, per se, or humiliation, per se. It was about bearding fear: do you have guts enough to face the most frightening thing?"

"Like?"

"I don't know. I wasn't there but that once—"

I sighed. I could have throttled her. "But you do know. You didn't say, 'Tia once did something brave.' You said, 'She was the most daring person I know.' That means you know more than one thing she did, and you know what others did. So, tell me."

"I can't."

"You're afraid to tell me?" I asked, swallowing my anger and trying to look sympathetic.

She didn't answer, which was as good as an answer.

"You're scared? Listen, this is your chance to face that fear—an easy way. So, take the chance. Come on."

She remained silent, trying to decide if I was sufficiently sympathetic, trustworthy. Clearly, a hard decision.

"You're probably thinking I don't understand what it's like to have a fear that straightjackets you, right?"

Hesitantly, she nodded.

"I was terrified of trees. Trees, for heaven's sakes! Trees are everywhere! I couldn't leave the city, couldn't visit friends in the country, couldn't even drive to another town. Driving through Golden Gate Park almost made me throw up."

She was nodding.

"So, see. I've got my demons, too."

She hesitated. "Okay, I guess. But we can't go to the Caffè; we have to talk here."

"Here is fine. Tell me about the group."

Something in her subtly shifted, and decision in itself seemed to calm her. "I did my thing, or, rather, didn't. I mean I got halfway—I can't bear to tell you what I wanted to face."

"I used to be afraid of large wooden objects with leaves on them. So, unless you think that fireplug's gunning for you, whatever you're dealing with can't possibly be more humiliating. Spit it out, Sister!"

She almost laughed. "Snakes. I'm terrified of snakes. It's so prosaic, *so* Freudian; everybody tells me that, especially guys. They love telling me. I see snakes everywhere, twigs on the sidewalk, pipes. Every time I hear stories about them coming out of the sink, the toilet, I'm terrified. I can't—"

"That's okay. I understand. What was your dare? Did they lock you in a room with snakes?"

It was so soft, I could barely make out her answer. "Yes."

"And?"

"They told me the room was a cabin, a one-room cabin, in the Sierras. They blindfolded me, stuffed earplugs in my ears, put me in the front seat of a van, and drove for hours. Then they marched me to the room. They left me alone, with the blindfold and the snakes."

"Omigod! That's horrifying." I could remember my panic about the forest, and how quickly I went to mush, how beyond control was my reaction. "An hour in a cabin with your fear could be an eternity."

"I couldn't get the blindfold off! I know that sounds crazy, but I was too panicked. The snakes slithered over my legs. They were on me! The people must have smeared something on me to attract them. It was"—she was really whispering now—"awful."

"Slithering across your skin!"

"I couldn't get the earplugs out, but they ended up falling out. And that was worse, because then I could hear them. Even when they didn't touch me, I could hear them moving, coming toward me, coming from everywhere."

"What did you do?"

She let out a shriek of a laugh. "I screamed. Of course that was useless. Then I lost it."

I put a comforting hand on her arm and waited a moment. "How long was it till you realized where you were?"

152

She shrank back into the wall. "You're one of them, aren't you?"

"No, no! I just put things together. Like you did, right?"

Slowly, she nodded, but she still wasn't sure about me.

"So how are you now?"

"Now? Okay. Okay, but I'm still terrified of snakes, and of closed rooms, and them."

"Why them?"

"They warned me never to tell anyone. Never. Never say anything."

"That's outrageous. Who the hell are they? They threatened you? You can go to the police."

"And tell them what, that people I only saw once, that I only knew by their first names, told me they'd put snakes in my bedroom? That I would never sleep again?"

"Couldn't you have moved?"

"No! You don't get it. They love these trials; it's sport to them to over-come this fear, then that one, and then this bigger one. It's an addiction! The more danger the better. They can't have the cops knowing about them or they could never do anything. The members, they're all over. I don't know where. There's no central group, just like cells, people who know other people, here in the city, but all over the country. They fly all over to do these dares. They're like bamboo, you think it's just in your planter, until there's a stalk under your stairs, in your neighbor's garden, coming up through the floor. I don't know how they know each other, but I know there are other groups."

Suddenly, she was trembling so much she dropped her purse. I put my arms around her and hugged her tight until the shaking subsided.

"You did a brave thing this morning, you know that, right? You walked back in that room. You sat there with your back to the room for forty min-utes. You must have been terrified the whole time."

153

For the first time her lips quivered into a hint of a smile. "I was. I'm still terrified remembering it. I could 'hear' the slithering the whole time, even though I knew it was crazy. That it was just in my head. When we stood up for an instant I 'saw' the boarding over the windows."

I was shivering with her now. I'd been so sure the cabbie was making up his story about the "bad vibes" and the wailing and the snakes escaping, here in the middle of the city. "That was incredibly brave. I really am impressed."

She stepped back and stared, eyeing me for signs of sarcasm.

"No, I mean it. You will be too when you look back on this day. But I have to ask you, why? What made you speak up?"

"Tia's dead."

"Omigod, you think they murdered her?"

She stiffened, looked like she couldn't move.

"No, listen, what I mean is, are you afraid they killed her, or—pay attention—do you logically think so? Are you coming from fear or logic?"

"I don't know. I just don't know." She began to cry.

I started to pull her back into the hug, but she backed away.

"Okay, then who are they? Who, besides Tia?"

"I only saw two others. Guys. One was older, dark-haired, white. The other was young, long brown hair." She gasped for breath, squeezed her eyes shut against more tears, and said, "I didn't plan to say anything today. I didn't even know there was going to be a memorial service. I just wanted to sit there because I knew Tia died there. But when I saw Renzo, something came over me. I had to, you know, speak."

"Why Renzo?"

"The long-haired guy in the group. He was Renzo's son."

CHAPTER 19

MY IMPRESSION was that Renzo's Caffè was open from early morning till after dinner and that Renzo never left. But he sure wasn't there now. Coincidence? It was too early to ask Jeffrey Hagstrom about him; his shop wouldn't be open for hours. Leo wasn't back either.

I needed time, and a safe space to make sense of what I'd learned about Tia Dru. Tia as part of a daredevil group, that was easy to imagine. Renzo's son? Who knew? Maybe he lived in the city. I had my phone out to call information, but what was I going to say: *Hi, Information, give me Renzo's son?* I didn't even know Renzo's last name. I also had to figure out what was going on with Leo's whereabouts, the zendo knives, and why someone had tried to kill me! And Tia, it all came back to Tia. A cab rolled slowly down the street. I hailed it.

"Where to?"

"Around the block."

"You have to do better than that, lady. Oh, it's you. 'Around the block.' Of course it'd be you."

"Just loop around a couple of blocks and up Columbus."

"What is it with you? You think you need a passport to cross Market Street?"

"Hey, your meter's running, drive!"

"Okay, okay. But listen, I've been looking for your guy but no joy!"

I was losing my mind.

"You know: the guy who looks like you."

That cabbie! The big, round-faced guy I'd given the twenty and asked to keep a lookout for Eamon. How could he have avoided seeing Eamon? He must have spent the last two days in Oakland.

"Okay, okay. Listen, I'm still looking for your guy. I've been by your building back there every spare minute."

"Really? What did you see?"

"Not him."

"So, what else then for my twenty?"

He shot across Columbus into Chinatown, a traffic-clogged district no cabbie not aiming to pad his meter would enter. I braced my feet against the seat and tried to read him in the rearview mirror.

"Okay, so I wasn't there every minute, but twenty bucks is nothing."

"Fine, then, give it back." I half expected him to toss a bill at me. But, apparently, it wasn't that close to nothing.

"You know the street was blocked off because of the movie, right? So that was hours gone right there. Before that, around noon I made a pass by—it was going to be the first of a bunch—but Jeffrey hails me—"

"You know Jeffrey?"

"I went to his Barbary Coast lecture. Lot of cabbies do extra stuff like that. You let a fare know you can be like a guide and you can get a whole-day gig."

If carting strangers around six hours was a good day for a not naturally friendly guy like him, he had to be living on the edge. It made me take another look in the mirror and see him a whole lot more clearly, and as one of my tribe. Movie companies were ever more squeezed for cash and the first place cuts came was on location sets. If it could be done in the studio against a blue sheet or with animation, the company saved tens of thousands in housing, food, equipment, salaries, and fees to cities. I had been very lucky to get the two gigs on *Barbary*, but that wasn't going to be the norm. Soon I could be waiting tables or driving a taxi, too. "So, Jeffrey hails you and . . . ?"

"So he wants me to drive him to the Presidio, and then to Fort Point, and to Divisidero and Broadway. He says he's testing the wind, like he wants to see where the wind goes, but that's crazy. He had a couple of balloons, but what good is that? You let 'em go, and they go. You're not somewhere else to catch them."

"Maybe he was working with someone else."

"Nah. He never called anyone. How would they know where to be? You ask me, he's depressed. Guy's depressed, what's he do? Gets in his car and drives. City guy, cab's the best he can do. The balloon thing, here's what I think. He had balloons. Maybe he had an opening at his store and had some left over. So he grabs a few. It keeps me from asking how he is. Weirdo stuff in this city isn't exactly a surprise, and any cabbie who's hauled hack more than a day knows to just keep quiet and hope the nut's got the fare."

I nodded. I'd believed Jeffrey when he said he was Tia's shoulder-to-cry-on. But that kind of intimacy can foster hope, even in a guy who knows better. If he nurtured hope, he had good reason to be depressed. But enough to slit her throat?

"Webb," I said, reading his name from his hack license, "did Jeffrey ever say anything about Tia Dru?"

"The broad who got killed?"

My friend, who got killed, I wanted to say, but I wasn't about to censor his comments. I swallowed my outrage and waited.

"Like what?"

"Like was he hot for her?"

Webb made a throaty noise I took for a laugh. "Well, yeah. Who wasn't? But he wasn't her type."

I flashed on her at the reception, her disgust when Jeffrey refused to go into the tunnel. "Did you ever get the sense that he was trying to change to suit her, trying to be something more than he was?"

"If he could've, he would've, but, look, I like Jeff and all, but him with Tia Dru, that'd be like a mole with an Afghan hound."

I felt bad about it, but I couldn't stifle a laugh. It was the perfect description. "Here's the odd thing, Webb. You know there's a tunnel under the zendo?"

He nodded.

"Tia was thrilled at the idea of a tunnel when Jeffrey mentioned it. She couldn't wait to get down there; she ran to the dark end, so fast she smacked into it. When Jeffrey said he wouldn't go there, she was disgusted, but he still didn't go. And yet, he pushed Eamon to buy the building because of the tunnel. Why—"

Webb shook his head. "You gotta give it to Jeff, he kept trying! He knew he was a mole, and he still kept hoping. He knew she'd leap at it. He got it for her." He was watching my reaction in the rearview. I nodded slowly, and he mirrored it, larger and emphatic. He yanked the wheel right onto Broadway, and in a manic burst ran the light at Columbus, creating a roar of horns and hollers.

"Brilliant."

Webb grinned as if I meant him, or maybe his driving. I let it stand.

"Hit Renzo's again."

Still riding his success, he yanked right and right again onto Pacific. As soon as we passed the zendo I spotted movement in Renzo's. "Stop! Here!"

"Hey—"

I held out two twenties to forestall the familiar whine. "Come back in a quarter hour."

"Hey, you're not my only fare. What if—"

I was out of the cab and racing to the Caffè.

Renzo spotted me in time to brace the door. "Go away!" His long, narrow face that had seemed suavely serene now was lined with the sort of unstable emotions that could blow either way. He'd seen whom I was running out to chase.

"Renzo, I'm sorry, but I can't."

He didn't move. On Columbus cars screeched away from the traffic light, sending a gust of cold, gritty air at me.

"I won't ask you about your son. That blonde woman—I don't even know her name—"

"Georgia."

"Georgia told me he was involved with Tia and the dare group."

His shoulders slumped. "'D,' that's what they called it. Like they were so 'in,' they only needed a letter. 'It's a D thing,' Marco'd say. There was no 'T,' no truth, just the dares, the bigger, more dangerous, more stupid the better. I bit my tongue. You're going to say that's not like me, but I did it that time. I knew better than to say, 'If they told you to jump off a cliff, would you do that, Marco?' Because I knew the answer." He let go of the door and stepped back. "Maybe I should have. Maybe."

I put a hand on his arm and nodded. I knew what it was like to have strangers poking the sore of grief from a son or a brother. I hated to be the one digging into the ever raw flesh. But I pressed. "I said I wouldn't ask—"

"Yeah, well, thanks." He poured two cups of espresso.

I accepted one gratefully, taking a sip and willing it to sharpen my wits as I searched for a decent detour. Vaguely I wondered how many cups a day

Renzo downed. "Jeffrey urged Eamon to buy the zendo building because he knew Tia'd be fascinated with the tunnel. You knew that, right?"

His hand tightened on the little cup. "I did."

"She wanted it for D, right?"

His face went tight. For a moment I thought he was going to slam the cup down on the glass table, but he placed it on its saucer so slowly it made no sound. He squeezed his hands into fists and stared down at them as they trembled next to the cup. "I couldn't stop it. I grabbed Eamon, gave him every argument I could come up with: property's way overvalued here, no foot traffic, rats in the tunnel, attractive nuisance lawsuits. I said, 'Eamon, you open that tunnel, someone's going to get killed.'" He stopped abruptly as if he heard his prediction with the ears of a stranger.

"Jeffrey thought the tunnel would bring Tia to him, but it did the opposite," I said, mulling aloud. "It threw her to Eamon. If she wanted—"

"There was no 'want' about it. Girl, you're looking at D like a game. It wasn't a game to these people; it was an addiction. And she was the worst. My son, he was in it for the high of running across the freeway, of swimming out into the Bay at midnight. He'd come home like he'd scored all the coke in Alameda County. But Tia, I kept in touch with her after the accident." He squeezed his hands as if he couldn't squeeze hard enough. "That's how Marco met her. Here. If I had known, ever suspected—"

"But you didn't, right?"

"No. How could I? Why would I?"

I took a sip of the espresso. There's a distinct moment in the day when coffee turns sour on your tongue. "It wasn't a game for Tia?"

"She had to do the dares. She had pain. She never told anyone about it, but I could see from how she walked, how careful she was where she put her foot down, how she sat. I could see it in how she braced her shoulders against the next stab of pain. She tried everything—never told people about that, either. She didn't *tell* me, but I cared about her, I was rooting for her, hoping this therapy, this drug, this surgery, this healer, this exercise, something would stop the pain."

I nodded. I understood all too well. "Being able to defeat the dares, that was what allowed her to beat back despair, right? Despite everything, she could still defeat fear—"

"For a while. I knew when she did one of them by how she was after. Not like Marco—not high, but calm, like things were in control again. The D's, they were a drug to her."

"It was more than that." I knew Tia, too.

He nodded, slowly, sadly. "She lived for them, for the thrill of making the impossible hers."

The ultimate orgasm, I thought, but did not say to Renzo as he sat looking down at his coffee. "It's what allowed her to be her," I concluded. He nodded. "Do you know what her dares were?"

"No. She never said, and I never let on I had any idea. But I do know this: I know what she planned to do with that tomb. The only question is whether she was going to seal someone in down there for hours or seal herself."

The espresso tasted toxic, but I drank it anyway. I looked down at my hands on the cup and felt a huge wave of gratitude just to be able to see them in front of me.

Renzo opened his and laid them flat on the table. "I'll tell you this, and it'd be true. If Tia had a key to that tunnel, she wouldn't have been able to keep herself from going down. She'd climb down that ladder and pull the gates closed after her and stand in the dark for longer and longer until she died down there."

I went cold all over. The thought of her . . . There was nothing to say and, somehow, neither of us could move.

Jeffrey's plan was brilliant. The tunnel would draw Tia back here time after time. Premature burial was the ultimate fear. And every time she climbed out shaking, Jeffrey would be right there to comfort her. At any price, it would be money well spent, but clever Jeffrey, he hadn't turned loose a dime of his own.

I didn't mention that to Renzo either. We sat together in the timelessness of horror until, thankfully, a man in jeans and a leather jacket burst in demanding a triple, which he grabbed as soon as Renzo poured it, and was out the door with a speed that belied his need for caffeine.

"Renzo," I said, standing up. "Georgia said there was an older man involved—older than your son, a guy with dark hair. Who is he?"

He was holding a cleaning rag. It fell out of his hand. "You don't know?"

"Tell me."

He shook his head. "You did me the favor of not prying off the scab about Marco. I can do this for you. I won't say more."

"What do you mean? You can't leave it at that!"

"I can."

"No, you cannot!"

"Look beneath the obvious."

"Obvious as to what?"

A black-clad couple hurried in to the counter, followed by an under-dressed woman wrapping her arms around herself. I don't give up, I postpone. I lived half a block away, I'd catch him later. "Look beneath the obvious!" Damn, I might as well be talking to Leo!

I went outside and was relieved to see the perpetually annoyed face of Webb Morratt, behind his running meter.

"Where to?"

I said the first thing that popped into my mind, "Romain Street," the address of my dark-haired brother who'd been so seduced by Tia, my brother whom Renzo knew.

"Upper or Lower?"

I hadn't been to this address, only knew it from Renzo. Who'd have thought there'd be an upper and lower? I pictured Gary. "Lower."

So much for postponing.

Webb Morratt made a few locals-only turns and landed on Broadway headed west, crossed Van Ness into Pacific Heights, near where Tia had lived. He hung a left on Gough. "I had an early airport call this morning. I swung by your place after, and picked up the producer and that little stunt girl he's hot for," he said, as if there had been no break in our conversation.

"You mean Benton Stallworth?"

"Benton Stall-worth? Didn't know his name before. Stallworth. Took them back up to the set."

"Are you a screenwriter?"

"Nah. I was thinking if I could get on with one crew as a knowledgeable gofer, I might have a nice sideline going. But they've got Jeffrey for research. Maybe I should've pushed him off the bridge when I had a chance." He pulled left onto Market Street, under the freeway, and past the Safeway.

In a couple of minutes we would be at Gary's house. When I faced him I would need to be a lot clearer than I was now about him and Tia, and D. But something the cabbie said was jabbing at me. Benton Stallworth hot for Lori Okira? That wasn't a news flash. She had sure been as petulant as a trophy lover. No, it wasn't that. It was . . . "Oh, shit!"

"What'd I do? The light's green."

"Nothing. Not you. The woman with Benton Stallworth, did you say she's a stunt double?"

"That's what she said. Said it three times, like she was trying to explain to a slow learner. 'I'm a stunt double, not an extra,' that's what she said. 'I was hired to do stunts.'"

"Did she say why she wasn't doing them, then?"

"Didn't say. I don't know why."

But I did. No wonder she was so hostile to me. Now the chill on the set came clear. Second units are close-knit. Of course they resented one of their own being shoved aside for a stranger. The gags I'd done were doubling Ajiko Sakai, small, slight, and Asian. Lori Okira was Asian American. Makeup and camera angles can compensate for a lot. But even I had found it odd that I, a five-foot-six redhead, had been picked to double a slight woman not much over five feet tall. Of course, Lori had been the stunt double. Had she sabotaged my stair fall, or was it that the animosity of the crew just made it possible for someone else to attack me?

"Where do you want out?"

"The brown house over there." It didn't matter, so I just pointed. I plucked another twenty from my wallet and waived the change. "Give me your cell number. I may need to get back from here."

"At your command."

I took the card. "Thanks, Webb."

The wind snapped my hair as I climbed out. If Jeffrey had loosed a balloon here it would have sailed southeast across Noe Valley and the outer Mission District toward Candlestick Park. As Webb drove off I wrapped my fingers around the keys in my pocket. Gary's keys—I'd forgotten to give them back last night.

There were two questions. How was I going to get my brother to tell me about a secret group devoted to extremely dangerous and sometimes illegal events? No sensible person would admit such knowledge, much less participation in it, certainly not an attorney. And there was the more pressing question: where did Gary live?

CHAPTER 20

THE WIND SNAPPED my hair against my face. The fog was gone, but the sky was only a dull blue and the wind was making me wish I hadn't ditched the long coat I'd lived in back in New York. At the end of the street I crossed and started up the other side, looking for someone I could reasonably ask where my own brother lived.

I didn't have to ask. Suddenly, in front of a gray stucco bungalow, I spotted a big, chartreuse, very tacky ceramic frog on a stake, a creature poised to leap for a ceramic fly. I smiled. Mike had given it to Gary when he started law school and it had achieved mascot status. But I didn't quite know what to make of its display in a spot where it could be stolen, vandalized, or scorned. For form's sake, I rang the bell, then opened the screen door, and started trying keys. How many times had Gary grinned at that kitschy frog? Like John, Gary hadn't forgotten Mike. How could I have imagined they would? The key turned stiffly and I pushed the door open.

It's odd to see your brother's house for the first time. Gary had either lived at home or at school, or I'd been away from San Francisco. His occupying an entire house surprised me, even a small square one like this. The place was a Victorian, but a very modest one with a central hallway separating a twelve-foot-square living room and slightly larger kitchen from bedroom, bath, and a sliver for an office. From the front door I could have done two cartwheels and been out the back. The living room was spare: red sofa and two black leather chairs around a craftsman table, a place where friends could eat and drink and not worry. The bedroom was almost filled with an overlarge double bed under a tumble of sheets and blankets that suggested Gary was having great nights or terrible ones. I was so tempted to crawl in, just for an hour. If he came home he'd never know I was there.

But I had to find out if Gary was the one Renzo couldn't bring himself to reveal. Logically Gary'd keep nothing at all connected to D. But when you've conquered the ultimate fear, maybe more than once, wouldn't you want a memento? Climbers atop Everest know every moment's delay increases the odds of their death, and still they stop to take snapshots. Surely, Gary would have a piece of freeway median, a strand of Golden Gate Bridge cable, something. He would have it, but not in sight. Not in the living room, but tucked away in his office where a guest wouldn't go.

I opened the office door and almost gave up. A large desk faced the window, and deep shelves came out from the opposite wall so that there was just room for him to roll the chair back and put his feet up. Or there would have been room had the floor, desk, and every shelf not been covered with stacks of papers, books, folders. Had Mom ever seen this? She would have been so gratified; it was exactly what she had predicted.

I cleared a file off the chair and sat, trying to put myself in Gary's place and think where he would keep a memento. It could be any size, any shape, a screw, a note, anything. I mulled the question.

I was asleep! I shook myself awake and made myself stand up as I rooted through the files in the right-hand desk drawer and then the left. With such limited space, it made sense that it wouldn't be there in a place of current importance. The shelves held plastic milk crates crammed with files. The ones on the floor and lower shelf were labeled with name and number.

The middle shelf—shoulder high for the sitter—was awash with papers. I started at one side and leafed through, hunting for anything not on letterhead or legal pleading paper. After twenty minutes, I conceded defeat.

Above were the heavy cardboard bankers' boxes favored by lawyers for storage. Gary had labeled them in magic marker. On the eye-level shelf were taxes, bills, and boxes with names I didn't recognize. On the top shelf, above my head in this high-ceilinged Victorian, was Dru . . . Dru . . . The whole shelf contained records of Tia!

The lawyer who got Tia that very fine settlement was Gary! The boxes were dated—three years of them. Three years was a long time for a lawyer to have a case he didn't get paid for until the settlement, a case he'd have to front money for court fees, experts, perhaps doctors. Did he do it because he was half in love with Tia from the start? He'd been an associate with a big firm back then, one that didn't handle accidents. So he'd have done this case entirely on his own, which meant on his own time after his seventy-hour week.

Like almost everyone in the stunt world, I had worked many part-time jobs, some of them temping in law offices. A plaintiff who leaps cable cars does not have a good case. Eight boxes. Gary hadn't sloughed off; he must have tried every angle known to law. He would have been battling batteries of insurance lawyers with deep pockets and slews of assistants. They would have buried him with interrogatories, demands for production of documents and things, requests for physical exams, requests for mental exams, and motions up the wazoo. How had he pulled it off?

I was balancing supposition on supposition, about to be buried under them. I didn't dare sit down; I'd be asleep in an instant. Real sleep was the only answer. I walked back up the hall to the bedroom and slid under the heap of covers, without straightening them, without even taking my shoes off. Untying each set of laces, pulling at the shoe, the effort, the effort was too great. I'd wash the sheets later. I pulled the covers over my head. The last thought I had was to promise myself I'd come back to the question of why Gary had taken Tia's case to begin with.

I woke feeling that I had been kicked out of the Room of All Answers. I lay still, struggling to find the door back in, but the room swayed and thinned, leaving whiffs of itself just out of reach. Nothing was left but noise: crunching now, like tires on gravel, like footsteps.

Footsteps! My eyes shot full open. Footsteps? Gary walking in? I hadn't expected him so soon. Whatever time it was, it was too soon. I needed to pull myself together. My head was under the heap of covers. He hadn't even noticed me. I took a deep breath.

Hey! Wait a minute! Someone had tried to kill me just today! And now I was no longer alone in the house! Now I was awake. Holding the sheets up to prevent noise, I slid slowly out of the bed. There was no sound of flushing or water running. I peered around the doorway into the hall.

Still no sound of water. Gary, the burglar, my attacker, whoever it was, must have gone straight through to his office.

I moved down the hall. A board creaked; I froze. The office door was closed but not shut. I peered around the edge and stifled a gasp.

The man in the office, rooting through Gary's drawers, was not Gary. He wasn't here to attack me, either. He was hunched over a drawer, fingers moving quickly, too quickly for a colleague Gary might have sent to find a document. This was no colleague; it really was a burglar!

I was so relieved, it took me a minute to process: a burglar rooting through Gary's papers!

How did he get in here? Did I leave the door unlocked? What was he after? Something to do with Dare? Something about Tia? Breathing through my mouth, I moved closer to the door.

His broad back blocked my view. From the size of him, he would find his prize and swat me out of the way as he strode down the hall and out with it.

The police! Where was my phone? Where was Gary's phone? I had no idea.

Carefully, I backed away from the door. Could I hide in the kitchen? Not if I wanted to see what he had. In order to see . . .

The hallway had open beams. I suddenly realized open beams could be very useful. I grabbed the second from the end, lifting myself up. The rough plank scraped my hands. The wood squeaked. My ribs thumped down on it. In the office the shuffling sounds stopped. Keeping my ribs in place, I pulled my legs up behind me. My glutes screamed; my hamstrings started to cramp. I stretched through my heels and willed the hamstrings to release until I could brace my feet against the beam behind me.

The edge of the beam cut into my ribs. I lay like roofing up there, breathing through my mouth, straining to hear him. Ready to spot whatever he had when he came out. The shuffling of paper had stopped. Now it crunched. He was folding it. Cloth swished. He was stuffing the paper under his jacket. No time now. He'd be gone. I tightened my fingers on the beam.

The door opened. He put a hand on the side, as if he was about to swing the door back and forth. He was thinking. He wasn't looking up, but he was worried. His shoulders were hunched as if he sensed someone else close by. Or maybe he was worried he'd left a full handprint in something. The beam was cutting into my hand, sawing my ribs. My legs weren't shaking yet but they would be any second.

He tapped his foot.

The beams were thick with dust. I squeezed my eyes against it. It was in my nose. I jammed my teeth together to keep from sneezing.

He fingered the door.

I couldn't wait. I swung my feet down hard, sideways into his throat. He gasped and fell.

He didn't move. Omigod, was he dead? Had I killed him? I didn't mean to— He writhed. I dropped to the floor and stared down at him, horrified, then perplexed, and then outraged. "Webb Morratt! You drive me here and then you come back to burgle? What's the matter with you?" As hard as I had kicked, with the full swing of both legs, as near as I'd come to his jugular, I'd come way too close to killing him. I was almost as shaken as he was. While he was still gasping, I reached into his jacket and pulled out the envelope. Thirty-seven dollars. "Thirty-seven dollars! You broke and entered for thirty-seven dollars! Are you crazy?"

He grunted something close to yes.

"Burglars burgle empty houses. You dropped me here!"

"Up . . . street."

"You dropped me at the top of the street."

"I hit the dead end. Turned around. You were walking down the street. It was clear you didn't know where you were going. I figured you were house-sitting, that someone had given you a key and you were looking for the place. I saw you come in here. That was hours ago. Fares were terrible. I got one to Twenty-fourth Street, not enough for a beer. So I came back by here on the chance I might spot you needing a ride back. There were no lights on. I figured you'd left."

"And so you'd rob me."

"Not *you*. I'd rob the owner, the person with enough dough for a vacation. What are you doing here, anyway, with all the lights off! This is the city. People use lights!"

I almost laughed at his outrage. "Thirty-seven dollars!"

He was pushing himself up, painfully, to a sitting position.

"Webb, this house belongs to my brother, a lawyer. My other brother is a cop. You do understand that now I own you. Right?"

"I just need—"

"I don't care. What you need to do now is to give me enough to make it worth my while to keep you out on the street. It's going to be easy. I know you drive down Pacific more than you let on. So what did you see that you were holding back?"

He shifted, bracing his right arm against the desk, trying to get purchase with his left hand and push himself up straighter. He would be okay, I assured myself, no lingering nerve damage. But it scared me nevertheless. I watched him sitting there trying to think.

Trying to think of a lie! "Webb, you've got to come clean! This is your freedom we're talking about." Chances were it wouldn't be his first offense either. "Who are you protecting? Jeffrey, isn't it? That fantasy about him and the balloons! Jeffrey, your source of tourist amusement and of tourists, right? What did you really see him do?"

His eyes shot to the left; his face tensed. Then he shrugged. "Jeff has an old car. His father left it to him. He doesn't drive it much. It's old, finicky, and dies on hills. He takes cabs. But the day after I let you off, he was pulling up by his store in it."

"When?"

"Early afternoon."

"And?"

"Tia Dru got out and she slammed the door so hard it bounced back open."

The day after he dropped me. The day I went to Tia's for lunch. Early afternoon, right after she vanished.

"Did he follow her?"

"He was in the car when I passed."

"Did you go back?"

"Why would I? I had fares to hunt. I didn't know she was going to get killed."

"Did you see either of them later?"

"No. The next time I came by, the street was blocked off for the movie." He now shifted onto all fours and clambered up. He was a big guy, but the effects of driving eight hours a day showed. Even standing, he was bent forward a bit from hip flexors that had tightened from years behind the wheel. If he came after me, he'd never catch me. If he did catch me, though, I'd be in big trouble.

"So, Webb, what did Jeffrey say after the murder?"

"Huh?"

"When you went by his house?"

"I didn't—"

"Of course you did. You were sitting on this prime piece of evidence. A scoop that could have turned into a sale to the media. You would have been a fool not to try to fill out the story before the cops got on to it."

For the first time a grin played at his lips.

"So?"

"He wasn't there."

"And?" Was this guy holding out, or could he possibly have just given up?

"And I got hailed for an airport fare."

"Please!"

"No, really. Jeffrey lives near the Presidio. He's right off Lombard Street, near all those motels."

"Motels where the desk clerks never call for cabs themselves, just leave their customers to hail you on the street?"

He was wise enough not to attempt an answer to that.

"Okay, let's go."

"To his house?"

"That house you couldn't be bothered checking out. Let's just see what Jeffrey has to say about the afternoon Tia Dru died."

CHAPTER 21

WEBB MUTTERED about lost fares, but it was from habit and even he couldn't whip up a quality whine. And one chorus of our theme song: *You Broke into the House of a Brother of a Cop*, cut his protest dead.

We shot down Market Street past the Castro District and Dolores Street, where the first mission church in the city, Mission Dolores, had been built in the year of the American Revolution. Subsequently, a huge basilica had been erected next to it. In the great earthquake and fire, the basilica was gutted, but the little wooden mission survived. There's probably a lesson somewhere in that.

I wouldn't have been surprised if Jeffrey lived above his shop in the neighborhood he'd so clearly made his own. However, had he been alive in the era that so fascinated him, he would have steered clear of our lewd and lawless street and that would have been a life-lengthening decision. At the zendo reception when he had assigned himself the role of bar and bordello owner, he'd credited himself with a toughness seen only in his imagination. For Jeffrey Hagstrom a house near the Presidio made sense. All the adjoining neighborhoods were upscale and safe.

Webb hit each red light on Divisidero just as it turned. At the spot where he'd told me Jeffrey stopped to play with his balloons, he crested the hill and began the steep shot down, screeching to halts at stop signs, in the manner of the most novice stunt driver. But I didn't point that out. He pulled up in front of a house on Baker Street, one block from the Presidio. Like so many houses in San Francisco, Jeffrey's was attached to its neighbor. Each had a three-pane bay window in a living room that sat atop a two-car garage. The main entry stood between it and what might be a study.

Drop cloths covered the shrubbery. Splotches of various tans marked the pale green stucco.

"Did Jeffrey just buy this place?" I asked as we got out of the cab.

"Inherited it from his father. He worked at the Presidio, got a deal on the place from someone transferred out in a hurry. Jeffrey's dad hooked him into some kind of scut job in the lab there when he was in college. Jeffrey hated it. Hated the military, hated the lab—you can just imagine, right?"

"Still, his father did him a big favor, leaving him this house."

"Damn straight," Webb grumbled.

The last time I saw Jeffrey, the night of the reception, he'd given me a story about just being Tia's good friend. Now my question was, had he intended to fool me, or was he deluding himself? "Just friends" rarely have women slamming out of their cars. And then disappear.

I pushed the bell. There were a lot of questions I was dying to ask, not the least of which was why Tia had abandoned me at lunch to go off with him. Did he drive up and lure her, somehow, into his car? Did he call and entrap her? Or—this possibility startled me—had she called him? Was she going *with* him or getting *away from* me? What had I said before she left? I tried to remember, but all I could come up with was some prattle about a case of John's I'd used to cover her awkwardness getting out of her chair. Maybe she assumed she was driving around the block to settle something and that she'd be back before I even poured the wine. Or maybe she just forgot about me. So many questions that he could clear up in a sentence. I rang again.

"He's not here," Webb grumbled a full thirty seconds before I would have given up. "Let's check the neighbors."

"Huh?"

"Trust me. I get calls; I show up; no one answers. They've changed their mind. Or, once in a while, if they've had long enough since they called, they've overdosed. Either way, I go to the neighbor's and ask them to call for me."

"Couldn't your dispatcher—"

"Yeah, but not nearly so effective. Lemme tell you, when a guy gets a call from a worried or pissed neighbor, he hauls himself to the door."

"Okay. There's a rental unit, right?"

"Yeah, downstairs."

"Let's try there first."

The entrance, halfway down the walk on the side of the building, was a weathered green utility door, the kind that might lead to a storage room— no window, bell, or knocker. Webb's fist was almost on the wood when I caught it. "Wait! I want the tenant to answer, not hide! Let's try a gentler rap first." I rapped softly. A minute passed. I nodded at Webb and he hit the door in something between a bang and an earthquake.

The door opened a crack. A woman with blonde hair looked out warily, her expression one of pre-set annoyance. As she surveyed Webb her mouth hardened. But when she spotted me, she did a double take.

I was every bit as startled. "Georgia! What are you doing here?"

"I live here."

"You rent this flat?"

"My department does," Georgia said.

"Your department?"

"CDC."

"The Centers for Disease Control? You're an epidemiologist?"

She laughed uncomfortably and I could feel my face flush as she read my amazement that the woman quivering in the alley this morning could have a responsible job with a front-line agency fighting epidemics. She hesitated, as if I had caught her with her bathrobe hanging open, and then added, "CDC does plenty of mundane things. It's not all about anthrax and Ebola. I'm here checking wind patterns for vector distribution."

"I'd guess an evening wind would distribute vectors all over the city."

"You'd be wrong, but not that wrong," she said more confidently. She looked like the sane twin of her morning self. "On an average night one biological error could infect a third of the city."

"Hey, you hired Jeffrey, didn't you?" Webb said.

Georgia gasped. I'd forgotten all about him standing in the shadows. But her reaction went beyond surprise. She'd gone as pale as she'd been this morning.

"Makes sense," he charged on. "You rent his apartment, right? You need a guy with time to turn loose balloons. Your balloons. He's got the skinny on where to set them off."

"How did you know?" Her voice was barely above a whisper.

"He hired my cab."

"When?"

"Couple of days ago."

"Where . . . where did you take him?"

"Broadway and Divisidero, out by the Cliff House, Fort Point, Sutro Tower, and one other place. Can't remember that. It was one long fare."

"Why do you care, Georgia?" I asked, mostly to make her focus back on me.

"Please don't let this go beyond us." She was focused on me, imploring, counting on the bond forged between us earlier. "CDC doesn't want to alarm civilians. If people even thought we were thinking about biological elements in their wind, it'd be a total nightmare. We're not just checking here, we're in every major city. But if word leaked—"

"But why do you care where Jeffrey went?"

She sighed. "He hasn't turned in his report. I advanced him the expense allotment. The agency is generous; the protocols were set in the days when it had to include enough for baksheesh and bribery. So it was three hundred dollars. I didn't expect it to tide Jeff over as long as it appears it has. I've got stuff stacked up waiting for that report and I have to account for the expenses."

"I could take you around again," Webb offered, a bit too eagerly.

"If I had time to drive around the city, I would have done it in the first place. If I'd known, I would have. By now, dammit, I've spent that much time making excuses for the delays." Bureaucratic indignation trumped fear.

"If you need the report so badly, why don't you just go upstairs and bang on his door until he answers?" I said.

"Jeff? He doesn't live upstairs. He used to live down here. I rented this place after he moved out."

I glared at Webb.

"He used to own it," he insisted. "He told me a couple of times. Honest."

"Do the people upstairs own the building, Georgia?"

"I pay them the rent."

"If Jeffrey doesn't live here anymore, where does he live?"

She shrugged.

"You hired him to do your survey. You issued him money. You must have gotten an address for him."

"Of course. Of course, I did. It's just so much a formality for my part of the work I didn't connect it. But of course." She went to the metal table in front of the window and fingered through a stack of papers and pile of scraps held down by a little jade frog. The address was on one of the scraps. "Here." She handed me an address on Eddy Street.

"That's the Tenderloin!"

"It's not as rough as it used to be," Webb said.

But, I was thinking, *it was a huge step down from here.* It was the kind of step an addict might make.

"I suppose you're expecting me to drive you there, too," Webb grumbled.

"No."

From habit, his face scrunched into a pucker of offense.

"Go," I insisted. "All these motels here, filled with eager tourists."

"Yeah, well, you'll get home on your own. I got a living to make," he said, as if clinching an argument.

He left at a fast lumber, glancing over his shoulder twice in case I was gaining on him. When he was out of sight, Georgia's shoulders relaxed and she let out a huge sigh.

I put a hand on her shoulder. "Georgia," I said, "surely you don't assume I believed your story."

CHAPTER 22

GEORGIA'S HANDS were shaking violently. She pressed them into fists so tight it looked like her bones were about to pop through.

I knew all about fear: the nausea, the humiliation, the paralysis of body and of mind. Feeling the way Georgia quavered wildly under my touch, I was horrified. And I was furious. "Don't give me this act. You're not having a panic reaction. And you're no great actress."

She jolted back, stared at me.

"You may be frightened, all right, but your fear is that you've miscalculated, and that's no phobia. Unless you tell me the truth, right now, I'm going to be into every facet of your life. Anything you ever worried about being exposed, it will be. Got it?"

"But the room with the snakes, it did happen!"

"And here you are back in the city where you were set up for that awful experience. Here you are living in the apartment of a crony of the woman who set up that harrowing encounter. You chose to move into a place Tia knew well, that she had or could get a key to. She could've walked in here anytime with a box of cobras. Georgia, this is the last place a terrified woman would choose."

She drew back; dark brown eyes flickered up and settled back like an opaque shield.

I said, "You came here to prove you're not afraid anymore."

It wasn't a question, but she took it as a challenge. "Right. But this time it was Tia who was afraid."

"How come?"

She turned and strolled into the living room, very much like a woman in control. "What I told you this morning was true. After that week, I fled. Didn't even give notice on my job. Left the landlord a check and a note but no forwarding address because I had no idea where I was going. I was just getting out of San Francisco. Forgot most of my clothes. Ended up in Atlanta because I missed the connection to wherever I'd bought the ticket. It didn't matter where I was going, or where I was. One cheap motel was like another. I thought I'd . . . I didn't think. I just sat there.

"But here's the odd thing. In a while—it seems like it was only a few days, but I really had no sense of time, so maybe it was longer—I came out of it. I saw an article about the CDC honing in on an outbreak of Ebola and I knew—I just *knew* that that was what I wanted. I'm no scientist; I had no background for CDC, but I wanted to be a part of that. A month earlier I would have chalked it up to a pipe dream and checked the want ads for clerk jobs. But then it was like I could see into the future where the job was mine. So I figured out what I needed to apply and I got a temp job while I took the classes I needed. I did the whole thing without hesitation. It was exactly what Tia had told me would happen." She looked at me now unblinkingly.

"So you came back here to thank her?"

"Oh, no. I came to panic her."

"How?"

She leaned forward and put a hand on my arm. I could hardly believe it was the same woman. "Honey, I represent the major medical investigative agency in the country. You don't want me focusing on you."

"You could focus on me from now to Christmas; it wouldn't faze me."

"Yeah, but you're not Tia Dru. You haven't tried every pill and potion hoping for a miracle."

"Still, it makes no sense—"

She laughed. "And you say you know all about fear? Sense has nothing to do with it. I told her I'd put her on our watch list, that we call the shots with Homeland Security when we have to, and there was no way she'd ever fly again without her baggage being fine-combed and the police alerted in any city where she landed. I told her she would never even taste the substance that could heal her."

"Why? You got what you wanted. Why the vendetta?" But I knew the answer and it made sense.

She inhaled, shivered, and then said softly, "I could have died in that room. She had no right."

"That's not the reason, is it?"

Her hand slipped off my arm. "No."

I waited.

"I ran into her at a pharmaceutical conference. I was liaising with a research group looking into a low-dosage curare derivative used topically, and she—well, I don't know what her excuse for being there was. She probably talked her way past one of the guards. But she spotted the curare group and she wanted samples. She walked right up, put her hand on my shoulder, and took over, like she owned me! Because she thinks she owns me. Because . . ."

"Because *you* think she owns you, right? Because you're not sure your whole life isn't a house of cards."

She sat dead still, as if there was nothing more to be said. And then she added, "Of course they gave her a sample. They had no business handing out a drug like that, but she's Tia, and so of course they did. And then . . .

then she held out her hand to me . . . and . . . and I gave her mine, because . . . she owns me."

She was staring blankly, all hint of bravado gone.

I sat, equally stunned. All these years I had assumed Tia left her lovers with a gift greater than herself, but maybe I'd been wrong, 180 degrees wrong. Maybe when she left and deprived them of her body, she also took their souls. Did the men Tia set on the path to their dreams have the nagging fear that Tia owned them? Did Gary fear she could somehow undercut his law practice? Was Jeffrey afraid she'd expose him as a charlatan posing as Barbary Coast authority?

And Tia herself, had she known what she'd done? Had it been intentional? Or did she live in the fantasy of conveying the great gift? Had she ended up as hollow as Georgia? I felt a rush of grief greater than at any time since her death. Finally, I said to Georgia, "When was it you faced down Tia?"

"Tuesday afternoon. I found her address. I went there. She was just getting out of the shower. I leaned on the bell till she dragged herself there. I told her and I left, just left her to think about it."

Georgia's pale face hardened into a shell of triumph. The hungry ghost has a stomach as big as the ocean, a neck as small as a pinhole. I was stunned by the absolute cruelty of it all.

Tuesday afternoon, when she was starting to get dressed for the reception.

"Jeffrey," I said, "why did he let you have this apartment, his apartment? Were you two in this revenge together?"

"Jeffrey? You're kidding. With Tia, Jeffrey never gave up hope."

"Jeffrey isn't a fool; he knew Tia used him."

"He just didn't know how much. But even if he did, he wouldn't care. If he can give her what she's desperate for, he'll do it, no matter what he has to sell."

"Do you mean he's buying some illegal drug?"

"No, not buying."

"Planning to steal?"

She stood up. "Look, I don't know. He didn't tell me his plans."

"Not intentionally, but he told you enough for you to figure things out. There's no vector survey that requires a guy driving balloons all over town, is there? What kind of fourth-grade project would that be? CDC is a bit more sophisticated than that. You didn't hire Jeffrey to find out anything; you paid him to be gone from his shop so you could search it."

"How could I get into Jeffrey's shop?"

That one took me a moment, but the answer was right there. "Renzo's got the key, just like Jeffrey's got his. Renzo, whose son kidnapped you and left you blindfolded. Renzo's not about to say no to you. That's why his son is gone, isn't it? He's hiding from you."

She stepped back and lifted her hands as if to shove me, but they were shaking, this time for real. She stared at them as if they were the first telltale mark of relapse.

"What did you find in Jeffrey's shop?"

"Nothing. Nothing, because he saw through my plan."

Nothing, because he'd moved it to the first place he could rent.

I raced out, down the block to Lombard Street by one of the motels, and flagged one of the airport-hopeful cabbies. He drove silently, but the sharp turns and abrupt stops signaled that he had the same opinion of short fares as Webb Morratt. He pulled up by a hydrant near Jeffrey's new address. I paid and barely got both feet on the pavement before he screeched away.

Light bars on three police cars flashed. The double-parked cars blocked the lane. The sidewalk was jammed. For an instant every single person there stopped and stared. I straightened my shoulders and strode toward them like Helen Mirren in *Prime Suspect*.

The crowd was arrayed in three concentric semicircles like waves lapping from the entry hall. The outermost, and thinnest in density and commitment to drama, was made up of passersby. Some were tourists, glad for an acceptable reason to stop and catch their breath in a city that had turned out to be much hillier than they had assumed. Be-jeaned locals milled among them with even less commitment. Police raids on Tenderloin apartments were not news; for them the payoff would have to be quick. Those in the middle circle were pressed closer, murmuring in groups, huddling in inadequate shirts against the afternoon wind. They had the look of tenants rousted when the police charged in. The center was, of course, the cops, milling like extras in a crowd scene. It was John who'd coined that comparison, but he wasn't complaining about the plethora of squad cars responding to a run-of-the-mill call in a reasonably safe neighborhood. "You never know when safe'll turn into Baghdad," he'd pronounced, following it with "There's no such thing as too much backup." His gripe had been the guys who hung around after "in case."

"Hey, lady, no one's allowed inside," a young blond uniform announced.

"I'm going—"

"You're Lott's sister, aren't you?" a short guy with a shaved head asked.

I couldn't read him well enough to figure out whether that was a plus or minus. I nodded and kept moving up.

"He's not in there," the cop yelled.

"Not yet? Tell him I'll be upstairs."

"Hey, I don't think—"

I turned, caught the kid's eye, said "It's okay," and moved faster, buoyed by the knowledge I wouldn't be facing John inside.

The building was usual for this area. Shabby now, it must once have been a stylish address, with its oval staircase winding up the three floors to what were now two flats on either side of the building. They'd be tiny studios with kitchen alcoves. The front ones sported bay windows; the rear ones would have views of the alley. Bare wooden risers squeaked under my running shoes. The carpet—a mottled brown chosen in prescient anticipation of stains—was so thin the landings squeaked beneath it. Here tenants would take the squeaks as not a nuisance but a warning. It was a temporary dwelling for those on their way up or slipping fast, where children entertained themselves with leaning over the railing to spit and run. I couldn't imagine Jeffrey Hagstrom here. He'd be like the white-collar fraud prisoner in *Shawshank Redemption*, the guy who hanged himself after his first night. People in his Marina neighborhood where Georgia lived would never even walk down this block.

The doors on the first floor were shut and I made it to the second-floor landing before it struck me that the cops might be here about something— someone—unconnected to Jeffrey. I could hear them on the floor above. I also realized I had no idea where Jeffrey's flat was. What I needed was a dark alcove—better yet, a closet—to slip into and reconnoiter with my brain. Why were so many cops here to question him? He'd be a suspect in Tia's murder, of course. But this army of blue? And the building emptied? Did they think he'd flipped out?

No. If he'd flipped, I'd be hearing "Police! Open up!" and the door snapping open, maybe gunshots. So, either they were here for answers or for something else, and his living here was coincidence.

Or there was a third possibility. But it didn't occur to me until I'd opted for the decision I always made in situations I had no chance of reasoning out: in for a lamb, in for a sheep.

"Jeffrey! Jeffrey, you up there?" I took a breath and headed up the stairs.

Chapter 23

I ROUNDED onto the third-floor landing. Cops were everywhere. Without pause I swung onto the steps and made it to the fourth floor before a stout officer with a brown ponytail hanging from her regulation blue cap barred the way. "This is a police scene. No one's allowed up here."

I peered around her into the living room. It looked empty. No people, no carpet, no furniture in sight. "Where's Jeffrey?"

"I *said*, 'No one's allowed up here.'"

I'm less intimidated by police than the average person. Strident rookies only raised memories of John at his worst, bullying Mike, who cared enough about him to pay attention. The sound of what Mike had called that "TV toughie-cop voice" transformed me into the four-year-old who'd flounced past John and laughed. "Who's in charge here?"

"I'm giving you one more chance to turn around and walk back down the stairs."

I wasn't about to get into a physical battle with the police. I'm not that much of a four-year-old. I also wasn't about to leave. She took a step toward me. I shifted to the right and snagged a clear view into the flat all the way to the bay window. Korematsu! There is a time to avoid the cops and a time to give in. This was the latter. "Detective Korematsu!" I didn't call out to him, merely said his name loud enough to catch the attention of a man who had to have been aware of the problem out here.

187

He turned and walked, rather than strode, to the doorway. He was wearing a tan suit, one too light a color for police work. It set off his too-long-for-a-homicide-detective hair, his dark eyes, and that odd flicker that might have indicated amusement or irritation. "Darcy, what are you doing here?"

"I'm looking for Jeffrey Hagstrom. What are *you* doing?"

"Discovering he's not here, apparently." He motioned me inside. "I've been looking for you."

"I know."

"You *know!*"

"Yes. I didn't want to talk to you until I had something worth discussing."

"That's not the way it works."

"Except when it does." I laughed, and I could see he was tempted. "I heard you outside the zendo, but I certainly wasn't about to get in between you and my brother. You can understand that."

Now he did laugh.

"But I'm trying to find out why it is Jeffrey Hagstrom chose this place to rent." I did a quick survey of the fourteen-foot-square room. "Are you sure he lives here?"

"He's on the lease."

"It doesn't look like there's anything of his here. Clothes?"

Korematsu nodded toward the closet. His dark thatch of hair was hanging so low over his forehead the ends seemed to be teasing his eyelashes—teasing *me*—creating a B-movie plot I could barely tear myself away from. But I'd seen enough actors with come-to-bed eyes. Still, I couldn't figure out Korematsu. Was he a straightforward cop in a fine body of which he was sweetly unaware, or was he trying every gambit? Or was the problem me?

I looked into a closet that held two pairs of jeans, two dark jackets, two black T-shirts, two pairs of shoes, and no drug samples or anything else worth hiding. "Interesting."

"The clothes?"

"The dearth of them, the precision of arrangement. They could be just back from the cleaner. Or they could be new, bought by anyone. Did you find anything else?"

"Nothing." He glanced toward the doorway, obviously, waiting for me to play my next card.

I believed him. A drug stash here would have been too ordinary a discovery to keep from me. Georgia could have been wrong. She was like the blind man feeling the elephant's tusk. Maybe Jeffrey's connection with Tia had nothing to do with tusks. But then what? And why was Korematsu here with half the police force? Was he going on the assumption Jeffrey killed her for some other reason?

I said, "I'm here because the new tenant in Jeffrey's last apartment gave me his address. She was in the zendo this morning. You remember her, the blonde woman in the suit?"

He nodded, but not in time to cover the small lift of eyebrow that signaled interest. So, he hadn't followed the same route here. How had he found out about this apartment? Had Jeffrey paid with a credit card? Korematsu would have done the standard checks on Tia by now—credit cards, phone, back accounts. Was Jeffrey leading the suspect list? Or had Korematsu run the credit cards of all witnesses? Leo's? Mine? I looked from him into the hallway and back. "This is a big operation here for a peripheral witness. The detective in charge of the investigation. Half of SFPD. You must be thinking Jeffrey killed Tia." It sounded ninety percent like a statement, about thirty percent more than it was.

"We're not labeling anyone a suspect yet."

So, Jeffrey *was* big in the running. But why did Korematsu think so? He had to know Tia had dated him. Former lovers always move to the head of the line. But even that wouldn't merit the lead detective and eight backup. There had to be something else.

The ponytailed guard at the door stepped inside. "Sir?"

"Higgins?" He followed her back into the hallway.

I was tempted to ease myself against the wall near the door for a listen, but chances were large I wouldn't be able to get back here fast enough to avert discovery. The only currency I had was Korematsu's sense of camaraderie, tenuous as it was; I didn't dare blow it. I stepped into the kitchen and pulled open a cabinet. Plate, bowl, cup. One pan and one pot sat on the stove. Either Jeffrey was just moving in or he was planning for a short stay. Or he'd never been here at all. In the bathroom, a single towel hung over the shower rod where a curtain should have been. The tub had been washed but the enamel held the ground-in dirt of every tenant since the great earthquake. The only thing that suggested anyone had been here longer than the time it took to hang the hand towel was a garbage pail with a few of the kind of paper napkins you get with takeout orders, as if someone had wiped clean a tube or bottle with the only thing they had on hand, and then tossed the napkins. No tube, no bottle, just napkins. Damn!

I stepped back into the main room and made one final survey. No land line.

"No phone?" I asked as Korematsu stepped back from the hall.

"No."

In the hall Higgins was lumbering away. A better woman wouldn't have held her tough cop tone against her or inwardly bad-mouthed her butt. I watched as she and her partner moved down the stairs, leaving Korematsu alone with me, and wondered what he had in mind.

The walls were dark beige. One held a faint rectangle—a tenant a few years back had hung a picture, and his successors had let the bland bare paint fade. Furniture consisted of two Swedish modern armchairs, stained mahogany. I settled in the one with the orange striped pad. "You got a copy of Tia's cell phone records, right? Was Jeffrey the last person she called?"

He pulled a matching chair to face me and sat. "Could be."

"Just ask; don't tell?"

He leaned back. That almost smile flickered. "That's the PD rule."

"Rules are made to be broken when you want something." It was such a corny line, I was embarrassed.

He struggled to keep a straight face and covered the struggle by swiping his thatch off his forehead.

"Enough!" I said. "Seriously, we both want to find Tia's killer. She was my friend. I only met Jeffrey in passing. If he killed her, get him. I'm just saying cop games get my back up. I'll tell you about the call, but I want something in return."

His hair was back over his eyebrows, but his eyes had hardened. "What?"

"Tell me what's going on here. Why so many officers just to sign off on Jeffrey's not being here?"

"You want to talk to the officer in charge of them?"

"That's not you?"

"Not me."

"I trust you," I lied. "Tell me."

"You first."

"Okay. Tia's phone call was just after noon. A short call."

"How do you know that?"

"Nuh-uh. Your turn. Why this big police presence?"

He didn't appear to move. His thumb and first finger rested together and I had the sense that he was just barely rubbing them together as he considered. "I'd say it was a coincidence, except in investigations coincidences have to be disproved."

"The coincidence? A whole different case?"

"Right. A homeless man who fell over the banister on the floor below."

"The one who lay on the ground floor till rigor set in?" The case that had so outraged John.

"Yeah, that's what they thought at first. It's why it sank to the bottom of the stack. That and the fact it was Saturday night, when we do a big business."

"So, what made it rise again?"

"Turns out the corpse hadn't been dead for hours at all. Guy went stiff before he died. Not the same as rigor. Guy died because he went stiff. The neighbors were being straight all along. A kid saw the guy fall over the railing 'like a chopstick,' that's what he said."

I cringed. Jeffrey's apartment, where Georgia said he was keeping the drug for Tia—and a stranger goes stiff and dies in the same building? I inhaled slowly. "Cause?"

"Some kind of neurotoxin; coroner's still trying to pin it down. That's why there're all these officers here. Guy's so stiff he falls over a railing and we just have no clue about what caused it. Whatever it is, it's not a substance we want in our city."

But I *did* know. If Jeffrey'd heard about the guy he'd have known, and—oh shit—Tia knew because she'd heard about the case. She'd heard it from me. That was why—

"Your turn. How'd you know about the phone call?"

Korematsu had upheld his half of the deal; I owed him. But I had to think about this—me innocently repeating the story to Tia, her grasping the connection, and how that death threatened any chance she had to get the toxin.

I'd already answered Korematsu too fast once today, when he sprang the question about the zendo knife. I wasn't about to do it again. I needed to see the choreography of what had happened, to play it in my mind like I did before a gag. But I needed to get away from Korematsu to do that.

According to Georgia, Jeffrey rented this apartment to keep the drug safe. "I know about the phone call because Tia had invited me for lunch. She went to the garage to get something and never came back."

"What?"

It was a moment before I realized he was reacting not to the oddity of her vanishing on me, but was asking about the item. "A diary." The image banged down between us. I had to give him some explanation. "We were in high school together, remember? She'd kept a diary one year and we were going to reminisce."

"About?"

"School, friends," I said, all the while puzzling about Jeffrey. *Jeffrey rented this apartment to keep the drug safe, not for Tia, but from her! So he could dole it out to her and keep control of her.*

Outside an ambulance hit its crescendo and squealed down. "A diary? Not a picture album or a yearbook. A diary is thought to be a rather personal item."

I nodded. Damn, why hadn't I said *yearbook*? Yearbook would have been perfect.

"Were you close friends back then?"

This was headed in a bad direction. I had to divert him. "Close in a competitive way. Close enough for me to know who she was and to have kept up with her. And here's the thing: she was the golden girl, the one who charmed everyone. I assumed she'd be the chancellor at some university now, or own a fabulous restaurant, or a startup—no, too ordinary.

Something spectacular. But the truth is I don't know what she did after high school."

"Tried to heal."

I felt like I'd been punched in the stomach. I could see Tia trying to swing herself out of her chair, trying not to let on how hard, how painful it was. I felt that same helplessness as I had watching, torn between easing her pain and saving her pride, choosing the latter and looking away in that eternity before she maneuvered up onto her unsteady legs. Making conversation to cover the awkwardness. Telling her—omigod!—about the homeless man falling over the railing stiff.

Jeffrey rented this apartment to keep the drug safe from Tia, so he could dole it out to her and keep control of her. The homeless guy fell off the landing after being poisoned with an unknown neurotoxin.

Korematsu leaned forward, glaring. "I guess you don't know how bad the injury was."

"I do know. Tia fell under a cable car."

"Right. Trying to leap across like you had done."

My body went taut. He knew that much? What else did he know? How much was he playing me? I willed myself not to move, and I waited.

"I'm sure, with the kind of business you're in, you're aware that some injuries don't heal. Some people are lucky, like you; they break bones, tear muscles, and end up good as new. But others, like Tia Dru, don't heal. No one knows why."

He knew a whole lot more about Tia Dru than I would have guessed. How much? He'd been the cop on the scene at her accident. Was he a little bit in love with her, too, like Renzo and Gary and Jeffrey? Had he kept tabs on her ever since, so that now this case was personal? To get his reaction, I offered the view I had had of her two days ago: "She always appeared so accepting and moving on, so not with her head in the past, you know?"

"That was her persona. But you ask your sister, the doctor. I'll bet she knows about the failed surgeries, the unaccountable relapses, the things that didn't heal, and those that healed wrong."

Grace was exactly the person I wanted to ask, about this, about Jeffrey's father, about bioweapons research, and how easily Jeffrey's father could have walked off with some weapons-grade substance that could send a man so stiff he fell over a railing and died.

Korematsu was staring, as if he could see me thinking, not revealing.

"Grace never said—" I began, then stopped.

"She probably didn't want to make you feel bad. You ask her." He leaned forward so he was almost touching me. "Ask her."

"Is that what this is all about, me asking Grace?" I waited until he looked directly at me. "Or is it something more personal with Tia?"

He started to reach toward me but caught himself. "Listen. Your family is in this neck deep. I'm not saying you Lotts are responsible for her murder, but your family has been involved with her since her accident. Gary, Grace, John. Gary spent years on her lawsuit and I have to give him this, he got her a settlement no one else could have. They settled to be rid of him."

"Insurers don't—"

"They knew he'd never give up. He hired an investigator to dig up every unsettled claim against the Municipal Railway. He was ready to hunt down plaintiffs, resurrect their claims, do class actions, whatever it took. He wore them down.

"Your sister, the doctor, got Tia experimental surgeries twice, got her into a very exclusive and very expensive pain clinic, and who knows what other protocols."

"Really?"

"You didn't know any of this?"

"I've been away. But surely you knew that, too."

He nodded.

"And John?" I asked hesitantly. John, who had insisted Tia was a liar.

"Nada. Strange, considering the family."

I didn't like the familiar way he was fingering my family. "You're very sure of that."

"I've checked. Trust me."

"Listen, I know you and John are not friends. But much as you don't like my brother, he has standards. Just because Gary and Grace are involved with Tia doesn't mean the whole family is. I have other sisters. You're not talking about them, right? So why bring John into this? Because of your vendetta?"

"Because there's something he's not telling me. Something you're not either, even though you have to know the truth."

"Which is?"

He hesitated momentarily, then leaned forward in a way that announced this was the point he had been aiming at. "Tia Dru said when she was hit by the cable car she was running from a man. Where did he go? John turned up at the accident scene before the closest beat officer. How did he just happen to be there? Coincidence, as your brothers and sisters insist, as they go to extremes to help this woman?"

"I—"

"None of them put themselves out to help her before the accident. Then, suddenly, your brother devotes years of his life to a one-in-a-million-shot lawsuit, and your sister puts her career at risk to get this near-stranger into medical trials. But John, he does nothing except be first at the scene of the accident."

I forced myself to maintain my gaze, to cover my shock and the realization that I had suspected it all along, what I had shoved back from consciousness, what I couldn't face. John, who told me Tia had lied to him.

"You Lotts closed ranks. But Tia's dead, and Darcy, now you are going to help me expose the truth."

I took a deep breath and made myself listen to the sound of it as I exhaled, to the grinding of the traffic. I made myself be aware of the hard, smooth, slightly sticky surface of the narrow wooden chair arm my hand was clenching. I looked straight across at Korematsu. "No, I am not. You want to go after my brother for your vendetta; you won't be using me."

He raised his fingers in the air in a parody of ease. He said, "You will help me."

"Why would I?"

"Because—and this is what I went out of my way to try to tell you this morning when you were playing hide-and-seek with me—the main suspect in Tia Dru's murder is the owner of the knife used to kill her in his own room."

"Leo! You think Leo—"

"The evidence points to him."

"The knife? That's just circumstantial."

"Circumstantial evidence is evidence," he said. "Does he wear flip-flops?"

"*Shower shoes?* Of course. I'll bet everyone in California has them. Why?"

He shrugged.

None of this made sense. "Leo didn't even know Tia!"

"Is that what you think? Ask him."

"You can believe I will. This is crazy! How can you even think Leo would kill someone? I saw him put his life on the line for a student once. This is crazy. Yeah, I'll ask him. I'll ask him right now. You can drop me at the zendo!"

"Better yet, I'll take you to the station. Visiting hours are over, but I'll get you an exception."

CHAPTER 24

"Leo! How long have you been here? I just assumed . . ."

Korematsu had dumped me on the desk sergeant, who'd passed me off to a rookie, who'd plunked me in a tiny, airtight interview room. I sat on one of those plastic chairs made to be as uncomfortable as metal and assessed Korematsu's accusation. My brother, John, had been sure Tia was hiding some clue about Mike's disappearance. He would have been furious and desperate but also righteously irate at her failure to cooperate with a police officer, a newly minted one. It took no leap of imagination to see him chasing her down the street, and her thinking she could handle the leap I'd made look easy. As for Grace and Gary, it was easy to see how they'd gotten hooked. The question I was left with was why John had let them shoulder his guilt all these years. Why was he still doing it?

If only I'd been able to call Grace or Gary or even John. But, of course I couldn't—not in Korematsu's car, not in the cop shop.

If only I'd been able to ask Grace to find out what bioweapons material Jeffrey Hagstrom's father had access to. But, of course, I couldn't. Where had Jeffrey gone with that substance? Obviously, the police didn't know. Maybe Leo, who'd been there in the zendo, across the street from Jeffrey, for days before I arrived had some clue. Maybe. My head was swimming, washed by the odor of stale smoke and sweat and the Clorox that failed to cover them.

No one would have smoked here for years, but the chairs, plastic table, and the walls were infused with the smell. The glass was one-way, and I didn't even see Leo's outline until the guard opened the door and let him in. His orange jumpsuit was almost ridiculously too big; he had the pants rolled so they made pouchy cuffs, and the short sleeves hung like grocery bags over his bare white arms. He sat and let out a sigh. I had the feeling there was plenty he wanted to say, but that he was concentrating very hard on his breathing. Finally, he said, "They only give you one call, you know."

"Did you call me? I didn't get any message. Did you leave a message?"

He inhaled slowly and spoke very slowly. "Yes, I left a message."

I pulled out my phone.

"I called the zendo."

"The zendo! Oh, Leo, I haven't been there except for morning zazen. I slept at Mom's. I had a four A.M. call this morning. I just made it to the morning sitting. I never thought to check your phone there."

He laughed. He could have been watching *Revenge of the Pink Panther*, chuckling at the miscalculations of Inspector Clouseau. Whatever he had been holding back was gone. "It hasn't been bad here. Being an abbot gives a prisoner a certain cachet. I'm leading a zazen group tomorrow. By the time I'm out we may have a few new members."

"I'll call Gary. He'll get them to lower your bail."

"No."

"He won't mind."

"No! I'm okay here. I'm doing some good. Bail's an unnecessary expense. What you need to be doing is whatever helps find Tia's killer." He had a way of squeezing his eyes for an instant so that you wondered if he really had been about to give you a conspiratorial smile, but then caught himself just in time. "You do have a surprising knack for investigating."

I nodded. "I'd better, Leo, because this is bad."

He looked at me as if to say: things are as they are, merely that. Don't make more of them.

"Tia was stabbed in your room, with the zendo knife, the one for trimming the candles."

"We don't lock up the altar supplies. They're right in the hall closet. Anyone who opened the door would see the open box. It means nothing."

"To you, it means zip. To the police it's *your knife*. Police look for means, motive, and main chance. You had the main chance because it's your room she was killed in."

"And motive?" he said, with infuriating equanimity.

"They're hot on the trail of it. They're not going to need much. This is very serious. There've been a lot of scandals involving the SFPD; they could use some good press. Solving a high-profile murder in three days would burnish their image big-time. Leo, they can't find Jeffrey, but they've got you; they're looking to get enough evidence to take to the D.A. They're looking for motive. Detective Korematsu hinted that you knew Tia before yesterday."

"Oh yes. That's why she came up to my room."

We could have been in parallel universes—him calmly announcing he had invited a woman to his room where she was stabbed to death. Me trying to make some sense of this man I knew so well and not at all. Six months ago I hadn't been aware of his existence. Three months ago I was stranded at a monastery trying to protect him from a murderer, while he, just as calmly, focused not on fears but on facts. He had an uncanny ability to see through to the core of an issue, while ignoring the fruit and the skin. It was a skill that engendered deep love and overwhelming frustration. I took a breath and tried to control the latter. "Tell me what happened."

"If I know Tia, she figured she'd come up, see how I was living now, and surprise me."

"You're surmising, right? But, Leo, what *did* happen?"

"Right. Things as they are." One of those Zen truths Leo kept coming back to in lectures. Things are what they are, no more than that; the rest is just unreal thoughts. "I saw Tia at the reception, but there was no chance to talk, not with all the flurry about the tunnel. There was just a moment for her to squeeze my arm and say, 'Later.' I rather thought that *later* meant later that night, but then when she left with Eamon, I remembered how quickly things change for Tia." He squeezed his eyes in that almost-smile.

"Were you and she—"

"An 'item'?" Now he did smile. "Once, almost. A nice almost."

"Why not?"

"It's a long story, but we've got time."

"No, we don't. That's what I'm trying to tell you, there *is* no time. Every hour that passes they're building a case against you."

He exhaled slowly and I watched his shoulders sink, his chest relax, his hazel eyes sink inward. But when he focused on me, his brow furrowed with concern. "You know, Darcy, there are things in my past. One of them is alcohol. I met Tia at a retreat. I can't even remember who or what was in charge, but the program was a week long. The place was isolated, though nothing like Redwood Canyon Monastery. It was in the Sierras, a couple of miles from a tiny town."

"You were there to dry out?"

"No, I'd had to do that before. This program was to help you focus on your life, you know the kind of thing. The participants weren't all alcoholics, or all anything. We didn't know what brought the others there.

We must have had meetings, but I don't remember. What I remember is Tia."

"Why was she there?"

"Like I told you, no one had to say. And Tia never did talk about her past. If I'd let her she would have focused on me entirely, when we were together. But that was the last thing I wanted. I was playing the same game. Once we realized that, the game shifted to gaming the system." He grinned. "Of course it was childish. It was a waste of whoever's money and time, and ours. But, what can I say? We—particularly Tia—were pleasant, cooperative, and the people in charge ended the week viewing us as successes. But Tia was a master at breaking rules, thinking fast and not getting caught, charming her way out if she *did* get caught, and ending up with whatever it was she wanted—which in our case was vodka. I still don't know the details of how she managed that. The nearby town was only a post office and gas station. But we watched the sun set with a bottle every night—Belvedere, Stolichnaya, Chopin, Grey Goose."

"But you weren't lovers?" It was an impertinent question to ask one's teacher, but I couldn't stop myself. And Korematsu would certainly be asking.

"She was too fragile; I knew better. Maybe it was the vodka—of course, it was the vodka—but we eased off not talking about ourselves. Tia didn't say much; mostly she spoke of dealing with the limitations from her mashed-up pelvis, handling the pain and the fear of pain, and her spurts of desperation. I don't know what I said, but by the end of the week she had me believing that I was worth talking to, that I'd helped her deal with the pain. I left there feeling that maybe I could still become a Zen priest. I hadn't even realized that that was my question."

She left him the way she'd left every boyfriend. "Did you see her again?"

"No. First, I needed to dry out again, and that took a lot longer than

I'd deluded myself into assuming. Afterwards, I was in the city some. I could have called, but the moment was over. It wouldn't have translated into coffee or a movie. The first time I saw her since the retreat was at the reception."

"But Korematsu knew you knew her."

"I told him."

What else had he told him! I knew the answer all too well; he had answered every one of Korematsu's questions with the truth. Korematsu would respect him, all the way to the gallows. It was foolhardy to be so open, I could tell him that, but he would smile and remind me about the precept of Right Speech. I would remind him about death, and he'd say, *Death is another part of life.* Inadequate fear of death has its drawbacks.

"So, Leo, then what happened when Tia was killed? I called you from my cell phone when I was running back from her flat, after lunch, after I'd looked all over her neighborhood for her and given up. That was late in the afternoon. When I got to our block of Pacific, the police had barricaded it for the movie. I ran into Robin, the second unit director; he was all excited about seeing the tunnel and so I showed it to him. By the time I got out of the tunnel it was too late to race into zazen—"

"Shouldn't race into the zendo."

"What?" I felt like a running dog yanked back by his collar.

"You shouldn't *race* into the zendo. You are like the bell. You don't ring the bell when people are still settling in for zazen, wiggling on their cushions, adjusting jackets. Then the bell would be just one more distraction. Instead you wait until everyone is still, then you ring the bell. The bell rings into silence. It brings the people into silence within themselves. When the bell rings that way, it is clear that the ring, the ringer, the hearers are one."

"Yes."

"Same with you. Do your wiggling around outside. Walk to your cushion in silence." He paused till I looked at him and nodded, then he grinned. "But you were asking me . . . ?"

Our talk here shifted from the aura of intimacy of a dokusan room, where a candle burned and incense cut the air, back to the police interview room where our every word probably was not being taped to use against Leo—probably. I was half here, half desperately trying to figure out what to do next. Leo sat here in the endless moment while I jolted ahead in time—his time—which was short. "Where were you? I went upstairs to wait for you, but you weren't at zazen at all. Tia was dead. Why weren't you at zazen? What happened after I called you? I need to know."

"I got a phone call."

"From?"

He hesitated, and just as I was about to make the case again for dokusan not being legally privileged discourse and the urgency of our situation, he said, "There were sirens in the background. Panting, a lot of other noise. All I could make out was 'Jeffrey' and 'Golden Gate.'" I ran—*ran*—to the corner. Luckily there was a cab there."

"Luckily, indeed."

"The night before, I saw Tia dismiss Jeffrey and leave with Eamon. It surprised—shocked—me. I hadn't been undone by her. But only because I had my practice and I wasn't battered around by every thought. I missed her, I ached, but I felt those aches, I saw my thoughts as thoughts. I made a point not to let myself be dragged into a great drama. But Darcy, that was after years of zazen, an entire year in Japan. Jeffrey isn't me. He doesn't have anything to fall back on. Not yet. Maybe if his Barbary Coast history lectures take off he will. But now all he has is the hole Tia left."

"The hole between the past and the future?"

Leo shrugged. "Hope is the enemy of now. When hope is so strong, reality doesn't matter. You can see why I dropped everything and caught the first cab out there."

"What did you find?"

"Nothing. It took me over an hour to be sure. I walked across the bridge to Marin, checked out the parking area, asked people looking across the water at the city, then I walked back and checked the approach to the bridge. It was dark by then. If there were any sirens they were long gone. Then I had to catch a cab back, which meant I had to walk back to the Presidio, find a phone, and call, because cabs don't circle around out there."

"And the cabbie who drove you out was gone?"

"He had fares to get. I couldn't afford to have him wait. By the time I got back to the zendo, it was almost ten. No one was there but the police. They were waiting for me."

"How could they arrest you? You had an alibi!"

"So I told them, but I was asking people about Jeffrey; I wasn't asking for their names. It was dark and cold out there. No one was focusing on me. Someone might remember me, but I have no way of finding them."

"But the cab," I said desperately. "Taxi drivers keep records of fares."

"That's the most damning thing of all. There is no record."

"Leo, do you remember what the cab driver looked like?"

The big bald guy he described might not have been Webb Morratt. Crows might not fly. I told him Webb Morratt's tale of driving Jeffrey around town to let loose balloons, and how Webb broke into Gary's house and drove me from Jeffrey's old house to his new flat. "The first morning I was in town, on a set on Broadway, as soon as I finished—and you remember how early that was, barely dawn—I caught a cab, a cab that was waiting at that hour by the set, and took it to the zendo. The driver was Webb Morratt. The guy's in the middle of everything. But the question is, who the hell is he?"

Leo just shook his head, not that his lack of answer mattered because at that moment the guard opened the door, and our time was up.

"Just one more minute. Really, one," I begged.

He pointed to his watch and shut the door.

"Leo, did Tia ever mention dares? A group that seeks out the most frightening dares?"

He leaned back, as if to let a memory flow gently into his mind.

Outside, the guard's watch was ticking.

"No."

"No? What do you mean, 'No'?"

"She didn't mention it. She specifically avoided mentioning. She asked me three or four times, at the retreat, if I could keep a secret. She meant if I *would* keep a secret, and I said no. I wouldn't make that commitment in ignorance. She gave me broad hints. She wanted to tell me more. Maybe I should have agreed, but refusing gave me power and I was still into liking that. And with Tia, I knew if I didn't keep some authority, something in reserve, it would be easy to be swept away. Even Jeffrey knows that."

"Did she mention anyone else involved in the dares?"

He leaned back a bit more, shifting the chair to the point of instability. If he tipped over, the guard would be in here in a flash and that'd be it for this interview! "No one specifically. But the impression I got was there were people all over the country, a loose network. It was almost like a religion, or a cult. They didn't share money, but they were expected to finance their own 'events,' as she called them. Money was an issue for her."

"If she had a very desirable site, like the tunnel, then she could sort of rent it out, right? Or swap it for other dares? It would increase her status in the group."

"I don't know enough to say."

But I did.

CHAPTER 25

THE HALL OF JUSTICE is not in a safe neighborhood. Jails so rarely are. Dusk had come and gone. The wind had picked up. I was still in a sweater and loose pants, garments two seasons short of adequate for this winter night. My sleeves and pants flapped in the wind, creating an extra-cold backlash. Cars, trucks, and enough SUVs to add a degree to global warming whipped by. Not one cab! I dialed Webb Morratt. The suspiciously omnipresent Morratt didn't answer.

A horn blared.

Had I misjudged Webb?

No. A bright red Mini Cooper screeched across four lanes of traffic to the curb. "Give you a lift?" Korematsu asked.

"Do you think brains gave out in my family after the sixth kid?"

"I'm off duty."

"Good for you."

"Get in. This isn't a good neighborhood to be standing around in."

"It's not a good neighborhood to get in a car with a dangerous man."

He pushed open the passenger door. "Listen, we're on the same side here. I want to help you."

"Fine. Release Leo."

"I'd like to. Give me a reason."

"You've interviewed him. Surely you don't believe he's a murderer."

He started to speak but caught himself and his silence inflated all my fears about Leo. Leo had the means. Opportunity walked into his room. All that the cops needed was a motive—a melodrama of renewed romantic anguish and long-suppressed revenge would be plenty.

Still, Korematsu'd been waiting for me, which meant he might be open to other possibilities. I swung into the car. "Take me to Jeffrey Hagstrom's shop."

"We've had a uniform on the shop since morning, you know." He pulled out and cut across two lanes.

"Of course, you've searched it."

He didn't answer. Which meant yes.

"No suspicious vials or little bottles?"

He didn't answer that either, not that I'd have expected it. Mostly I was thinking aloud and he was happy to listen in. The answer was no. If he'd found any hint of the toxin Jeffrey had procured for Tia, he wouldn't be tooling around listening to me.

He veered back into the middle lane of Bryant and I exhaled slowly. Even in light traffic there were a million dangers lurking. I'd done the setup for a car gag on a street like this, choreographed trucks backing into lanes, motorcyclists whipping between cars, cyclits jaywalking their bikes, old ladies collapsing in crosswalks, kids running out between cars, and projectiles of all descriptions shooting off every flat spot. If I had to be in this car with Korematsu, I just wished I could say: let me drive.

"You still want to go to Pacific Ave?"

"Let me think. Jeffrey wasn't in his new place or his old one, so where else would he be?"

He focused on the road. I was the anxious one here, desperate to find some lead that would clear Leo. All Korematsu had to do was wait. The angrier I got, the better his chances. Seeing that didn't calm me down, not hardly.

"What do you know about Webb Morratt—cabbie—shaved head? He's spent more time with Jeffrey than most, drove him around for hours a few days ago. He was waiting for Leo right before Tia was killed. I've had first dates who are less attentive. Run a make on him. See who's bankrolling him. Find him, he's our best lead to Jeffrey."

He slowed, hung a left on the Embarcadero.

"Do you have a better lead? Why are you waiting?"

He looked straight ahead, pressed his teeth together between parted lips. Finally, he said, "Morratt's strange all right, but Darcy, he's got nothing to do with Tia Dru. He's just on your case. Not that that's not a problem. You could ask your brother—"

"Why would I do that?" I stiffened and assessed his face for a quickly controlled twitch of glee or some more subtle eye shift. I wasn't going to like his reply.

He clicked his teeth slowly, lowers against uppers. "Morratt's in John's stable."

"What does that mean? He's a snitch?"

"He doesn't have connections worth ratting on. He's just a guy out for a buck. John uses him, for off-the-book things."

"Like?" I snapped.

"Hey, I'm sorry. He's *your* brother."

"He *is* my brother. Just what are you accusing him of?"

"Maybe you're better off just asking him."

"Oh, no, you tossed this accusation out; finish what you've been gearing up to say all along. Like what?"

"Like picking up suspects in the cab, suspects' families, witnesses, and reporting their conversations."

"That's hardly illegal."

"I didn't say illegal, I said off-the-books."

"What exactly do you mean?" *Breaking and entering?* My heart was hammering against my ribs. If Leo's freedom hung on John, Leo'd better like jail a lot.

"I can't tell you anything definite. I can only say that Morratt's been accused before of battery, trespass, and assault, but he's never been charged."

"You're the king of circumstantial evidence! Sometimes guys aren't charged because they *aren't* guilty. Or there isn't hard evidence. Sometimes cops have legitimate dealings with civilians and those civilians do things unconnected to those dealings during the rest of their lives. Sometimes a murderer picks up the knife lying in the zendo and follows Tia to an empty room and kills her and it has nothing to do with Leo."

He turned toward me and shook his head. "You know why circumstantial evidence is called that? Because it's evidence. When it pulls the question beyond reasonable doubt, it's as good as an eyewitness."

"You're so sure you know who's paying Morratt? Let's go ask him."

Korematsu just stared.

"Hey, he's a cabbie. He's working tonight. Call the cab company."

Nothing moved but his eyes, which were shifting back and forth as if visualizing a tennis match between the competing choices. For a guy so controlled, it was a huge breakdown. Hadn't anyone ever said, "Dude, you are showing yourself bare!" Maybe it wasn't the kind of unsolicited advice one police detective offered another. But in a minute he had his cell phone at his ear and was talking to someone named Ed. In another minute we were shooting north. In two more, the surprised, then appalled face of Webb Morratt looked toward the source of squealing brakes and watched first me and then Korematsu hoist ourselves out of the Mini.

The cab was in a white zone near Pier 39, one of the city's most crowded tourist spots. A decade ago I had been here when the last private pleasure boat had relinquished the last slip to a herd of sea lions. San Francisco Bay has a short but plentiful run of smelt, an attractive entrée for the sea lions. Their bellies filled with this delicacy, the adolescent males shoved their way up onto the slips to sun between meals. Soon they topped the tourist attraction chart. I had once seen an outraged boater, separated from his craft, charge down the slip at the nearest male. It was as close as I'll ever come to seeing a sea lion laugh. Morratt's expression was akin to the boater's as he scurried back onto the pier. But Webb had nowhere to retreat and no metal mesh door to lock behind him.

Korematsu moved toward Morratt, but I slipped in front of him and began to list for Morratt the times he'd so conveniently happened by where I was. "Who paid you to keep tabs on me? Save yourself time; don't bother lying."

He looked behind me, as if checking escape routes.

"We're not talking anything illegal, Morratt," Korematsu prompted. "Anyone can pay a cabbie to make himself available."

Webb's brow wrinkled.

"We're just asking for information. Information we will appreciate," Korematsu spoke softly, as if truly requesting a favor.

Webb looked from the detective to me and back. His shoulders relaxed. "Okay. But I didn't tell you, right?"

"Sure," Korematsu said automatically.

"Who paid me?" He looked down at me. "Your brother, woman. John Lott."

Korematsu nodded. No glance passed between the two of them, but fingering John was a win-win for them. Maybe Morratt was speaking the truth, maybe not.

"What did he want to know?" I asked.

"The usual. Where you went; who you saw."

"And?"

He hesitated. "And he wanted to be sure you were safe."

I laughed. This from the guy who broke into Gary's house.

Korematsu was smiling like he understood the ludicrousness of this, too. But, of course, he didn't know about the break-in. That meant his pleased expression was the result of something else. The triangle I'd created to squeeze Morratt was squeezing no one but John, and Korematsu couldn't hide his satisfaction. Morratt got to shovel dirt on John, and Korematsu got to sift through the pile. Meanwhile, Leo sat in jail.

I put a hand on Morratt's arm. "Give us a moment, Detective."

I motioned Webb back a couple of steps. The crowd filled in the space. "And the break-in? You searching Gary's office? Who was paying for that?"

He turned and started walking out on the pier. I matched his pace. The pier was the length of two city blocks, closer to a mall than a working wharf. The crowd surged around us, pushing to cross the wooden thoroughfare to fast fish shops, T-shirt outlets, pearl jewelers.

Webb looked straight ahead, concocting his answer. "No one paid me."

"It took you that long to come up with such a lame lie?"

"No, I—"

I grabbed his arm. "You broke and entered the house of the brother of the guy who's paying you! While he was paying you. How do you think John's going to take that?"

"He's not going to sue me!" Webb snorted. "Not going to press charges, is he?"

"So you're saying a cop has no other means of making your life unpleasant? A cop with a very long memory? Listen, Webb, I've known John many more years than you; he is not a guy to turn the other cheek. I honestly don't know what he would do if he found out that you broke into his brother's house while his baby sister was asleep there . . ."

Shaking loose, he quickened his pace.

"If I told him . . ."

He leaned toward me but kept walking, veering around the little merry-go-round that lit up the dark. Once we were past it, the crowd thinned and the air was suddenly colder. "If?" he bartered.

"What were you after?"

A guy in a blue hoodie, arm around a girl shivering above her bare midriff, cut in front. Webb stepped away as if to let them join up with another couple wearing the same shade of blue. Beyond them a man hawked cable car kitsch from a kiosk. The pier would be an easy place to disappear, even for someone the size of Morratt—even with Korematsu tailing us, as he surely was.

"What, dammit! Okay, let me guess. Not money, right? Certainly not thirty-seven bucks."

He dismissed that with a glance.

"Something in the office. You went right there, like you knew Gary would have his office back there. Like someone—"

"No one told me the layout. Those houses are all alike. You drive the city long enough, you know there're only five layouts."

"Tia's case is long over. No point in going through legal papers. No other interesting files." I eyed him in time to spot a small, inadvertent nod. Korematsu had nodded like that when he'd suggested John had been chasing Tia before she leapt the cable car and that Gary and Grace had bent over backwards to help her because of it. But suppose Korematsu had it wrong. What if it was the other way around? What if John thought it was Gary who'd been involved with Tia all along?

The frog! At lunch, Tia had been fingering a little jade frog. Georgia had the same frog on her card table. And by Gary's front door was the big green frog Mike gave him. Why all the frogs? Coincidence? What were they a symbol of?

Mike's frog meant nothing, surely. Probably. But if Gary had a little one, too . . . "Small green jade frog."

Webb started.

Bingo!

"What was John going to give you, if you found it?"

"How'd you know I—"

"—didn't?" *Because I searched Gary's office before you,* but I wasn't telling him that. "You wouldn't be sitting out in the cold on your cab hood if you'd made that kind of score. So, what was the deal?"

Ahead of us shouts erupted. Suddenly there were a dozen guys in blue hoodies and another dozen in orange, yelling at each other. Gangs?

I pulled Morratt into an alley between shops. The screams bounced off the walls, pushing us forward toward the unlit slips. At the end of the alley I turned right, moving behind the back walls of the stores, toward the open water. We were alone, except for the sea lions, their barks plenty loud enough to cover any splash or scream. Webb had to be thinking the same thing.

He'd given me next to nothing. I didn't have much time. I stepped in front of him and stopped. "Did John make you an offer, or did you just figure John would be very grateful, or very indebted, if you found proof his brother was caught up in the dare group?"

He didn't bother answering but shifted and blocked any escape.

"You broke into Gary's house so you could blackmail John, right?"

To my right, dark mounds of sea lions shifted on slips. Ten feet behind me the walkway ended, and the railing was broken. There was nothing to keep me from backing right into the Bay. Webb moved toward me.

I stayed where I was and braced my legs. "Where's Jeffrey?"

"What?"

"Jeffrey. Where is he?"

"I don't know. I told you before, I don't know. Last I saw him Tia was slamming out of his car and he was just sitting there looking empty. Get off my case." He moved closer.

I inched back. "What about the drug? The stuff Jeffrey got for Tia? Where is it?"

"What drug? I warned you: get off my case." He was so close I could see his brow wadded in tension, or anger, or fear.

I kept moving back. I was so close to the edge I could see the warning signpost out of the corner of my eye. If he pushed me into the drink, no one would hear me. I shifted forward; I was in his face. "Looking empty? Why was Jeffrey—"

For an instant I thought the roar came from the sea lions. Mouth open, red-faced, Webb leaned back, came at me with the full force of his weight, and shoved me off the pier.

I caught the signpost. He sailed by me into the Bay. I heard his scream, but I didn't have time to worry about him finding the ladder. I knew why Jeffrey had looked desolate the afternoon Tia was killed. And now I had a good idea where the drug was.

CHAPTER 26

"THE DRUG Jeffrey had. It's in the tunnel," I said, as soon as I found Korematsu on the edge of the melee halfway down the pier.

"The thing is, Detective, Tia Dru didn't take something out of the tunnel. I thought that was why she wanted to go down there—to get something. Wrong! She put something in there, hid it. Hid her purse," I said, as we double-timed it toward the street. "Tia never leaned on her cane if she could help it. But at the reception, she used it once, when she walked over to Jeffrey, put her arm through his. I thought she was comforting him. A minute later she put her hand in his pocket. She was wearing a shawl. It covered her hand when she moved it. She lifted the drug out of Jeffrey's pocket. There was only one place to slip it—her own purse."

"So?"

"She was the one who was so eager to get into the tunnel. She ran so fast into the pitch black that she smacked into the far wall. But when she climbed back out, she didn't have that purse. She put the purse, the drug, in the one place Jeffrey wouldn't be able to get it, because he's afraid to go down there."

"She hid her purse in the tunnel?"

"It sounds crazy, but listen, the purse was small—easy to push into a corner. It was a mud brown that'd blend in. The tunnel—it was dead dark down there. It's not like it's a popular spot."

Korematsu hesitated only briefly, then unlocked the car, and in a minute we shot into traffic. He drove with one hand, phone in the other, calling for a crime scene team.

"Lights!" I said. "Tell them we'll need major lighting, like they use for a night shoot!"

"What?"

"On a movie set. Filming after dark."

"Oh. That kind of shoot. I thought—"

"Of course, you would."

As the traffic light turned from yellow to red, he hung a left.

"We're going to need a key to the grate. We should call—"

"No need. City's got masters."

"To grates leading to private property?"

"Grates in or near public sidewalks. When there's an emergency we can't be running around after every property owner asking him to hunt up his key. We've got grates all over town." He cut right onto Pacific and whipped down the few blocks to the zendo.

Brakes screeched. The red flashers from the light bar turned the macadam bloody. Patrol cars. The crime scene van. Techs and investigators poured out. I raced into the courtyard and pointed to a potted tree and the metal cover underneath it. "Entrance is there."

The tunnel would be warmer than out here, but I shivered at the prospect of climbing back into it. Tia was one daring woman, to descend and run so confidently into the dark to hide that purse. Then to look like she was about to collapse back at the ladder and force us all to help her up the ladder and out. You had to hand it to her.

Korematsu pulled open the grate. A tech moved in beside him and shot a spotlight down into the hole. The tunnel, with its mud-over-stone walls, sucked the variations out of the light, so that what we saw, as before, was undifferentiated muck.

An African American guy with a miner's cap moved in closer. The tech called for another light. Someone leaned over the entrance and began clicking pictures. The metal ladder attached to the wall was barely visible, but I remembered its location and was over the top, down the five rungs, and onto the gummy ground before Korematsu started shouting.

"Lower me a flashlight!" I grew up with a cop; I should have remembered it's a waste of time giving them orders. Korematsu yelled something about staying still. The tunnel's mud walls slurped up as much sound as light. Voices called out, but words were sucked away.

Tia had dropped to the soft floor in here, then run so fast she hit the far wall. People lumped us together, but she and I were opposites. She lived for danger met head-on; I choreographed it so I'd never be taken by surprise. Now I stepped into her world, out of the circle of light into total black. I blinked, but my eyes did not adjust. Normal life fell away. I put my fingers on the damp mud wall and forced myself to step forward. The ground squished under my feet. The smell of rot filled the air. I tried not to think of the young girls entombed in rooms like this a century ago. I failed.

Behind me metal clanked. Someone else climbing down the ladder. "Smells awful!" a man yelled.

I moved faster, guided by the wall and the slope of the ground as Tia had. I needed to be close enough to the wall to get a clear look before Korematsu ordered me back and the crime scene crew blocked everything off. With every step the air became thicker, more putrid. I wished I had a scarf to cover my nose and mouth. How had Tia . . . ?

". . . lights down!" the man yelled.

I ran. My foot caught. I fell.

On something soft. Gases whooshed. The smell was shocking, overwhelming, sickening. My face was in the mud. My breath wouldn't come.

"What's going on there?" the man yelled.

"Get me light!" I forced out. I pushed up with my hands and feet, forming an inverted V. Flies buzzed my face.

"Don't touch anything! We have to preserve the scene. You've got no business being down there. What's going on?" the voice kept yelling.

Lights burst on. The mud glistened. I looked down on legs. Legs splayed to the sides. Legs in brown pants. I squeezed my eyes shut a couple of times to clear them. Then I screamed.

The body was Jeffrey Hagstrom. He was lying on his back, arms flopped to his sides.

"It's Jeffrey; he's dead!"

The ladder clanked.

His eyes were open, brown eyes, but they were sunk deep in the sockets. His mouth hung open, too, like he was merely surprised, not dead.

"Don't move!"

"Don't throw up! We have to protect the scene!"

"Get her out of there."

His skin was both dry and glistening, and white like the underside of a fish. He looked like Jeffrey and not like him, like a much older version with sinking skin.

Blowflies circled his chest.

Bile shot up my throat. I was going to retch. I couldn't retch, not here. I swallowed hard, bent my knees, and pushed with my arms. It took all my strength to thrust myself up to standing. That's when I saw the knife protruding from his chest, from the hole the blowflies had zeroed in on. It was the other zendo knife, the duplicate of the one that had killed Tia.

"Darcy. Get out of the scene!"

I jolted up and half staggered, not toward the voice but to the dark corner of the tunnel where Tia had gone. In my memory this end of the tunnel was like the end of a mud-walled boxcar with sharp corners. In reality it was an uneven mass of rock covered in mud. It looked like a giant fist had smashed into it. The corners were not sharp, the wall was not flat, and the bottom edge was not tight. The light was dim down here. The purse had to be there, pushed into the corner, hidden by the shadows.

But it wasn't. Nothing was there but rock and mud.

I peered down at the empty corner. That position, here in this spot, was familiar. I felt it with body memory. When had I stood like this? Why?

I glanced from the corner to the dark hole beside it. I remembered when I'd shown the tunnel to Robin Sparto that something down here had jarred loose. I'd taken it for a big clod of mud, or a rat. But it could have been a small purse. It had slid slowly down that chute.

The purse, and whatever was in it, had to be that dark chute.

If Tia hadn't acted on impulse, if she'd had time to plan, she could have chosen a better spot. But she didn't. She was Tia.

I took a breath and slid my hand into the hole.

"Darcy!"

I felt something. Leather? Or muddy rock?

"Darcy!"

Rock.

"She's in shock. Come on, we have to get her out of there before she fucks up the whole scene."

"I'm okay." With an enormous rush of relief, I pulled my hand out of the slimy hole. The police could get the purse. They had equipment. That's what police were for. I stood a moment, looking down at that hole where I would not have to go. I'd been in worse places than this, but none had so viscerally upset me. Desperate as I was to see the purse, to be positive it was here, I was relieved beyond reason to get out of here and let the police go down that wretched hole.

"Keep to the edge. You'll destroy as little evidence as possible that way."

"If there's any she hasn't already trampled," I heard someone mutter.

I moved slowly along. Korematsu would be occupied with the murder, so I'd be able to wait till things were under control and then point out the hole. I'd have plenty of time to think while I waited. Plenty of time to remember that only two days ago Jeffrey'd been regaling half the guests at the reception with tales of this very tunnel, with Tia tossing him easy questions. And now they were both dead. Both stabbed to death.

At the ladder, I turned for a last look at Jeffrey. What I saw was not him but Leo's knife. I grasped the ladder and started up. The air cooled with each step. The sounds changed from the techs' back-and-forth instructions in the tunnel to sirens and brakes and Korematsu saying words I couldn't make out.

This time, Korematsu couldn't suspect Leo. Leo was in jail.

The top of my head was level with the street. Cold fog-laden air played with my hair. I took another step.

Leo was in jail *now*. Unfortunately, Jeffrey had been dead long enough to have blowflies around him. Long enough to have been stabbed before Leo was in custody. Korematsu could suspect Leo. When he discovered the murder weapon was Leo's knife, he damned well would.

Korematsu extended his hands and pulled me out of the tunnel, landing me in front of a gray-haired white man in civvies that hung as if they were his uniform. He stood, feet apart, gaze surveying the area and me, as if he owned the scene, as if he owned me and Korematsu.

"Acting Chief of Detectives Broder," Korematsu said.

"You're Lott's sister," he said, in a tone that suggested he'd heard a lot about me or about John, none of it good. Listening to my theories was going to be the last thing on his mind. But I had to make them get that purse before they saw the knife and locked in on Leo.

"Tia Dru hid her purse in that tunnel, at the far corner, by a chute, and it got dislodged and slid down."

"What would she do that for?" Broder demanded.

"To hide a highly toxic painkiller she got from Jeffrey Hagstrom at the reception."

"In the tunnel?"

It did sound crazy.

"In the one place Jeffrey wouldn't go. He was claustrophobic."

"He gave her a painkiller, and an hour later she's hiding it from him? What makes you think—?"

"I saw her run so fast to the dark end of that tunnel that she hit the wall. Later I saw something slide down that hole!"

"How deep is this hole of yours?"

"It's a hole!" My breath was coming fast, my shoulders were tight, and I squeezed my hands into fists against the urge to strangle him. "Maybe it's a small hole; maybe it's a chute. Maybe there's a bottom, maybe it empties into the sewer, and if you don't get that purse soon it will be spit out into the Pacific and you'll have to go call the Tokyo police."

Broder simply turned away, as if from a small yappy dog. It was clear I was banished.

I had blown it. Furious with them, with myself, I strode off down the street to Columbus and raced through traffic into Chinatown. I hurried along Grant Avenue, past darkened windows of butchers where freshly killed chickens hung in the windows, and tchotchke shops with gaudy laughing Buddhas, flower-bedecked flip-flops, and T-shirts from last year's rock concerts. I cut around families, past elderly women dressed in drab clothes schlepping stuffed woven bags, past straw-thin young women in saucy fashions.

I needed to think. I needed to talk to Leo, but he was the one person I couldn't possibly reach. I could call Yamana-roshi, my old teacher in New York . . . No, wait, it was the middle of the night in New York. It was verging on the middle of the night here. I needed to . . . get calm and think. The Buddha said: put no head above your own. I had to trust my own head. If Yamana-roshi, or Leo, or the Buddha were sitting across from me in dokusan, what would he say?

Sit down.

I almost stumbled down the steps of a tiny restaurant six steps below street level. Even at this hour two tables were occupied, one by a couple of plump and serious Chinese men, and the other by a younger couple. At a third table I sat down and ordered noodles and a pot of tea.

My interviews with Leo had been casual and his teachings had often taken me by surprise. But Yamana-roshi, who'd been a priest in Japan, retained the formality of the dokusan interview, and it was his form that filled the chair opposite me here.

Leo is already in jail. As soon as Korematsu realizes Jeffrey was stabbed with Leo's zendo knife, he's going to be hard-pressed to look any further than Leo.

This is the reality you create in your thoughts, Darcy.

I felt the same jolt of annoyance I had every time Yamana-roshi had said that. Now I was annoying myself!

The illusion of Yamana looked at me and insisted: *What is real?*

The tea arrived, not in the standard white pot but in a small black iron pot, a miniature of the one at our reception. It was odd to find a tetsubin in a Chinese restaurant, but then it was odd to be a Caucasian doubling a Japanese actress playing the part of a Chinese prostitute. *What is real?* I sipped the tea.

Exactly.

I smiled and felt the hot liquid flowing down my body.

What is real?

Rats. I knew the tack Yamana used. How could I know what was real when I could only see through my own eyes?

Exactly.

I didn't bother to smile, I waited.

What do you not *see? What is it you are avoiding seeing?*

That was an unusual detour into the psychological for Yamana.

Not psychology. Fact: the police are on a detour to Leo Garson. What will bring them back to the true road? What are you avoiding?

The noodles came. I slurped noodles, drank the hot, salty, spicy broth, and ignored the ghost of Yamana.

What is real?

Dammit, the only thing that was real was the drug Tia took from Jeffrey.

Exactly.

I didn't need a ghost to tell me what I was avoiding, what was down a tunnel where a man had died, down a narrow hole into the dark and who knew what?

But the police would have the scene cordoned off for hours. There was nothing I could do. What I needed now was some sleep. And someplace safe to do it. I needed someone I could trust.

Suddenly, in a way that was not a thought but was real, I knew who that person was. I called my sister Grace.

Then, punching the phone off, I lifted my teacup to Yamana. I wished he were here and I could pour him a cup.

No need. I'm not a hungry ghost. He laughed and laughed.

CHAPTER 27

FRIDAY

GRACIE'S ELDERLY station wagon, in which she'd hauled families of patients, groups of medical students, towers of boxes, and probably substances I didn't want to know about, clanked up, and I climbed in. The time was nearly 2 A.M.

"I'm surprised you remembered the Lott Spot, Darcy."

"Considering the amount of time I spent shivering on this corner waiting for the unlucky sib Mom corralled, it's no surprise. You, at least, came. More than once, Gary forgot me."

"You're hiding out? Some things never change." She drove up Washington, turned left on Drumm, and made a loose right two blocks later, heading for the familiar night route up Sacramento, through Chinatown, over Nob Hill and Russian Hill, to Pacific Heights, taking advantage of the late hour and the one-way street. "I suppose you think I'll protect you, huh, Darce?"

"That's my plan."

"You and Mike, you got such a free ride. John used to grumble that if it weren't for him, you'd have had no discipline at all."

"Yeah, well, he sure filled that void. When I left, he must have had hours of free time every day."

Grace laughed that small sly laugh that said she understood and was with you but, still, she had to watch her back. "Mike was bad, but you were awful. The monkey." She pulled into the intersection at Polk Street as the light turned red and rattled slowly across. Grace was notorious for her absent-minded driving. For her, time in the car was rare time alone to ponder and mull without interruption. Watching the road, much less her own speed, was an interruption. With Grace driving, you could observe death moseying toward you as she elaborated on the specifics of the municipal emergency plan she was working on.

I turned to face her. "Gracie, I had lunch with Tia the day she died. Do you know what the last thing she said to me was?"

"No."

"She asked me for your phone number."

"She didn't call me."

"Right after that, she walked outside, got in Jeffrey's car. He drove her back to the zendo and she was killed."

"Your point?" Grace snapped.

I had forgotten this defensive side of hers. "My point is that she wanted something from you. That was the reason she invited me to lunch, to reconnect with you. She said, Gracie, that she didn't want to talk to you about her health—something else. Her voice—you know how it is when a person tries to sound like they're just dropping in a casual question, but it's the whole point?—well, that's how this was."

"I—"

"No, let me work this through. She'd already stashed a drug she'd been desperate to get; she'd lifted it from Jeffrey Hagstrom at the reception the night before and hidden it away—"

"Why'd this guy bring a drug to the reception?"

"I can't say for sure. Maybe he was going to dole some out to Tia later and she got tired of being doled to. It's not like he could leave it in the apartment he rented in the Tenderloin. But the thing is, Tia still needed something else, something from you, *you* specifically. She didn't want, she *needed*. She was tense the night before for obvious reasons. But she was still tense at lunch and it all came to a head, in a tightly controlled way, in her question about how to reach you. Gracie, why you?"

"I was with her after the accident. She was grateful." Grace put out, as an opener.

"But why suddenly now? She made the decision to call you the night before, after the reception. She invited me to lunch then."

"Why didn't she just ask for my phone number then?"

"She started to! She said, 'Do you have her phone—' But then she shifted to invite me to lunch and so I didn't pay any mind to that. The thing is, we weren't alone. She must not have wanted anyone to know she needed you." I looked across the dark at her small sharp-boned profile, her hands at ten and two o'clock on the wheel. "What did she want from you that she wouldn't want anyone to know about?"

"I can't imagine."

"Gracie, she was stabbed to death the next day! This is the last thing she asked for. It's important! Think! What do you have, what do you know?"

"Well, I'm a doctor."

"No, you're a particular kind of doctor, an epidemiologist."

"And?"

"Where does *your* medical knowledge—whatever it is, maybe not your specialty—intersect with Tia, past or present? That's what you have to be thinking about."

"Sorry. Okay, give me a second. Well, when I first met Tia, in emergency, her pelvis was such a mess I didn't think it would be possible to put it back together. I didn't think she'd walk. But she did. She had more focus, more ability to make herself endure pain than anyone I've seen.

The thing is, Darcy, pain wears you down; it programs the neural pathways. You can't endure it forever. It's not mental weakness that makes people take more and more painkillers; it's that the pain debilitates the body. It narrows your world."

"Do you think she'd ever have asked you for illegal painkillers? Maybe to tide her over till she could use what she'd just gotten?"

"No!" Grace snapped.

"How can you be so sure?"

"Because, Darcy, we'd already had that conversation. She was willing to take her chances with the law, but I can't do that."

"When was this?"

"A couple of years ago. Before my divorce. Before I moved back in with Mom."

I nodded. That would explain Tia's not knowing Grace's phone number now. "Maybe she thought you had something new, something experimental? Something to do with suppressing epidemics."

Grace laughed. "Like what? The silver bullet for epidemics? There is *nothing* on the horizon; that's why we're still talking quarantine. The only biological agents I know about are the pathogens themselves."

"Well, is there such a thing as an organism with a split personality, a Jekyll and Hyde pathogen? Could one also have a palliative potential?"

"No."

"Are you absolutely sure?"

"Well, of course, there are always people who want to believe that apricot pits cure cancer and poison darts are the way to heaven. But—"

"Poison darts? Why did you mention that?"

"Just an example—"

"No, Gracie, it's not just any example, it's the one that came to your mind. Something brought it to mind. What?"

"I don't know—"

"What do you know about poison darts?" It was the wrong question to ask when she had to make a left and cut across four lanes. Behind us brakes squealed; a horn honked. Gracie waved as if to acknowledge . . . something.

"Poison darts. They were used by the natives in Central and South America and parts of Africa. Some poisons are made from bark, like ouabain in Somalia or curare, others from poison dart frog secretions. The military was hot after golden poison dart frog for a while."

"Golden poison dart frog? Is it green and gold?"

But my sister was in full exposition mode, not about to be diverted. "The frog is so poisonous that just touching its tongue to something the frog has walked over is enough to kill a small dog. The poison is absorbed through mucous membranes. One frog carries enough to kill ten people. The army researchers figured they could reduce it to the essentials, tweak the format, and come up with weapons-grade extract. Then they'd add an accelerant and bingo, thousands dead."

My breath caught. I could barely get out the words: "How does it kill?"

She hesitated. "It's a neurotoxin."

"Specifically?"

"The nerves stop transmitting impulses. The muscles are contracted, but they're inactive."

"So patients just go stiff? They're alert but stiff?"

"Well, yeah. But there's no research on that; it's not like the dogs report in after they die." She drifted into the slow lane on Geary Boulevard and turned to assess me. "Why are you so interested in this?"

"Remember John grumbling about that case in the Tenderloin, the guy who fell over the railing and John thought the neighbors had let him lie on the ground floor till rigor took hold?"

"Yeah?"

"Turns out the guy went stiff before he fell. That's got to be why he fell."

Her hands tightened on the wheel. The car had slowed to ten miles per hour. "You think he dosed himself, somehow, with golden frog dart poison? It's incredibly dangerous stuff. Word is, the military researchers gave up on it because of its toxicity."

"How so?"

She turned toward me. "Three researchers died. Two trapping the frogs and one guy who'd gotten some in his eye. All this is rumor; the whole thing was high-level hush-hush. But why do you care?"

I jabbed my finger toward the road. When she was facing forward again, I said, "Suppose you used it, sufficiently diluted, on your skin, on your torso, not near a mucous membrane? Would it numb your pain?"

"Well, yeah, maybe. But—"

"And because the muscles are contracted you'd be able to get around?"

"Yeah, not flexibly, but—"

"You'd be okay walking, but to do something like hoist yourself out of a chair would be hard?"

"I guess. But no one's using it for pain. Haven't you heard anything I said? It's way too dangerous."

"For Tia, danger would only add to the benefit. And at least, in theory, it could work for pain, right?"

Grace tapped her teeth together very slowly. She didn't disagree. The engine coughed; the speedometer looked to be at seven miles per hour. "In theory. But it's not like you could pour it out of the bottle onto your skin. It would need a lot of work, by researchers who were committed and insanely careful."

"But where would she find that kind of researcher?" I mused aloud. "The military? You said they gave up on it."

She hit the brake, unnecessarily. "This country has tested all sorts of pathogens. The headquarters was Fort Detrick, Maryland. But our government ran tests, on civilians, all over the country. Dugway Proving Ground, Utah; Edgewood Arsenal, Maryland; Pine Bluff Arsenal, Arkansas; Rocky Mountain Arsenal, Colorado. And lots, lots more. When they finally officially halted the program in the seventies, they kept samples of the pathogens in Fort Detrick, so, presumably, they could test preventatives."

"Fort Detrick, where Jeffrey's father worked. Tia was back there. Eamon told me he saw Tia there. He said she'd been on an adventure weekend with one of the guys on staff there. An adventure weekend for her would have been a Dare event."

"What?"

I told her about the Dare group. "The thing is, that she came back from the dare to Fort Detrick, with one of the scientists."

"You don't know that he was a researcher. Not for sure. You're only guessing."

"If not him, he'd know researchers. Gracie, I've seen little green jade frogs—green with gold—in Tia's house and in another Dare woman's house. The Dares cost money; members have money. They live for risk. The golden poison dart frog is a perfect symbol for them. And then, for Tia to realize the poison might dull her pain . . . How could she not find a researcher in Dare? How could a Dare researcher refuse her?"

The car sat in the lane. Grace let out a sigh and turned to face me. "For money, that's how! Painkillers are big-money drugs. Find a way to tame that poison and you're a multimillionaire."

"Tia had that capsule in her purse when she went into the tunnel. She didn't come out with it. Turn around."

Grace pulled the wheel right. Only then did she realize the car wasn't moving. She hit the gas and hung a U.

"So, Tia heard about the frog dart—"

"Golden poison dart frog, *Phyllobates terribilis*. It's not named *terribilis* for nothing." She shot through an intersection.

"I tried to get the police to look for it, but they're caught up with Jeffrey's murder. Korematsu won't back me up. And the guy who seems to be in charge thinks I'm a fool, and I don't think he cares much for John, either."

"The capsule's in the tunnel?"

"I'm almost positive."

"Almost?"

"Tia stashed it there. But it wasn't there tonight. Here's what must have happened. It slipped down a chute at the end of the tunnel."

"Chute to?"

"Who knows?" I said, bracing against the dashboard as we sped across Van Ness.

"Who knows! *Who knows!* The Bay, the drinking water? We're not talking about merely the deadliest of frog dart poison, we're talking poison that's been amped up as high as possible, reborn as weapons-grade. This could be a disaster. A disaster that could hit tomorrow or six years from now. We have to get it out of there."

"I'm not totally positive—"

"Odds are it's there, right? In a leather purse that could get eaten by rats. The vial could get broken and spill and . . . We can't take the chance."

If I wanted someone to keep me from going into that tunnel and down that hole, I was riding with the worst person in the city. Just the thought of it filled me with fear, but I knew it had to be done, and if I didn't go down that hole, my sister would, and she, who had had no physical training, might well die down there.

CHAPTER 28

THE CRIME SCENE van and what looked to be the last patrol car were pulling away as we passed Pacific and parked on Columbus, where there was less chance of anyone spotting Grace's beat-up-into-uniqueness station wagon.

I said, "I need to picture the reception, to place where we all were. I'm trying to remember where Eamon went to get the key."

"Think, now."

"I am, but you can't just summon a memory, Gracie. It's not like—"

"Close your eyes."

"Fine, but—"

"But what? Why are you stalling? If you don't want to go down there, I'll go. We're talking about an epidemic that could wipe out the entire city." She slid out of the car and strode off.

I followed suit, catching up with her quickly on Pacific. "You've got your reputation—"

"Yeah, it'll be a great comfort while I watch people die. Listen, I'd call in the authorities if I could. Believe me."

"I'll call Korematsu—"

"Darcy, if he was going to go back down there and get the purse, he wouldn't have cleared off."

"Maybe they even have it already. Maybe he listened to me, after all."

"If he'd found something as dangerous as frog dart poison, the whole area'd be cordoned off. So, the key?"

"I'll have to hunt." We were in the courtyard now. I stepped inside the zendo. At the reception, when Tia insisted on seeing the tunnel, Eamon had stepped into the vestibule. He hadn't been gone a full minute, so the key had to be in the closet. I opened the door and spotted it in the back. If I moved it, Grace would never find it and neither one of us would have to go down that hole. If I—

My thoughts shocked me. Didn't I care about the epidemic? What kind of person was I? I was the perfect person to do this. I'd had years of training to handle hard situations. I had done car rolls and blind drops into catchers four stories down. I'd been worried, but not shaking. Bad as those gags were, there'd been rescue crews on the set, paramedics standing by. Bad as they had been, they were over in less than a minute.

But this hole was an entirely different thing, and it viscerally terrified me.

The thing was, giving in to fear frightened me more. I wondered if this was what Tia felt. Only half; her high came from beating back the laws of ordinary life. I grabbed the key and the emergency torch and stepped outside. How bad can it be? I asked myself. Grace will be right there at the top of the hole. If there's any problem, she'll get help. She'll be inches away the whole time.

The fog had thinned, but the circles and ovals under the streetlights still glistened wet and cold.

"Odd, there's no crime scene tape around the grate, no uniform left on duty," Grace mused suspiciously. For Grace there was always an underside; confidence merely meant someone overlooking the pitfalls.

"What were they going to tape off? Pedestrians had walked over that grate for two days before we got there. And it's been hours since I was here." I glanced at my watch. It was almost four in the morning! "They've had plenty of time to get what they need." I inserted the key. It moved surprisingly easily. The grate did not. I had to brace both feet and yank. In the dim light the ladder was barely visible.

"I'll go first," Grace said.

"No." My throat was so dry I had to swallow to get out the rest of my admonition. "You'll stay up here."

"Darcy, I can handle this."

"What if someone comes along and shuts the grate? No one will know we're down there, ever!"

I swung onto the ladder before I had time to think about Grace not being at the top of the hole, not being actually in the tunnel at all, not being near enough to hear me scream. The flashlight illumined a tiny circle. How had it seemed so much more adequate when we were down there after the reception? Had it just been the party atmosphere, the sense of adventure, like a movie set where wrong can only happen within limits? Then the tunnel was crowded and small. Now I was alone and it was huge. Before, it was a party game. Now it was Jeffrey Hagstrom's tomb.

My feet hit the bottom. The mud grabbed them. I turned and shot the light down the wall, along the floor, and made myself walk, hand on wall, as I had earlier tonight, away from the ladder, past where Jeffrey's body had lain—Jeffrey, who I desperately wanted to believe had been dead before he was dropped into this place he so feared.

Jeffrey had to have been thrown down here. Nothing else made sense. By the time the killer had forced Jeffrey to swing himself onto the ladder and climb down, Jeffrey would have screamed so loud half the city would have gathered around. Pacific is a quiet street after hours. It's an ideal spot to carry or drop a body, but a terrible one in which to move a screaming hostage.

The tunnel had been quiet before, as if the mud sucked out the sound, but now my feet swished with each step, raising the whispers of the sailors, drunk, unconscious, or dead, who had been dropped through trapdoors into waiting carts. The putrid smell filled my lungs and I thought I was going to cough and cough until there was nothing left. The radius of my light was so narrow I had no sense of where I was in the tunnel; it seemed endless.

My foot hit the wall. My nose was inches from it. I coughed. Spray hit my face. I blinked hard against it. "Grace?"

"You okay, Darce?"

"Sure," I forced out. "Just checking. I'm kneeling now, looking down the hole. I'm flashing the light into it."

"What do you see?"

"Nothing. I'm sticking my hand in, rotating the light."

"Do you see anything now?"

"No. Just black." I waited for Grace to speak again, but she didn't. There was nothing to say. We both knew it. I stuck my head in the hole.

It was black. The walls were rough, the chute narrow. I couldn't see the bottom. And then I could, way down, and at the base something tan against black rock. The purse! Relief washed over me; a new wave of terror washed it away.

"Find anything?" Grace called.

"I don't know. I'm . . . I'm going to have to look again." I needed to take a deep long breath and calm myself; I couldn't stand to pull this awful air that deep into my lungs. I plunged my head back in. The walls narrowed but they were too dark, too irregular to show by how much. Space in darkness is deceptive. I could see the purse now, definitely a purse. It lay where the walls came together, maybe ten feet down. Around it were white sticks. Sticks?

Or were they bones? What was this chute?

Maybe they were just sticks.

"Darcy? How's it going?"

"I found the purse. Down a chute. Ten feet down. I can get down there."

"I'm coming in."

"No! You've got to stand watch up there."

"Shine the light over here. I'm on the ladder. Jeez, this is slippery. What is this place? It's revolting."

I laughed. It was such an inadequate word. I aimed the light and spotted Grace's green loafers, already mud-splattered. She should have stayed up top, but I was so very relieved to have her down here with me. "Keep your hand on the wall as you walk. It's easier, no matter how awful it feels."

"Hey, I'm a doctor. I don't do squeamish."

"You're wearing a belt, aren't you?"

"Yeah, why?"

"I'm going to take mine off and give it to you. If I get stuck, loop them together and brace your feet to pull me out."

"Okay." Her voice was tight, but did not carry the fear that shot through me. I had doubled the lead once in a script about a child stuck in a well for days, the air getting ever more fetid, his little body weakening, sinking, getting more wedged in. With fire departments from six counties unable to— I shook my head, hard.

"Hey, keep that light steady!"

"Yeah, like when you were squatting on the beach outside our tent that time and you were so busy carrying on about the flashlight you toppled over and rolled into the water?"

"What about you on the boardwalk in Santa Cruz?" she said, with a forced laugh. She understood the need for a little distraction. "'Hold me! I want to stand up! Hold me while I stand!' And the roller coaster hadn't even left the gate!" It wasn't the same thing, but this was no time to get critical.

"Okay. You're here." I handed her the light, noting, not for the first time, how small she was, not letting myself dwell on whether she'd really be able to pull me up in an emergency. I hugged her, harder than I had intended, then bent, braced my hands on the sides of the chute, and slid my feet in. I leaned forward to use the lip for traction. My feet dangled in air; the mud was useless to stop my fall. I thrust my arms out. The fall stopped, for the moment, but even my arms were sliding, my body was dead weight. Carefully, so I wouldn't create more momentum, I moved my feet out to the sides. The chute had looked narrow, why wasn't I coming up against wall? My arms were slipping. I couldn't fall, not onto the poison! I split my legs wider, moved my feet back and forth. Was the wall there and I just wasn't feeling it?

My arms jerked, slipped inches at once, they were almost vertical, near useless. I couldn't keep on hunting for the walls like this. I thrust one foot back, one forward, and then caught wall. The back-forth wedge wasn't as reliable as the side-to-side, but it was better than freefall. I slow-skidded the back heel until it found something that might be a ledge or a pimple-sized bulge; there was no way to tell. "Please," I said to the outcropping, "just a little longer."

With side wedges you can press the edges of your shoes into the wall and do a very controlled skid. But front-back was too unsteady. Very slowly I wiggled my foot downward, feeling the rock through the rubber sole, trying to tell whether the space was narrowing. My arms slipped again, only this time I was braced. My hands were still outside the hole. The black was unrelenting; I couldn't see anything. The smell—must, brine, decay—forced me to breathe through my mouth.

"Darcy, you okay?"

"Mmm."

I wiggled my toe an inch lower. My rear foot was losing traction. Jamming the front toe hard into the rock, I slid the back foot. It went fast, too fast. I couldn't find purchase. It was slipping. My front knee was bending. I thrust my hands to the sides and caught wall. I was hanging on my outstretched arms now, feet dangling. The rock cut into my hands, and still there was too much mud; the friction was going. My hands were slipping. I rammed my feet out to the sides and caught wall again.

My feet skidded. I pressed the sides of my shoes into the walls, but that only slowed the skid. Something flitted over my face, but I didn't dare take my hands away from the walls. My hands slid.

The wall was gone. My hands were in air. My feet sliding fast. I covered my face and fell.

I hit bottom with a crunch. My feet hit hard, my ankle bones jammed against the sharp angles around me.

"What happened?" Grace sounded terrified, her voice miles away.

"I hit bottom. I thought for a minute I'd snapped my ankles. But it was something else breaking."

"You didn't land on the purse! Is it intact?"

"Oh, shit. Let me see. This is going to be tricky. It's too tight here for me to bend over. I'm going to have to see if I can ease it up with one foot. While I balance on the other."

"Be careful. If the bottle's broken and the poison spilled . . . If it gets in a cut, it'll kill you before you get out of the hole."

I shivered so violently I hit the walls. Then I couldn't move at all. I heard myself moan.

"Something the matter?"

A laugh, near-hysterical, shook me. "No, Gracie, it's fine down here now that I know there's not as much danger of being buried *alive*." Grace didn't know the half of it. If I balanced on my ankle and it was broken, I wouldn't be able to wedge my way far enough up to even grasp the end of the belts. If I bent over and got wedged in, I was dead. I would be stuck with my hands down and there would be nothing in the world she could do to extricate me. Even the fire department wouldn't be able to get me out.

"Darcy—"

"Let me think! This is what I do for a living, plan moves like this. Just give me a minute." Slowly I bent my knees. My ankles screamed, but I didn't dare move my feet. I sank, squatted until my back was against one wall, my knees against the other. Still, I couldn't reach the purse. Down here at the bottom, the chute curved in on all sides like a colander.

I shifted my shoulders. They touched wall on both sides. But I couldn't reach any farther than my ankles. If I could see the purse . . . If I had the torch . . . But I didn't. There was no way but to wedge onto one ankle, lift the other foot, and hope I could get the purse loose. I shifted; the ankle screamed. With my free foot I felt with my toes. Something moved. I didn't dare kick it up and break the poison container. Instead I moved my toe back and forth until it got under something, something I hoped was the purse, and inched it up against my braced foot. When it was ankle-high I caught my toe under, bounced it up.

"Got it!"

"Great." But there had been a little pause while she caught her breath and I realized that she hadn't believed the retrieval was possible, not really. Not that that had stopped her trying, or had me try.

"Lower the belt and I'll send it up. Shine the light down, at an angle, not in my face."

As soon as the purse was gone, I took as deep a breath as I could stand in this putrid air, ran my hands up opposite walls till I found the narrowest route, and began wedging my way up. My ankle ached, but it was on its own. Maintaining movement was vital. If I paused even momentarily, I would slide all the way back to the bottom. I wedged elbows and feet until the chute widened and it had to be arms and feet, touch, dig in, lift, touch, dig in, lift.

"Grab . . . me!"

"I'm ready."

Grace was so small I was afraid, but I was wrong. When I got my head out of the chute, she locked onto my shirt and gave me enough support to thrust my shoulders up. Somehow she pulled and I shot out of the chute like an easy birth. We both ended up in the mud.

It was a minute before she said, "I have good and bad news."

"What?" I forced out. I was shaking so hard I couldn't think.

"Good: you were right, the vial was in the purse. Bad: it's not there now. The purse, it's got a Styrofoam insert, whittled down to fit in. But the center, where the poison vial was, is empty."

I pushed myself up. "Worst possible. She had it and somebody killed her for it. Jeffrey realized it. It was the first thing he'd think of. And that got him killed."

"And the killer has had that poison for two days. Darcy, there's only one thing you hold on to something like that for."

I waited.

"To sell it. It's as bad as it gets."

But Grace was wrong about that. It wasn't as bad as it gets. Not for another ten seconds, when the grate to the sidewalk slammed shut over us.

CHAPTER 29

"HEY, LET US OUT!" Gracie yelled.

The only reply was the metal doors reverberating as they settled in flush with the sidewalk.

"We're down here! Open up! Hey!"

"Save it, Gracie. If there was anyone else around, whoever's done it wouldn't have slammed down the doors."

"Maybe it was a mistake? It could be, right? Someone sees doors open at night; it's just the neighborly thing to do, to shut 'em. It could—"

"No one's up there. It's four-thirty in the morning."

"People could come to work early. They—"

"Gracie!"

"Oh, God . . . I was supposed to be watching the door! That was my job! Darcy, I should have—"

"Stop! Just stop!" Her hysteria scared me almost more than our being trapped. I had the flashlight. "Look at the light. Put your hands out and walk toward me." When her arm touched, I eased her in and hugged her. I wanted to hold her till she calmed a bit, but there was no time—no time for guilt, explanations, no time to spare. "Do you have your cell phone?"

"In the car."

"Never mind," I said. "There's got to be a door switch in here."

"Why?"

"Because it makes sense. Put one hand on the wall; hang on to my back." Sliding my feet, I moved toward the slither of light under the metal doors. Grace didn't speak but her tight breaths—each inhalation broken off with a gasp—said it all. How could I have allowed my so good, so committed sister to come charging down into this tomb? All she'd thought about was protecting everyone else. Oh, Gracie! I wanted to say, "I love you, Gracie," but I didn't dare. Instead, I swallowed, controlled my voice, and insisted, "There'll be an emergency switch because it's a storage area, not a prison. We're not in the nineteenth century; this is now." I reached around for her hand. "Here's the ladder. Run your hand along the other side. Start at waist level, brush across. Be thorough, but don't waste time."

She didn't ask why, and I didn't tell her that the biggest danger was not the metal doors closing but the killer pushing those big planters over them. I spread my fingers, swathed my hand back and forth on the other side of the ladder, moving a couple of inches higher each time, desperate for a switch, a button, a chain, anything.

"Darcy, there's nothing here! We're fooling ourselves. There's no way out! That's the way they built these tunnels, so prisoners couldn't get away!"

"Shut up! Just shut up! What kind of role model are you?" I'd almost said, *What would Mom think?* But that would have turned her, and me, to mush. "Keep at it. I'm starting up the ladder. If the switch isn't down here, then it'll be at the top."

I felt along the right side, and then the left. No switch, no loop, nothing. Panic swirled in my stomach. Why would there be an exit when there weren't lights here? There was no electricity; what was I thinking? How could I have— Stop! In Zen practice we don't push away thoughts, we let them go. But I pushed them out now and focused on my breath. I felt the metal ladder cutting into my hands, my feet pressing against the step, felt the dank of the tunnel icing the sweat on my back. Felt the moment as it was. Watched the incipient panic recede.

Pencil-point lines of lighter dark outlined the metal doors. "Gracie, I'm going to push the door open. Stand to the side. I may fall."

She didn't answer.

The doors met to the right of the ladder. I climbed till my shoulders touched metal, braced my feet and pushed. The metal vibrated but didn't give.

I moved up to the next step, hunched over under the door. "I'm trying again."

Gracie said nothing. The only sound was her short, thick breaths. She was doing all she could just keeping quiet. I inhaled, braced one hand next to my shoulder, shoved with all my strength.

The door shifted; the light was wider, brighter. My feet slipped off the rung. I grabbed. Too late. I heard the metal clank as I landed on my back in the mud.

Mud splattered my face. I gasped for breath.

"Oh, Darcy, are you all right?"

"Uh-huh!" I forced out, and pushed myself up out of the muck. "Yeah. The mud cushioned my fall." My back throbbed. My head swirled, my vision was blurred, but maybe that was from the mud. I reached for the ladder. "There's something heavy on it, but it's not locked."

Grace gave an odd squeak, the shadow of a laugh. "Of course it's not locked, Darce, we took the key."

"We're so good!" I started up the ladder, ribs screaming each time I hoisted myself up. "I have to get more leverage. Come up behind me, brace my back so I can use both hands."

I climbed till I was squatted double like a power lifter. Grace grabbed the ladder around me.

"If I start to fall, jump. I don't want to kick you."

"You've finally grown out of that?"

I forced what passed for a laugh. Gracie was trying so hard. "Okay," I said, "ready? Go!" I exploded up with the fury of childhood. The metal shimmied, gave. Light came through as one door released an inch. But the weight atop it held, and I slammed back down into Grace. "You okay?"

It was a moment before she managed a yes.

She had held, but she was too small to do it again. Still, there was no other choice. I took a deep breath. "Again. Ready?"

I thrust up, catching the edge, pushing with strength I didn't know I had. Metal rattled; something shifted. I shoved my shoulders between the metal doors, twisted, braced it. "Climb around me. Quick!"

She was up and out in seconds, caught the door, and held it till I slid out. The big masonry planter from the courtyard was still caught at the edge of the door, still atop the metal. I let the door bang down.

It wasn't quite five in the morning, but light as noon. I could see everything, wanted to inspect every brick and stone. The air was cold. Rain was starting. It felt wonderful. I yearned to sit there on the grate and suck the clean air down into every inch of my body to let every cell know I was alive.

But there was no time. "We have to move. Come on," I said, pulling her up. "He's already stabbed two people."

"He?" she puffed as we ran for the car.

"He? She? Someone strong enough to carry Jeffrey's body and throw it down into the tunnel."

Grace opened the door of her car, climbed in, and unlocked my side. "Where to?"

"I don't know. Does this vehicle have heat?"

"It certainly does. And food." She sounded giddy. She gave the glove compartment a single hard rap. The door flopped and half the candy bars in the city fell out. I snagged a Baby Ruth.

"We could be dead!" Her elation had burst, her voice a monotone now, as if the reality of the tunnel had just intersected with rational thought. "Lying down there dead."

"Like Jeffrey. And Tia. The killer stabbed her, stole the poison, and then climbed down into the tunnel to stuff her purse back in the corner of the tunnel."

"How'd he know it was there to begin with?"

"The same way I did. Except he had a head start. When she jumped into the tunnel he knew what she was up to. So, all he had to do was watch."

"Wait a minute. Explain this," she said, in just the tone she had used when bailing me out of homework crises. "Tia's at the reception with Jeffrey. Jeffrey's got the vial in his pocket. Why didn't she just wait for him to give it to her? Why go to all the hassle of getting it out of his pocket?"

"She wanted the whole vial, but he'd tried to dole it out in portions. Jeffrey's goal was keeping her around. She didn't have time to wait. See, Georgia had shown up at her place earlier that afternoon and threatened to sic the CDC on her. So, she had to get the vial pronto." I fished around in the back for a water bottle. "Tia took it and hid it. Then, the next day at lunch, suddenly I'm telling her about some homeless man going board-stiff before he died—bizarre, right? Exactly what the poison dart frog toxin does. I barely had the words out of my mouth when she rushed off, suppos-edly to look for a diary in her garage, but instead called Jeffrey. You have to know she was asking herself: what the hell had Jeffrey been doing with that poison all this time? Was he *that* careless? And how long was it going to be till the police were all over it?"

"But how could she expect to get an answer from him? I mean, she'd just robbed the guy."

"Because, Gracie, she was Tia Dru. She could handle Jeffrey; she always had. And, in fact she did. He probably answered her questions, plus he drove her to the tunnel, and she got out, angry, but nonetheless safe and sound."

The car was warming up. We smelled like we'd been in a pigsty. Still, the heat felt wonderful. I leaned back against the seat, trying to put my finger on the mistake we'd all made. "You know, Leo was right."

"Leo! Darcy, what *are* you talking about?"

"'Don't assume!' That's what Leo kept telling me. I assumed it was Tia and Jeffrey who were the friends and then along came Eamon, but in fact it was Eamon and Tia all along and—"

"Eamon! Our Eamon killed Tia? Oh, Darcy, I just can't . . . No, that can't be. He ate at our table. He's slept in our house. How . . . how?"

"I know, Gracie, it's a shock. Eamon seems like a nice guy, but he's always got his eye out for the next move, right? He went from being a grunt in a lab to leasing property on Pacific Avenue, with no hint of a job or income."

"Yeah, but—"

"We *assumed* what they wanted us to think. But the reality is, from the time Tia spotted Eamon at Fort Detrick, the two of them set out to get ahold of the frog toxin. Tia was desperate for anything that might numb her pain. Eamon knew Jeffrey's father had brought the toxin here. When Tia pointed out his resemblance to Mike, Eamon saw his entrée in the city. Tia set out to cultivate Jeffrey—thus her temp job at Letterman, where Jeffrey worked. Of course, she got Jeffrey to give her the thing she desperately needed. Guys always did that for her. Hard to get better connections than that. And best of all, there was us."

I realized I expected her to be as shocked as I'd been when the realization hit, but maybe she was on overload. She just sat in the dark car, her small angular face backlit by the streetlight, and she nodded as I said, "It was because every one of us in the family was so determined to find Mike. Because of the articles Katy got into papers across the country, how she humanized the family to grab people's attention—the upright siblings involved in so much of San Francisco civic life and, of course, the pictures of Mike."

Grace's breath caught. Her face went stony. "Because," she said in disgust, "everyone—us, our friends, anyone who knew about Mike—really wanted to like this guy who was the next thing to him. They loved it that he fussed over Mom, spent time with John, took me to dinner. Everyone was rooting for him to be near enough to being Mike." She shook her head. "I had doubts. Really. But he was good to Mom and I didn't want to take that away."

I put a hand on her arm. "I'll bet John, Gary, Katy—all of them—could say that. But he's expert at playing people. Look, he was waiting in the house at four in the morning to drive me to the shoot. I liked him, too. Sort of."

"But—damn him!" She sat, looking straight ahead. "*Damn* him. Now he's going to sell that toxin to God knows who. He's probably already flying—"

Wheels skidded around the corner behind us from Pacific onto Columbus. Eamon Lafferty slowed, doing a completely freaked double take when he saw us in Grace's car. The engine coughed, as if in response to the foot of a shocked killer when he sees his victims outside their grave. He hit the gas before the engine stalled, then shot forward.

Grace and I stared, stunned.

"Slide over, Gracie! Let me drive!" I ran around and swung into the driver's seat.

"But why didn't he stop and just kill us?"

I turned the key and pumped the gas. "Because it's a quarter after five."

"What, too close to dawn to kill? Let the gas up slower."

Using my lifetime's quota of patience, I turned off the engine and started again. It caught, and patience gone, I hung a U and shot down Columbus.

"Hey, he went the other way!"

"I'll catch him! Find your cell! Call 911!"

"By the time I explain . . . let me call John."

I veered left on Montgomery, dead as a sepia-toned photo at this hour, and made the light to cross Market.

Her head bobbed. The phone music twittered. "Darcy! Have you lost your mind, or are you just trying to see how fast you can burn up my engine?"

I whipped down New Montgomery, doglegged Howard onto Hawthorne Street. "First flights out of SFO leave at six. They board at twenty of. He was already cutting it close. They don't hold a flight for you because you got delayed killing people. Even now, he'll be lucky if they don't give away his seat."

A van pulled out mid-block. I cut around it, the screech of the wheels almost covering Grace's plea to John. "He's headed to the airport! With the poison! Hurry!"

There were cars on Harrison. I honked, hit the turn signal, and cut off a white Honda.

"Damn! Can't you go any faster?"

"Can't you buy yourself a better car?" The light at Fourth turned red.

"Go! Run it!"

"We'd be dead!" I said as a truck lumbered through the intersection where we would have been.

"SFO's got three terminals, probably a hundred gates. John's got to go through layers of police and airport police. We can't be sure he'll get the word out in time."

"Right. We've got to catch him on the freeway." The light turned. I drove through, gas pedal floored, car moving sedately. "Don't you ever get this thing serviced?"

"Do you think I've got nothing else to do?"

I eased up the on-ramp to the elevated freeway, the engine catching a bit more as we picked up speed. I switched from lane three to two, heading south now on 101. Downtown was to our rear; ahead was the straight shot to the airport. "Check behind us . . . it'll be easy to spot him . . . he'll be speeding."

"What if he's not behind us? What if he's ahead?"

"I'll deal with that," I said with unmerited bravado. The best driver in the world can't make a rattletrap into a NASCAR special. I signaled left, then flicked off the light.

"What?" Grace was almost out of her seat, peering through the windshield.

"Up ahead. It's slowing."

"This is the West Coast, remember, Darcy? Brokers are already at work. The stock market opens at six."

"He behind us?"

"No. Nothing but two buses."

"Damn! It's stopping! A crash or—"

"Get off! Darcy, trust me. Now!"

I swung across two lanes and off at the Eighth Street ramp.

"Straight on Harrison. If we make the lights . . . there, okay, left on Tenth. See the entrance?"

I shot on back on the freeway. "You see him?"

"No! Dammit, what if he's not here?"

"He knows we saw him, knows we'd call John. He wouldn't dare take either of the bridges out of the city. The airport's the only choice." I passed Cesar Chavez, the street that had been Army when we were kids. "There he is!"

"Where?"

"Fast lane. Hang on. He's picking up speed. If I miss him here, he's gone. Call John. Tell him he's got fifteen minutes."

"Army Street! Green convertible!" Grace said into the phone. "I *know* you can't keep the line open, John!" She clicked off. "He's on it."

Eamon Lafferty shifted right, out of the fast lane into the center.

"We're losing him. Isn't there anything— I've got it floored."

He cut across two lanes.

"Omigod, he's not going to the airport . . . he's on 280. Call John!"

"I'm trying. I can't get through! Where's he going?"

The 280 freeway led to the western districts of the city, to the beach, to a choice of roads south to Los Angeles. No bridges to stop him. "If we lose him, he's gone!"

A truck blocked the middle lanes. I hit the gas, cut him off, ignored his horn blast. The green convertible was locked in behind a van. "This is our chance." I snapped off my seatbelt and stood on the gas. "Slide over, Gracie! Can you take it when I jump?"

"Yes," she squeaked.

I angled half a car length in front of him, pulled close, opened the door. "Now!" With both hands on the window frame I kicked off, swung, and landed in his passenger seat. The sports car lurched, slammed the median. Gracie's car was all over the place.

The truck's brakes shrieked. The sports car bounced off the median, skidded across lanes that somehow had no cars in them, spun full around, and scraped along the slow lane edge. Sparks shot. Eamon jumped out and ran.

The truck launched him twenty feet, into the exit lane.

I yanked on the emergency lights, leapt over the windshield, and raced to him.

Eamon's body was mashed and bloody. Lying there, he didn't look like

Mike at all. Thank God. Brakes screeched, gears scraped, wind from the traffic whipped my thin, still-wet sweater. He lay in the lane, struggling for breath. There was a slew of questions I wanted to ask, but only one I couldn't bear not to. I bent down close and said, "Which Portland?"

"Port . . . . land." I could swear a look of satisfaction crossed his face before it went blank.

For a moment I stood staring at this man who had so callously used us all. Then sirens screamed again; flashers cut the dawn sky. Grace was standing beside me, shaking. Highway Patrol cars squealed to stops, one ambulance, then another.

"Get away from him, Darcy." My sister had stopped shaking and was in command. To the CHP guy she said, "He's carrying an extremely deadly poison. That truck hit sent him flying. The container may have smashed. Call HazMat."

We moved off the roadway, watched the CHP block off the scene. Suddenly John was walking up behind us, resting his arms on our shoulders. A tech, covered in white from head to foot, bent over Eamon Lafferty's corpse. He checked his pockets, inside the lining of his jacket, examined his pants. He stood and walked over to the officer in charge. "Nothing here, sir."

"The poison's not on him? Did you look in his car? Or the road, the median, the shoulder?" I demanded.

"Not yet," he snapped. "We're going to have to close down the whole road south."

"Close it!"

The coroner hurried over to John and said something lost in the traffic noise. John said something about jurisdiction.

In the hour it was shut down I stared at the empty macadam, feeling as if I'd come full circle from the moment when I stood atop the turret on Broadway, before my high fall, before I spotted Eamon Lafferty.

The tech walked back. "Nothing, sir. Not in the vic's car, not on the roadway, not beside it. There's no sign of any substance. Nothing." He glared at me. The officer in charge glared at John.

I turned to Grace, but even she shook her head. "I never saw it," she muttered to me.

John inhaled very slowly. He was watching his career evaporate. "We closed the freeway; we created havoc in the airport. How could—"

"John, he killed two people. He saw us and ran. He was escaping!"

"But not to the airport, was he?" Behind him the other officers just watched, waited.

"No," I admitted. "No, because he didn't have the poison—"

"Now you—"

"Because the poison is somewhere else. Because he was racing to get to it and—"

"Somewhere else?"

"John, why would you cut off 101 from downtown onto 280? To go to Mom's, right? The morning after he took the vial from Tia, Eamon was in Mom's house. He's got a key, right?"

He hesitated. "After all this is cleaned up, maybe—"

"No!" Grace said. "You can't wait! Mom's coming back this morning. She'll get home anytime."

"I'll call—"

"No! Listen, she's bringing Darcy's dog. As soon as he gets in the door, Duffy will be into everything. You gotta go now!"

CHAPTER 30

JOHN HAS PULL, but not enough to convince the CHP to turn loose women who cost the city and state a bundle in money and more in bad publicity. It was an hour before John called back to the CHP here at the scene, and longer till an officer handed me the phone. In a voice tight with fury, John said, "He put the poison in Mike's room!"

Hours later, John, Gary, Grace, and I sat around the kitchen table. I pulled Duffy onto my lap and admitted, "It was the stupidest thing I've ever done, that car chase."

"Gracie could have been killed," Mom insisted, standing behind Grace on the other side of the table.

"You're right. I'm sorry."

"She's not athletic like you, you know."

"I know."

"She doesn't think before she rushes in to help. She's not a good driver; she's a terrible driver."

"I should have thought of that. I'm sorry."

Mom was patting the shoulder Grace's sling hung from, so she missed Grace's grimace.

"You, Darcy, you I never worry about. Your father, he worried about you. He claimed that worry for his own from the day you were born. He worried when you took your first step, worried that you hadn't crawled first, worried that you weren't talking, that you were talking too much. So, I never had to worry about you at all."

There was too much family history in that statement; I'd have to deal with it later. Meanwhile, stew was heating and glasses of Powers had been poured. Grace used her good hand to lift her glass and swallow the Irish and her irritation. She knew better than to defend her own driving here among those she'd exasperated for years.

"You broke half the laws of the road, Darcy," John insisted. He sat, straddling a chair, his back to the wall, as if felons were going to sneak up behind him from the dining room. "You're lucky you were right about Eamon. Otherwise, they'd have thrown away the key." He took a swallow of Powers and let his gaze settle back on me. He wasn't finished with me. He shook his head.

But it was Gary who said, "I can't believe you haven't been served with a single summons. The truck driver alone, if he was my client—"

"May he only deal with lesser lawyers."

"You should have called me," John and Gary said as one. Gary held out a piece of stew meat to Duffy. Duffy ignored him.

"I can't believe that Eamon," Mom said, returning to the topic that had interspersed all others since she got to Grace in the emergency room. "He sat at this table, ate from our pot!" Ate from her pot of hope and trust and pain the sight of him caused every time he walked in and for a split second she saw Mike, before realizing each time anew that Mike was gone. He spooned up all her pot of kindness and threw it in her face. Now her mouth trembled, and for the first time she was in danger of losing control in a way she never had all these years. We all busied ourselves with our glasses until she could continue. Her voice was still shaky as she said, "And all the time he had planned the whole thing from the first time he saw Mike's picture in the paper."

Gary made a show of plopping Duffy's rejected meat in his own mouth. "Yeah, Eamon really played us. You gotta give him that; he was good! He let us believe he lured the zendo to his building to please John because Mom wanted Darcy back. Damn! It was all so he could be close enough to keep an eye on Jeffrey and snatch the poison. He got Darcy the stunt job so . . . ?"

"To keep me out of the way. And then, Gary, because he knew the people on the set, knew the location, it was a snap for him to sabotage my stair fall, to keep me out of the way. Plus—"

"Plus?" Grace said. "He did something else?"

"I don't know exactly what deal he had with Robin Sparto and the crew, but he kept stalling them. Of course they assumed I knew because I was there because of him. That's why they were fuming every time I was on the set."

I sipped the Powers, took in my brothers and sister and Mom there behind the red Formica table in the yellow and green kitchen, with the familiar aroma of stew hovering between us. I felt rather than thought of all the times we had sat at tables together, our talk so loud Dad would bang his glass when we were young, talk so stilted after Mike disappeared I could hear the slosh when he lifted it to drink. "You know, I thought I was the only one who never stopped looking for Mike."

They all just looked at me, and I couldn't tell whether it was with surprise or uneasiness. "Was that why you said Tia was a liar, John? Not because of her saying Mike had a Celtic cross tattoo but—"

"She did say that!"

"Yeah, John, to get your attention," Gary said.

"—but because she let people believe you were chasing her into the intersection when she had her accident."

"Yeah." John followed his comment by emptying his glass, so he didn't see Gary catch himself just as the 'You' of 'You didn't?' was almost out of his mouth. I noted Grace's raised eyebrows. I wasn't surprised that was why they had both put themselves way out to help Tia. I just wished John had some idea how much his brother and sister cared about him. I said, "I had no idea about the favors you called in hunting for Mike, John. I never saw the newspaper articles Katy got placed across the country, never knew what you and Gracie did, Gary. I wish I had.

"Or maybe I couldn't have handled knowing all the roads you all took hunting him and all those dead ends." I almost mentioned Eamon's tease about the Portland airport, but that would have been just another dead end.

There was silence. Then, as one, we lifted our glasses. For an instant I thought someone was going to toast Mike. But we were all just covering the awkwardness.

CHAPTER 31

THERE MAY COME a time when rain raps zendo windows and pale morning sun backlights the Buddha on the altar. People, perhaps in costume, perhaps not, will sit facing the other end of the room, where a card table holds bowls full of rice, oranges, almonds, walnuts, water, and rose petals. Incense will drift and vanish. Zen students from other centers in the city, in Marin County to the north, in Berkeley, will sit quietly on zafus. Maybe Grace or even Gary will be there. Or Mom might come to see what has hooked her youngest daughter. Even John might turn up to sit in a chair next to those new students Leo attracted in jail. With luck John won't know them.

When the zendo door swings open a procession will enter, two robed attendants followed by Leo Garson-roshi, in full robes, banging a heavy walking stick with each step. The children will giggle as the rattles hanging from that stick clatter and the cymbals clang. They will point to the mane of white hairs sprouting from the top. If the time is near Halloween, the zendo will be full of small goblins, witches, and superheroes. Everyone— priests, goblins, and their parents—will hoot and shout, blow horns and pound drums, to attract the hungry ghosts. The kids will love that.

Leo will say, "We call the hungry ghosts. They have huge bellies and pencil-thin necks. Their hunger is constant, overwhelming. Desperately they grab for food, but they cannot swallow what they've taken. No way can they sate their hunger. So we offer them small bits of food, food they can swallow. Traditionally, it is said we do this to help the ghosts fill their great needs and let go of their attachment to this realm."

"Aren't we all hungry ghosts?" someone will whisper a bit too loud. Leo will nod and smile.

We will sit in silence for a bit, and then, slowly, from all over the room, names of those who had died during the year will be called out. Their names will float in from beside us and behind, their friends, lovers, mothers offering all that is left of them to the silence. Their names will vibrate and then be gone.

We will walk to the table that holds the fruit and nuts and rice and make our offerings so the dead are sated and can go on their way. So we can let them go.

Acknowledgments

My thanks to Vice Abbot Alan Senauke of Berkeley Zen Center, to stunt double Carolyn Day, and to writer Linda Grant and editor Michele Slung. And, as always, to my agent, Dominick Abel.